Praise fo

D0286009

"Dan's likable first-person voice rings with authenticity… For those looking for books on the ever-important topic of bullying."

—*Kirkus Reviews*

"Blount's debut novel combines an authentic voice with compelling moral dilemmas… Raise[s] important questions about honesty, forgiveness, the ease of cyberbullying, and the obligation to help others."

—*VOYA*

"A morality play about releasing the past and seizing the present… The ethical debates raised will engage readers."

—*Publishers Weekly*

"With comedy, drama, and a wonderful message, *Send* is a superbly well written debut novel."

—*SeeItOrReadIt*

"An amazing and captivating tale of a teenager learning to live with his mistakes."

—*A Beautiful Madness*

"Emotional, dark, and real, *Send* will not disappoint… Fans of Katie McGarry's *Pushing the Limits* will thoroughly enjoy this contemporary novel."

—*Singing and Reading in the Rain*

"A book that will stick with me. The story packs a big emotional punch and it opens your eyes to the far reaching consequences of bullying."

—*Rainy Day Ramblings*

"A powerful story that will leave a lasting impact."

—Blogger Traci, *The Reading Geek*

TMI

PATTY BLOUNT

Marysville Public Library
231 S. Plum St
Marysville, ~~~~ ~~~~
(937) 642-1876

DISCARD

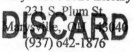

sourcebooks
fire

Copyright © 2013 by Patty Blount

Cover and internal design © 2013 by Sourcebooks, Inc.

Cover design by Elsie Lyons

Cover images © Thinkstock/Getty Images, Marie-Reine Mattera/Getty Images

Sourcebooks and the colophon are registered trademarks of Sourcebooks, Inc.

All rights reserved. No part of this book may be reproduced in any form or by any electronic or mechanical means including information storage and retrieval systems—except in the case of brief quotations embodied in critical articles or reviews—without permission in writing from its publisher, Sourcebooks, Inc.

The characters and events portrayed in this book are fictitious or are used fictitiously. Any similarity to real persons, living or dead, is purely coincidental and not intended by the author.

Published by Sourcebooks Fire, an imprint of Sourcebooks, Inc.

P.O. Box 4410, Naperville, Illinois 60567-4410

(630) 961-3900

Fax: (630) 961-2168

teenfire.sourcebooks.com

Library of Congress Cataloging-in-Publication Data is on file with the publisher.

Printed and bound in the United States of America.

VP 10 9 8 7 6 5 4 3 2 1

For my boys, Chris, Rob, and Fred,
who inspire me as much as they confound me,
who tease, support, sustain, and love me,
always.

Chapter 1
Meg

The eyes had no soul.

Megan Farrell flung down her brush with a curse. The eyes refused to shine for her. No matter how she sketched them, no matter what colors she used to fill them, they sat on her canvas, dull. Dead. She couldn't even get the color right and probably never would, not unless she asked Chase Gallagher to sit for her, and she could never do that.

Chase Gallagher wasn't part of her plan.

She stretched, cracking her neck, and stared out her window into the backyard that butted against hers. He was out there now, running around with his little brothers, trying to fix the snowman they'd built during a late-season snowstorm that hit Long Island three days earlier. Temperatures had risen to the fifties since then, but Chase would never tell the boys Frosty couldn't be saved. The Gallagher brothers scooped up every inch of snow that hadn't melted and brought it to Chase, who had an unlimited supply of patience from what Meg could see. Even through the closed window, she could hear the boys' belly laughs and screeches of pure glee. "My turn, Chase! My turn!" And Chase would pick up another brother and lift him high enough to pat handfuls of snow into place. Suddenly, he lifted his head and stared right at her.

She jumped back, her face on fire. Not smart, letting him catch her with her face pressed to her window.

She turned back to her canvas, and with a charcoal pencil, she crossed out the color mix she'd noted. It was too dark out to fix it now. The master bedroom was already striped in shadows. After her father died, her mother had refused to sleep here, so Meg moved in, loving that she didn't need to "Clean up that mess!" when she was done painting. The room was large enough for art supplies *and* her stuff, not that she had much. Just a twin bed shoved against one wall, a garage sale bookcase and desk for homework, an ancient laptop whose E button had long since disappeared, and a meager wardrobe that hardly filled one rod in the walk-in closet otherwise devoted to art supplies.

The way the light shining through the huge palladium window illuminated the paintings on her easel, and the paint splatters on the wood floor made her feel like a real artist in a studio.

Usually.

Today, it only emphasized her failures.

On stiff legs, she took her brushes and palette knife to the bathroom that adjoined the bedroom to wash them. A drop of crimson paint hit the tile floor and spread, seeping into the grout.

Her throat tightened. Her breaths got shallow. Her stomach pitched and rolled, and when her legs buckled, she slid to the floor in a boneless heap, whimpering the way she had all those years ago when it had been blood on the floor instead of paint. He'd been gone for ten years now, but she could still hear his voice.

"The future, Megan!" he'd always said. "Focus on the future. Set goals and don't let anything or anyone ever make you lose focus." Her father's plan. But he'd failed. So now it was hers—a promise she had to keep.

Minutes passed, or maybe they were hours. She sat on the hard floor until she was able to pull herself together. How long it had taken this time, she wasn't sure. She grabbed a towel and rubbed furiously at the spot on the floor until it squeaked. Then she pulled out the tie that held her hair back in a messy knot, wincing when a few rooted strands came away with it. She dragged herself to her feet and ran the shower.

Piece by piece, she shed her paint-spattered clothes. She stood under the stream of water as hot as she could take it. She really wished hot water could melt away all the anxiety that seemed to cover her like a thick coat of ice. The panic attack, the SAT scores that still hadn't arrived, the job she was about to lose when the movie theater closed its doors in a few weeks, and the bills—the endless pile of bills her mom cried over when she thought Meg was asleep. When the water went cold, she stepped out, wrapped herself in a towel, and stood in front of the mirror, scowling at the look in her eyes.

Bailey would notice.

She always did, and Megan didn't want to talk about it. It was old news.

She tugged on jeans and a T-shirt, detangled her hair, and coiled it in another elastic. Downstairs, she foraged for dinner but found only a brown banana and the heels of a loaf of bread. Mom still hadn't been grocery shopping. She slammed the refrigerator door, hoping there was enough money in her wallet to spring for a fast-food meal, and grabbed her cell to tap out a message to her best friend.

Meg: Outta food again. Going to Main St. Wanna go?

Bailey would say sure. They never discussed it, but Bailey knew there wasn't always enough money for groceries, so she often came over with leftovers that she'd put on the top shelf in Meg's empty refrigerator without a word. That was one of the things Meg loved about Bailey—she knew when it was time to talk and when it wasn't.

Meg grabbed her keys and the art show flyer she wanted to show Bailey. Outside in the cold March air, she drew her hood up over her wet hair and rubbed her knees together to keep warm.

After about five minutes, her cell buzzed.

Bailey: Not hungry. CU tom. XOXO

Megan's forehead puckered. Bailey always walked with her to Main Street...or sometimes drove since Bailey was the proud owner of a driver's license, even when she wasn't hungry. Said it was a great excuse to escape her mother. Meg thought for a minute and typed back.

Meg: What's wrong?

There was no reply, which was even stranger than the first message. Bailey always had to have the last word. It was a thing with her. Meg started the half-mile walk north, trying not to obsess. She had her learner's permit, but she had never been behind the wheel of car.

Pauline Farrell didn't have the time or money for lessons. Meg had started a driver's license fund, setting aside change from her part-time job for lessons or maybe the driver's education class her school offered. She'd need a license to find jobs, and she'd need jobs to be independent. But first, she needed money to earn the license.

At a table in the corner, she sighed and picked at her meal. French fries and chicken nuggets kind of sucked when you didn't have anyone to share them with. She unfolded the flyer that had shown up in today's mail and studied it again. Bailey hated museums, and Meg knew convincing her to go to Manhattan's Museum of Modern Art wasn't going to be easy. She'd go. Of course she'd go. But first, Meg would have to agree to a day of shopping—one of Bailey's favorite sports—and maybe do some extra character sketches for the video game Bailey was trying to develop. But Bailey's radio silence had her considering even higher stakes.

Maybe makeovers.

She ate her last fry and shuddered. For Bailey, she'd do it.

She checked her phone. Still no reply from Bailey. Maybe she'd had another fight with her mom. Meg emptied her tray and started the long walk home. Or maybe it was Simon, Bailey's latest boyfriend. Meg rolled her eyes. What a jerk.

By the time Meg got home and still hadn't heard from Bailey, panic had set in. She logged onto her computer, fired off a quick email, but it too was ignored. The next morning at the bus stop, Meg took one look at Bailey's flat curls, bare-naked face, and sparkless demeanor, and her panic jolted straight to redline levels. Bailey Grant did not leave the house without her makeup coordinated to her outfit and her hair perfectly coiffed.

"What's-wrong-did-somebody-die-oh-God-are-your-grandparents-okay?"

Bailey glanced up, her blue eyes dull, and shrugged. "Everyone's fine. Nobody died. Nothing's wrong." Her eyes narrowed when she got a look at Meg. "What's wrong with you? You look terrible."

Knew it. Megan pressed her lips into a line and shook her head. "The usual."

Bailey nodded, understanding. "Anxiety attack again?"

"Anxiety attack?"

The deep voice had them both spinning around. Chase Gallagher frowned down at Meg, worry filling brilliant eyes that defied her every attempt to render on canvas. Greens, golds, flecks of browns and grays, his eyes were a source of endless fascination—and frustration—for her. Before she could stop it, her face split into the stupid smile her lips somehow reserved just for Chase.

Damn it. She needed a reason, an excuse, an explanation, something that could explain the grin, something like—

A book accidentally-on-purpose falling on Chase's foot. "Oh! Sorry, Chase," Bailey sang.

That might work, Meg sighed in relief. While Chase bent down to pick up the book, Meg gave Bailey a barely perceptible nod of thanks, which Bailey answered with a barely perceptible nod of her own. Chase frowned at Bailey and then at Meg. She knew he wasn't going to let it go. Luckily, so did Bailey. She quickly handed Meg something wrapped in a napkin just as Chase opened his mouth. "Here you go, Meg. Strawberry." Bailey handed her a Pop-Tart. She shoved half of it in her mouth before Chase could interrogate her.

Meg's eyes slipped closed. It was still warm.

"So, Chase, why are you riding the bus with the rest of the terminally uncool?" Bailey asked while Meg chewed.

"Lacrosse practice today. My mother needs the car. My brothers have a birthday party, music lesson, and a doctor's appointment after school today. Blah, blah, blah." He rolled his eyes as he ticked the events off his fingers, and Meg's heart gave a little pang. She thought it would be cool to have a big family like Chase's.

The bus arrived and everyone piled inside. Bailey slid toward a window seat, and Meg took the aisle seat beside her, leaving Chase on his own. He grinned and held up a hand. "Later."

Meg shut her eyes and sent up a prayer of gratitude. Sitting beside Chase Gallagher all the way to school would have killed her. It would have set her on fire, she was sure of it.

The bus continued its route, but Bailey remained quiet. Meg dug out her sketch pad and handed it to Bailey. "I did some character sketches I forgot to show you. Can you use these for your game?"

Bailey flipped through the pages of pencil sketches, stopping at one. "Who's this?"

"Pope Sixtus. Not a particularly *nice* guy, but he liked art, so I figured you could use him for the Renaissance level."

Bailey nodded and gave the book back to Meg without a word. Something was seriously up. Bailey was always bugging her to work on her video game, and Pope Sixtus rendered in charcoal didn't even earn a grunt? Curiosity tinged with worry twisted Meg inside out, but she would give her friend some privacy.

This vow lasted until lunchtime.

"Did your mom start in on you again?" Meg asked.

Bailey blinked. "What? Oh. No. She went away for the weekend. I'll see her tonight." She waved a hand and went back to picking apart a chicken strip.

Right. Meg had forgotten Bailey's mother, Nicole, had gone on another hot date. So if it wasn't her mother and it wasn't Simon, it had to be something serious. Meg tried again. "Is it your SAT scores? Mine didn't come yet, but I heard a few people got theirs and—"

"God, Meg! Please stop. I don't care about SAT scores. I only took the test early because you did."

Meg stared at Bailey for a moment and then quietly put her sandwich down on her cafeteria tray. She knew Bailey didn't care about school much, but the SATs? Their entire futures rode on those scores! Meg hoped for a scholarship. Actually, her entire plan depended on getting a scholarship to a good college, where she'd study business or maybe medicine. She hadn't figured that part out yet. Or maybe she'd wait tables while she attended community college just like her mother. Pauline Farrell had just a few courses left to finish the accounting degree she was earning at night school. Meg couldn't wait. Maybe then they'd have enough money so that her mother wouldn't cry at night.

She sneaked another glance at Bailey and finally faced facts. Bailey wasn't going to talk until she was damn well good and ready. Meg cleaned up what was left of her lunch, piling the plastic containers back onto her tray, and hoped Bailey wasn't pregnant or dying or something. Her head whipped up when Bailey suddenly shot to her feet with a muffled scream.

Gatorade rolled down Bailey's jeans, leaving behind angry red scars. Her boyfriend held the now-empty bottle, and from the sneer on his face, Meg knew it was no accident. An instant hush interrupted the usual cafeteria racket while Bailey frantically blotted the mess with a stack of recycled napkins. Meg leaped to her feet. "What the hell is wrong with you, Simon?"

Simon Kane tossed the bottle onto the table and took a threatening step closer. "Shut up, Meg. This is all your fault. What did you tell her? What lies did you spread?"

So Simon *was* the cause of Bailey's mood. Why didn't Bailey tell her they'd had a fight? They'd known Simon since second grade, and Meg never understood what Bailey saw in him—except for his computer programming ability. Sure, Simon was cute. But ever since his parents had won the lottery, he'd become conceited and spoiled, teased Bailey often, and questioned everything she said. Worse, Bailey allowed it. Actually thought it was cute.

Gag.

Meg tossed more napkins at her best friend, who now sat in shocked silence. "I'm not the one hitting on cheerleaders when I'm supposed to be with someone else."

"I wasn't cheating!"

Meg laughed. "Sure."

Simon ignored her and turned to Bailey. "Do you believe her or me?"

Meg wondered about the answer to that herself. Last week, after she'd caught Simon hitting on Caitlyn, the head cheerleader, there had been no apology, no explanation. Bailey swore—she *promised*—she was through, but Meg never expected Bailey to actually *keep* that promise....or worse, keep it from *her*. Whatever. She and Bailey would discuss that later. Right now, she had more important things to do.

"Bailey, can I make him cry now?"

Simon's blue eyes went dark as he stared Meg down. "Just mind your own business. You did enough."

"Meg. It's okay. Sit down." Bailey murmured, tugging Meg's arm.

"No, it is not okay." Meg glared at both of them. "Those are fifty-dollar jeans, and Gatorade never washes out. You should buy her a new pair, Simon."

"Megan, stop," Bailey said.

"Oh, I *should*, huh?" Simon laughed once and his blue eyes narrowed. "I'd have bought her tons of jeans. I'd have bought her anything she wanted. If she were nice to me, I'd have been nice to her." He shot Bailey a wounded look.

Bailey looked at him like he was diseased. "I'm done, Simon. Get over it."

A muscle in Simon's jaw clenched. "You know what, Bailey? I *am* over it. I can get any girl I want. You're not even that hot." He high-fived one of his friends with a loud laugh.

Meg was about to defend Bailey when she saw the hurt in Simon's eyes. Well, jeez, she'd never expected that. She looked at Bailey. Had she caught Simon's expression too? But Bailey's face was frozen, her eyes just as hurt, and Meg knew Simon's insult had hit home. Bailey was curvy with long blond curls, huge blue eyes, and a smile bright enough to power a city block. She was the definition of hot, no matter what Simon Kane had to say about it. But Bailey never believed the compliments. Simon would know all about Bailey's insecurities, and Meg's eyes narrowed. It was a low blow, an arrow aimed straight at Bailey's Achilles' heel.

And it had pierced the target.

Meg gripped Bailey's hand and squeezed hard.

"Simon, get lost. Nobody here is impressed." Bailey retorted, her face pale.

Simon's male-model smile full of capped teeth went tight. Vibrating with fury from the soles of his high-priced tennis shoes to the tips of his designer haircut, he nodded slowly. "Yeah. Fine. I'll leave you and your little dyke girl-friend and go find a real woman." He stalked around the table and motioned for his pals to follow.

Meg's eyes met Bailey's and she gave her a signal she knew no one else would see, a raised eyebrow that said, *Is that the best you got?* Bailey acknowledged it with a tiny close-lipped smile and turned back to Simon to fire off one last taunt. "Simon, you should take lessons from Meg. Unlike you, *she* knows how to keep me coming back for more."

Everyone in earshot applauded. Someone's shout of "Burn!" rippled over the small crowd that watched like it was reality TV.

"You'll be back. You're crazy about me." Simon shot them both one last glare and finally strode away, his pals on his tail.

Onlookers went back to their meals, chattering loudly about the floor show, but Meg just grinned proudly at Bailey.

"Close your mouth, Meg," Bailey snapped.

"You did it." Meg giggled. "You really did it. That was…it was—*wow*—really impressive. But why didn't you tell me? I *knew* something was bothering you."

Bailey sighed and didn't answer her for a moment. "You didn't see Facebook last night?" she finally asked and grabbed Meg's water bottle to blot the stains from her jeans.

Meg shook her head. "No, I was painting. What did he say?"

Bailey put the water bottle back on the tray and pulled out her phone. "Here. Check it out." She opened her Facebook app and scrolled down, and there it was—Simon's attempt at being smooth.

> I've got two tickets to I-CON. One of them has your name on it, Bailey Grant. You know you want it. Meet me at ten on Saturday. Your welcome.

Meg snorted at the spelling error and figured Simon didn't need brains as long as he had money. Meg's amusement faded when she noticed the time the message had been posted. She'd been drowning French fries in ketchup and feeling sorry for herself. "Oh, my God, Bay, he didn't even post this on *your* Wall."

She rolled her eyes. "Or apologize. That's why I wrote this." She scrolled down a bit further and showed Meg the screen again.

> You no longer have anything that interests me even a little. Maybe Caitlyn's interested. Have you tried her? Oh, I forgot. You already have.

Meg laughed and took Bailey's phone. She scrolled down, read some of the other comments. "Oh, wow. This got so many Likes."

Bailey boiled. "Good. I hope it makes him see what an ass he is."

"Still, I-CON, Bailey."

Bailey lived for I-CON, the annual science-fiction convention held at a college campus on Long Island. It was a huge multiday event that attracted the biggest names in video and role-playing games, animation, comic books, and sci-fi/fantasy fiction. If there was one thing Bailey adored more than hair and makeup, more than going shopping, more than even boys, it was video games—something that made her very popular with the guys. Dangling

I-CON tickets in front of her should have made her putty in Simon's hands. Meg was even more impressed with her friend's sudden resolve.

She flopped back into her seat and blew a curl out of her eyes. "You can't stand Simon. Figured you'd be happy I finally listened to you." She covered her face.

Meg shifted in her seat but didn't say anything. True, she wasn't a huge fan of Simon's. But she certainly never wanted to see Bailey hurt like this. "I *am* happy. He treated you like crap, and it's about time you did something about it. I just wish you didn't do it so—you know—publicly. You have to think of your safety." Bailey wasn't a think-ahead kind of girl, so Meg usually did that for her. "Remember Josh from last summer? He followed you for two weeks. Oh, and that guy Ian from the stables! Didn't he like…threaten you or something?"

Bailey mashed her lips into a tight line. "Simon wouldn't do anything like that."

"No, he'd just run to a hot cheerleader behind your back." At Bailey's hiss of pain, Meg gave her hand a squeeze.

Several minutes passed.

"By the way, you might want to talk to Chase."

Meg tensed. Talk to him? That was never a good idea. "Why?"

Bailey handed Meg her phone again. "Take a look at his status."

Meg scrolled down and hissed in a breath.

 Chase Gallagher is in a relationship.

"I never accepted that request!" Meg's hand curled into a fist. Bailey pried her phone away, tucked it carefully into her bag.

"Meg, before you freak out, why don't you—"

"Bay, we've been over this."

Bailey snapped her teeth together and rolled her eyes.

Meg boiled in silence and then remembered the art show flyer. God, could the timing be any worse?

"Uh-oh. Your shoulders are doing that hunchy thing. What do you want?"

And there's my cue. Meg opened her mouth and then chickened out. "It's not important."

"Meg, come on. What is it?" Bailey nudged her.

Meg slid the art exhibit flyer over to her and girded her eardrums for the assault she expected in three…two…one.

"No." Bailey moaned the word out for one long beat.

"Come on, Bay! I'll go with you to I-CON if you'll come with me to the museum."

She sighed in misery. "Do I have to? I'd rather have flat hair."

Bailey hated art in all shapes and all forms, and dragging her to Manhattan's Museum of Modern Art to see the upcoming exhibit on printed art ranked right up there with asking her to wear last year's styles. In other words: So. Not. Happening.

"Please, Bailey?"

"Megan!" She hit a new high on the shrill scale, and Meg cringed. "I really hate when you do this."

"It's called a compromise, Bay. I'm willing to subject myself to guys wearing underwear over tights in exchange for you looking at art with me."

Bailey rolled her huge blue eyes. "That stuff's not art. It's a bunch of posters and advertisements somebody stuck on the walls and sold tickets to."

"Please?"

Bailey gritted her teeth. "Fine! But you totally owe me."

Meg shrugged and happily bit into her sandwich. When she looked up again, Chase was heading toward them, carrying his lunch tray. She quickly folded the flyer and slipped it into her pocket, hoping no one noticed her lame *Here comes Chase* smile, especially him.

"Hey." Chase jerked his chin toward the rear of the cafeteria, sliding into the empty chair across from them. "What did you do to Simon? He's crying all over Caitlyn's shoulder."

Uh-oh. Meg thought with a worried glance at Bailey.

Bailey nibbled a fingernail. "Crying? Like seriously crying?"

Chase rolled his eyes. "No, not really. He's just putting the moves on her."

"Oh—"

"So what did you do?"

"I broke up with him."

Chase nodded with approval. "Good for you. Guy should get a clue."

Meg huffed out a laugh and muttered, "He's not the only one."

Chase raised his eyes to hers, and Meg stopped breathing. She never got tired of staring at his eyes. They hypnotized her and taunted her to find the hue and tint on a color wheel that could accurately render them, but that color didn't exist. Flecks of beige, gold, green. Streaks of brown and gray with a rim of black—the colors seemed to swirl as he stared at her, and then Meg realized why.

She'd hurt him.

"Sorry," Meg murmured.

Chase lowered those variegated eyes. "Um. Yeah. Whatever."

Bailey took pity on him. "We're going to an art exhibit in Manhattan. Why don't you come?"

The words were out of Bailey's mouth before Meg could kick her under the table. She gave Meg a bright smile. "And I-CON. You should come to that too."

Meg's teeth almost cracked from the strength of her clench.

"Really?" Chase looked to Meg for confirmation, hope glinting in his eyes, and Meg sighed, unable to resist. She *hated* that.

"It's up to you." She shrugged, hoping he couldn't tell how much she really did want him to come. "You didn't like the modern art exhibit at the library. You said it all looked like finger paints to you."

"It did."

"And what about the last time we went to MoMA? You stared at *The Scream* and said you—"

"Yeah. I remember what I said, Megan." He cut her off with a furrowed brow that intensified the color of his eyes.

"I'm sorry. I just don't want to waste your time, so if you have something better to do—"

"Megan, I like hanging out with you. I don't care what we do." Chase shrugged, and Meg looked away with a wince. That's exactly what she was afraid of.

"Chase, it's not a date."

He looked away, and she swore she could see him physically deflate. "Why not?"

"Delete your relationship status," she said abruptly.

He straightened up and glared at her. "I thought we were—"

She cut him off. "We're friends, Chase. That's all."

He sighed and scrubbed his face with his hands, and she wanted to kick her own butt.

"Fine. I'll delete the status when I get home."

The disappointment in his voice rattled the gate around her heart, and she wished she were stronger, tougher, with a heart coated in steel.

She *had* to resist him. It was essential. He was graduating in a few more months and would go off to college. She and Bailey still had another year. She would not be the one who ruined his plans.

And he would not ruin hers.

"Megan?"

"Um. Yeah." Meg jerked when she saw Chase waving a hand in front of her face.

He smiled, and it was a toothpaste commercial kind of smile that had her looking for the little twinkle that always sparkled at the end of those ads.

"I gotta go. Later?"

Her face burned. However, Meg nodded once and he was gone.

"Meg—" Bailey began, but Meg cut her off.

"Will you *stop* doing that?"

"What?" She blinked, and Meg glared, not buying the innocent act.

"Stop pushing us together. It's not fair to him."

"He really likes you."

Meg's eyes dropped. She knew that, and that was the entire problem. She couldn't afford to like him back, and the more time they spent together, the harder it was to remember why.

"Bay, I don't want to let him down."

"Not all guys are like our dads, Meg."

Meg sucked in a sharp breath. Neither of their dads had bothered to stick around long. Bailey never knew her dad, but Megan had known hers. She missed him. Every day, she missed him so much she was sure she'd choke on the tears. Bailey's words were a slap, and they both knew it. "Bay, I don't want—"

"Oh, you are *such* a liar. If you really don't want him, why does your face light up like Broadway when you see him?"

It did *not*. Meg was so done with this conversation. "Shut up. I'm mad at you."

Bailey pouted and twisted a curl. "You love me."

She did. But she was really mad too.

Bailey pursed her lips and shook her head. "So. Spill. What did he say the last time you went to the museum?"

Meg frowned, remembering. In February, she and Chase had been partnered up on a research paper. They'd grown close—too close—during the month it took to research their topic, the objectification of women in modern art. She'd been excited by the assignment. Chase had been excited by his assigned partner. "We saw a print of *The Scream* by Edvard Munch. Chase saw it and said, 'Hey, this guy's an artist too? I thought he just produced horror movies.'"

Bailey blinked. "What's so wrong with that? At least he knew his name. That's more than I would have gotten right."

She spoke quietly, but there was a sting in her tone, and Meg squirmed under the sudden attack of conscience. "You're right," Meg said quietly. "That was snobby and mean and ungrateful and—"

"Meg, stop! I never said that. Look. I'm just saying, Chase is trying. You should too."

Bailey scooped her books from the table, snagged her tray, and left Meg standing in the shadow of her own ego.

Chapter 2
Bailey

In the girls' locker room, Bailey blotted and dabbed and rubbed and wiped at the red streaks all over her True Religion jeans that had cost *all* of her birthday money, which Meg would totally have a cow about if she knew, and Bailey wasn't about to press Play on *that* song. Meg never spent her money unless it was for art supplies. She was all about saving for college and the future and—and her freakin' retirement. Meg was always planning, planning, planning and wasn't happy unless she had plans for her plans. Hell, even breaking up with Simon was a Meg Plan!

Her heart hurt when she thought of it. Simon looked so sad under all that tough guy acting. Maybe Meg was wrong. Maybe Simon had a really good reason for flirting with what's-her-face. He was so pretty, with his blond hair, blue eyes, and movie star life. She'd believed him when he told her she was hot. She'd believed him when he told her she was the only girl in his life. He'd been the one who got her hooked on video games back in ninth grade—first *Halo* and then *Call of Duty* and, after that, *Portal*. When Bailey showed not just interest but actual skill, Simon finally asked her out this semester, and she fell with a splat.

He was so cool on their first date. He did all those gentlemanly things like hold doors open and pull out chairs, and he never tried any moves. He took her to a nice restaurant, asked her a bunch of questions, and really listened to her answers. He walked her to do her door, asked if he could see her again, and promised to call. She walked inside, hurried up the stairs to her room, and flipped on the light, and her phone buzzed. He told her he'd had a great time and couldn't wait to ask her to breakfast the next morning. Swooning, Bailey agreed. The next morning, he picked her up, drove to Bailey's favorite game store, and handed her a bagel while they waited for the doors to open. Meg thought that was lame, but Bailey deemed it the perfect date. That was when he kissed her for the first time. Oh, that kiss! She brushed her lips, not surprised they still tingled. It was amazing and romantic and perfect, and every date was just like that one. They'd been great together. Or so she'd thought.

And then somewhere along the line, he'd stopped respecting her. Little things at first. So little that Bailey hadn't even noticed them. Things like snapping at her, teasing her, rolling his eyes at the things she'd said. But Meg had noticed. And Meg didn't take any crap from anybody. It was one of the things Bailey loved most about her best friend—and also the least.

She frowned at herself for the traitorous thought. She'd first seen Meg's courage that day back in second grade on Bring Your Dad to School Day. There were a bunch of kids in their class who didn't have dads. Bailey didn't, so she asked Gramps, but he had to work, and there was no way her mom's skeevy boyfriend would show up, even if she wanted him to, so Gran came instead. Rather than being grateful, Bailey nearly threw a tantrum because she was the only kid there without a male guest. Abby had brought her uncle.

Karla had brought her big brother. Marc had his mom's boyfriend with him, and Shane, a pudgy kid with a buzz cut, had brought his grandpa, who was also chubby and had a buzz cut. Everyone without a dad had brought someone—except Megan. And she stood up there in the front of that classroom and told everyone her dad *was* there, even though they couldn't see him.

He was watching from heaven.

Bailey thought that was the bravest thing she'd ever seen and told Megan that at recess, when she'd shared her cookies because Meg didn't have a snack. Over the years, she'd come to rely on Meg's courage to say what needed to be said, even when she didn't want to hear it. But Simon wasn't that pair of yoga pants Meg warned her not to buy. He was the love of her life, and now…he wasn't.

Oh, she shouldn't have listened to Meg! She should have talked to Simon and worked things out, but it was too late. He'd never speak to her again. She'd been so sure Simon was "The One." Guys never stuck by her for very long. Meg said it was because Bailey was too nice and that guys appreciated a little strong will once in a while.

Bailey moaned in frustration. It wasn't fair! She just wanted to fall in love. Was that really asking so much? To find someone who loved and adored her in an Edward-loves-Bella way, only in a less stalker-y way, someone who she could fall head over high heels into love with—love song love, movie love. Real, happily-ever-after, to-die-for love.

She thought of Chase and moaned again. Meg had it! She had the kind of love Bailey dreamed about and wished for just a few houses away, only Meg just kept swatting at it like it was some hairy spider. If Chase ever looked at her the way he looked at Meg, she'd never, ever tell him no. He was no Simon, but Chase was strong and quiet and loyal and seriously cute, the way his brown hair dipped over his eyes. *Those eyes.*

Meg had a little shrine in her room dedicated to Chase's eyes. Sure, she never talked about it. But Bailey knew exactly what the various shades of green smeared all over Meg's easel meant. She had it bad for Chase but would rather paint those gorgeous green eyes instead of stare into the real thing. Meg was all about "The Future," and unless Chase Gallagher came with a Satisfaction Guaranteed! promise, there was no room for him in those plans.

The future, she snorted. The future was years and years away! Who cared about that stuff when they were seventeen? She pressed her lips together and sighed at her jeans. They were hopelessly stained. Gran would know some laundry trick that would work. Maybe she should call Gran and pretend she was way more upset than she really was just to get out of spending the rest of the afternoon in these jeans. That was as far into the future as Bailey ever dared to look. She much preferred the present.

Bailey's lips twitched. If Chase were part of *her* present, what would Meg think? If Chase liked *her*, would Meg mind? Would she even notice? Meg would never admit it, never talk about it, but she had a competitive streak in her as wide as Simon's shoulders. Yeah, yeah, it was devious. A little competition might be just what Meg needed to make her appreciate the things she took for granted, things that were right under the nose that was always buried in a textbook or smeared with paint.

Besides—and now Bailey smiled—if Meg was all wrapped up in her own love life, maybe she'd finally butt the hell out of hers.

23

Her mind made up, Bailey considered various ways she could get Chase Gallagher to pay her some attention. She and Meg looked nothing alike. Meg was athletic and brunette, while Bailey was blond and soft, so changing her appearance wouldn't help. And she couldn't produce a decent painting if it came in a Crayola package, so art was out. Bailey's mind discarded various ideas until she remembered Chase's brothers. She could help them with something, obviously not homework because Meg helped Bailey with hers. But maybe… wait! She smacked her forehead. She wouldn't need his brothers. Chase was a game geek just like she was. Plus, he was also into computer programming. Maybe she could convince him to help her build her video game.

She grabbed her phone to text him, even though it was against school rules, and he probably had his on vibrate anyway, but she didn't want to waste another moment. Bailey was totally committed to getting this game built, even though Meg thought it was dumb. She hated video games, though she frequently bounced ideas off her and even sketched some characters. But Bailey always felt like Meg would rather be doing a hundred other things instead of game design.

Bailey deleted her half-typed text message. Maybe she should just forget the stupid video game. It's not like it was going to be her career or anything. Wait. Why couldn't game design be her career? With her eyes rolling, she scolded herself for thinking like Meg. Okay, so she didn't know anything about computers or programming or graphics, but she could learn. She was smart.

Sort of.

When Meg forced her to be.

Bailey locked herself in a graffiti-marked stall that reeked of old cigarettes, sat on one of the toilets, and put her head in her hands. She didn't know—that was the entire problem! She didn't know what she wanted to do, what she wanted to be. Hell, she wasn't even sure of who she was. Just some kid without a dad. The result of another teenage pregnancy. Thankfully, her mother had Gran and Gramps. Bailey wasn't all that sure Nicole would have even kept her if her grandparents hadn't been there. Some days, she wished she had just one answer—just one—instead of nothing but big hairy question marks. She tried. Oh, people could say whatever they wanted, but nobody could say Bailey Grant did not try. She'd tried gymnastics for a while…and horseback riding. She'd even tried to like football (and still wasn't completely sure why anyone actually did).

But none of it made her happy.

And now she had the video game. Meg was always yelling at her for not sticking with things, so this time, she would. She would learn how to create a video game. There had to be something on Google, an app she could buy. Chase would know.

Maybe she wouldn't tell Meg she was working with Chase—if he even said yes.

She tapped out a new message to Chase asking if he'd meet her later and clicked Send. With a happy smile, she looked down at her jeans, which were still stained and now very wet, and decided she'd had enough school for the day.

"Hi, Gran. Can you pick me up? I had a little accident."

It took Bailey five full minutes to assure Gran she wasn't hurt, sick, or in the principal's office. But Gran was on her way. She zipped her bag, left the stall, gave her hair a flip in front of the mirror, and spun around at the sound of a slow clap.

"Oh, you're good. I thought you'd have to pull out the fake tears."

Caitlyn. Wasn't that just perfect? With narrowed eyes, Bailey sneered. "Caitlyn, don't you have a class or maybe someone's boyfriend to steal?"

"Been there, done that. This was a lot more fun." She waved a hand over Bailey's ruined jeans and turned to the mirror to reapply a slick of lip gloss over the dozen or so coats she was already wearing.

Bailey shrugged. "If the stains don't come out, I get to go shopping. It's a win-win."

Caitlyn paused, the gloss wand hovering over full lips. "They won't. Gatorade never does. That was my idea."

Bailey's heart gave a little flutter at that. She knew Simon wouldn't have thought to do it on his own. Even though he'd hurt her, she knew he wasn't cruel. But there was no way she'd let Caitlyn know that. "Then I owe you one." She straightened her spine and bared her teeth.

Caitlyn took a step closer and pinned on a plastic smile. "Isn't Simon just the hottest thing ever? His hands—oh, and the things he can do with his lips." She looked carefully from side to side and lowered her voice. "Well, I don't have to tell you he's got some mad skills seeing as how you were with him." She smoothed her sleek hair in place. "You were with him, right?"

She never gave Bailey a chance to answer. With a flip to the ends of her long blond hair, she headed for the door.

"Oh, well. Just means there's more for me. Bye!"

Bailey watched the door close after Caitlyn and unfisted her hands. *What a total bitch.* She stared at the crescent impressions in her palms and wondered why she was upset. It wasn't like Simon had dumped her. She'd dumped *him.* That was it, wasn't it? That Bailey used to have something Caitlyn now had. It was the way Caitlyn operated, making you second-guess yourself for every little decision. She'd always been that way. Back in first grade, Bailey traded folders with Kimmie Li. Kimmie had *My Little Pony,* while she'd been stuck with *Hello Kitty.* Hello—who wouldn't have made that trade? But Caitlyn put her arm around Kimmie and ooh'd and aah'd over *Hello Kitty.* Wasn't it so cute? Look how it matched her notebook. Did she also have the pajamas and sheets for her bed too? And the whole time—the *entire* time—her eyes stayed pinned on Bailey's.

Bailey never traded anybody anything after that.

If Caitlyn wanted Simon, fine. They could have each other.

She took one last glance at her jeans and sighed.

They really were trashed.

Chapter 3
Meg

Meg strode to the mailbox at the curb. Empty again. She cursed and hurried inside.

"Meg? That you?"

"Hi, Mom. Did you get the mail?" Meg dropped her backpack near the front door and headed for the kitchen.

"Yeah, it's on the table. I have class. I'll see you later." Pauline Farrell hurried past, wet hair ruthlessly scraped back in a ponytail, and patted Meg's cheek on the way by.

Meg rifled through the envelopes piled on the old oak table and froze.

"Mom, wait." Her voice squeaked. "My scores. They're here." She pulled out a chair and slowly sank into it.

Pauline joined her at the secondhand kitchen table, a smile brightening her tired eyes. "Well, what are you waiting for? Open it."

Meg put her hands on the table and drew in a deep breath. For three weeks, she'd been waiting for these scores, and now they were here—the numbers that would determine her future. With her blood pounding in her ears, Meg opened the envelope while Pauline twisted her hands.

She scanned the numbers.

Her shoulders sagged.

She moved her hand to her chest and tried to shove in more air, but it didn't work.

"Honey, it can't be that bad. Let me see."

Meg let the slip of paper fall from her hands and shut her eyes. Pauline took the sheet and gasped.

"Meg, these are good."

Meg thought about The Plan. "Not good enough."

Pauline took a chair beside Meg and pulled her hands away from her face. "Megan. A 1950 is a really great score."

Slowly, mechanically, Meg shook her head. "No, Mom, it's average. I needed to do so much better than average." *Average* didn't get the scholarship money. She'd been counting on it. She'd based her entire plan on it. No scholarship meant no degree. No degree meant no career. No career meant no financial independence.

Her dad would be so ashamed.

Pauline laughed once. "What were you expecting, honey? A perfect 2400?"

Meg gulped back a sob. Pauline didn't get it. The Plan was never anything more than just something Meg and her dad did together. It was never real to Pauline.

And now it would never be real at all.

Pauline's smile slipped. "Megan, look at me." She lifted Meg's chin with a calloused hand. "You're working so hard. But you're putting too much pressure on yourself. And that's my fault." Her tired eyes teared up. "A 1950 is an excellent score. It says here that's the ninetieth percentile. That's much better than I did, and I went to a good school."

"You're right, Mom." But in her mind, she was saying, *Yeah, such a great school and still no degree.*

"Crap, I'm late." Her mother glanced at the clock. "I'll see you later. Sure you're okay?"

"I'm fine." Meg managed a tight smile and even a wave. Only after she heard the front door slam and her mother's car start did she head upstairs to her room and give in to the tears that choked her. She cried until it sapped her energy, until she had nothing left to feed the sobs. It was obvious a really good school wasn't in her future. Her scores were good enough to get in but not good enough for a full ride. She'd need a whole new plan. She'd have to readjust and find one of the local colleges where her pathetic score might get her more financial aid. The degree is what's important, not the school. She just had to get her degree so she could get a high-paying job and never have to—

A light went on in the window across the yard. Her belly flipped and for a second—just for a second—she thought about calling Chase to cry or vent or whatever.

No.

She wiped her eyes, straightened her clothes, and picked up her paintbrush. She would not do that to him.

Instead, she opened oil paints and mixed Prussian blue with Flanders yellow. As a rule, she hoarded these paints. Artist-grade paint was expensive but so much better than working with student-grade materials. Plus, they took forever to dry. But she *had* to find the right green.

She needed to paint Chase. It was the closest she could ever allow herself to get to him. The rest of her plan may be shot to hell, but this—oh, this she would master.

She grabbed one of the small canvases she'd already underpainted and started layering colors. She began with a foundation color. A faint gray. On top of that, she added a circle of the green she'd mixed and then stepped back to critically examine it. Maybe...just maybe. She noted the color mix formula. She added a subtle rim of the black around the green iris and then dabbed on a pupil in the center. She mixed a few more colors—a soft brown for contrast, a warm gold for highlight. She switched to a fine brush and worked from the center out, blending and pulling, stepping back often to examine her results.

She glanced at her bedside clock and cursed. Where had the time gone? She was on the schedule to work tonight, so she quickly capped paint tubes, cleaned brushes, and found her uniform, doing her best to ignore the echo of her dad's voice.

What are you going to do with the rest of your life?

She shoved the thought away. Right now, she was due at the theater, so she fastened her name tag to her uniform, tucked her phone into her pocket, and wondered about what candy to take home for Bailey. Mondays at the theater were usually slow, which meant the time would drag. She should bring her backpack because she hadn't yet done any homework. One good thing about Monday was that it was payday. She needed a few tubes of acrylic paint. At four bucks a tube, she could easily spend her whole paycheck, so she would have to settle for the basics—red, blue, yellow, and white.

She also needed to eat. She frowned at the pathetic contents of the refrigerator. Still no groceries. Her mother hadn't stopped on her way home from work and was off to her class. Pauline worked full time during the day, went to night classes twice a week, and every other night worked as a waitress at the diner on Main Street.

Meg rinsed the coffee cup her mother had left on the counter and then searched for something to eat later. She sighed and smeared peanut butter and jelly on the two heels of the bread loaf left in the bag and then hunted for plastic wrap in the kitchen drawer.

Instead, she found a photograph, creased and stained, stuffed at the bottom of the drawer.

For a long moment, she stared at the picture, sandwiches and plastic wrap forgotten, her hands clenched into fists, her breaths coming in heaving sobs. She grabbed the knife, still smeared with peanut butter and jelly, and drove it through the face in the picture—again and again and again—until the snapshot was shredded, pieces of it glued to the knife. She raised the knife one more time, but a flash of movement caught her eye. She whipped her eyes to the back door.

Chase. Oh, God, Chase.

The knife clattered to the floor.

She shoved the door open and stood in the frame. "What are you doing here?" Her voice was raw.

He swallowed and brought his arms up but never touched her. "Um. I messed up. Big time. Brothers all hate me. Parents disappointed. My only hope for redemption is Happy Meals. Do you need a lift to the theater? I thought we could grab a burger or…you know…" He trailed off.

She wanted to say no. It was better to say no. But she looked at the sandwich on the counter and her stomach rumbled. Finally, she sighed. "Yeah," she said and blinked. "Yeah. Thanks."

Chase made a strange choking sound, stepped over the threshold, and tugged her close to his chest. For a moment, she melted and allowed him to hold her. She even raised her arms and thought about hugging back. But her dad's words replayed in her mind. Instead, she stepped back, set her face in her toughest expression, and bent to clean up the pieces of paper from the floor.

Chase knelt to help and gasped. "Jesus, Megan. What the hell?" he asked with wide eyes, and just like that, she knew he knew about her dad.

He *knew*.

She shot up like an arrow and stalked from the room. He didn't follow. She heard him moving around in the kitchen, the slide of the doors, the click of the lock, the slam of a cabinet door, and she was grateful for a few moments to settle herself down. She was tying on the black tennis shoes that were required with her uniform when he joined her.

"Um. I wrapped up your sandwich. You ready?"

Meg took the wrapped sandwich without looking at him. "Yeah. Thanks."

"No problem." He shrugged. "Why are you so mad at your dad?"

She scowled and rolled her eyes as if the answer was so obvious. "Because he left."

Chase shook his head and reached for her again. "Megan, he *died*. I know you miss him, but—"

She slapped his hand away. "I'm fine. Look, I'm just gonna walk. Thanks for—just thanks." She jerked open the front door and bolted out into the evening chill.

She heard her front door slam and cursed under her breath. She'd forgotten to shut it.

"Megan! Megan, wait," he called.

Meg's long legs ate up the street. She never slowed. Chase broke into a jog, caught up to her, and with an arm on her elbow, spun her around to face him. "Damn it, Megan. I said wait."

She couldn't look at him. She'd lose it if she did. "I'm gonna be late."

"Talk to me, Megan. We're friends. You can trust me."

"Trust you?" She laughed once, a "yeah right" laugh. "You're a guy." The last time she'd trusted him, she'd gotten a C- on a project! It was her lowest grade ever. A C- would never get the scholarships or the high-paying jobs. All a C- would get her is locked into the life she was trying so hard to escape.

He took half a step back, like she'd slapped him. "Megan, come on. You've known me how many years now? When have I ever let you down? Just talk to me. Tell me what's wrong."

She looked up at him, and for a second, she wished she could just unload and tell him everything. Tell him about her dad, about her plan, about the feelings she really did have for him but pretended not to. He reached out and—

"Meg! Chase! Hey, guys!"

Chase spun around to watch Bailey jogging over to them and groaned. Meg caught her eye for a second—less than a second—and took the opportunity to run.

Chapter 4
Bailey

Bailey bounced down the porch steps and hurried down the street to Meg's house just in time to see the fireworks.

"Megan! Megan, wait!" Chase was…well, chasing Meg from her house down the street. She ignored him and kept stalking. Uh-oh. Bailey had seen that walk before—a lot. She called it the Meg March. It rattled the dishes in Gran's cabinets. It could mean only one thing.

Meg was seriously pissed.

Bailey shrugged. It didn't take much to piss Meg off, and whatever it was, she was sure she would quickly get over it because for Meg, anger was a lot like a sugar high—it peaked fast, burned off, and then she'd crash. If she needed to talk, she'd text, but right now, she'd focus on her work because Meg always gave things 100 percent. Bailey, however, was between jobs. For her, jobs were like boys. She couldn't seem to hold on to either for very long.

With a mental kick, Bailey snapped herself out of her pity party and slowed up her steps when Chase grabbed Meg's elbow and spun her around. Wow. That was so romantic, and Meg didn't have a clue. She waited—neither of them had noticed her yet, and she wouldn't have said a word, not one peep, if she hadn't seen Meg's face.

Meg was on the edge of a complete blurt.

Oh, God! What should she do? Meg hated the Blurt—she called it verbal diarrhea—with the same level of intensity she usually saved for a bad grade. But this was Chase, the boy next door with the fairy-tale eyes who adored her and needed just one opportunity to show how her much. She could duck between cars or maybe dive behind those shrubs or—damn it!· She could see Meg take a deep breath. Blurt was imminent, so Bailey did what friendship demanded.

"Meg! Chase! Hey, guys!" she shouted and hoped nobody noticed how shrill her voice was.

They spun around. She heard Chase curse but saw the relief that flashed across Meg's face, and then Meg was gone, practically running down the street. *You're welcome,* she thought.

Bailey turned to Chase with an overbright smile. She'd really wanted to see *him,* not Meg. Her smile faded when she got a good look at his face. "Hey. You okay?"

Chase's worried green eyes rolled skyward and he shook his head once. "Not even close."

"What did she do now?" Bailey asked, already aching on his behalf. He was a good guy and Meg needed to start appreciating that instead of pushing him away.

Chase raked both hands through his hair. "Bailey, what the hell did her dad do to her?"

Bailey's eyes popped. Meg didn't talk about her dad, not with anybody, and that included her.

Bailey twisted a curl and considered Chase for a moment. She decided it was best to stick to the obvious. "Um…he died."

Chase spun around, muttered something she didn't catch, and then spun back. "Yeah, I got that part. Why the hell is she mad enough to stab pictures of him?"

Her mouth fell open. Stabbing pictures? There were no pictures of Meg's dad in her house that she had ever seen, so she didn't know anything about why Meg would be stabbing them.

Chase made a choking sound and bent over to grab his knees. Bailey stepped closer and patted him on the back because it was the only thing she could think to do. Then again, she didn't really know why he was so upset.

"Oh, God. Oh, my God, Bailey. Did he…did he, you know…*hurt* Meg?"

Of course he'd hurt Meg. She was only six or seven years old when he died, and Meg missed him. Bailey looked closer at the sick expression on Chase's face, and her eyes popped in understanding. "Oh! You mean—no. Eww. No." She shook her head. "No, it was nothing like that. She's just mad at him for dying, you know?"

Chase shook his head. "I've seen her mad lots of times—well, pretty much all the time—but not like this. She was—it was like she was burning with it. I mean, off the charts with mad."

Bailey smiled once. "Yeah, that's how she gets. I'm sure it's nothing serious, Chase."

"Nothing serious?" Chase stared at her like she'd sprouted a huge zit between her eyes. "Bailey, no offense, but this is like the most serious shit I've ever seen. I was about to pick up a flowerpot and heave it through the glass door."

Okay, this had gone far enough. If there was one thing Bailey knew, it was how to handle Megan Farrell, and Chase needed to understand he was doing it all wrong. "Chase, you need to back off. Meg hates people getting all up in her face when something's bothering her. She'll get over it on her own. The more you nag her, the more you try to 'be there for her,' the madder she'll get," Bailey said, making air quotes. "By the time she gets home from work, she'll be back to normal. Trust me."

Chase continued to stare at Bailey. She rubbed her forehead. Definitely no zit.

"What?"

"Bailey, you know what's up, don't you?" He folded his arms and frowned. "The anxiety attacks, the mood swings—you know."

Uh-oh.

"Bailey, tell me." He stepped closer.

Bailey shook her curls.

"I need to know." He grabbed her arms.

She shook her head again. "No, Chase. She doesn't talk about it. She doesn't want anyone to know. I don't even know all of it." There was only one thing she could say that he'd really hear. "You want to impress her? You want her to love you back? Let Meg keep her secrets." She smiled brightly at his look of confusion and barreled ahead. "I was heading to your place to see you anyway. Are you busy tonight? I want to talk to you about a video game."

Chase blinked and then lifted his brows. "A video game or *your* video game?"

"Um…yeah, my video game. I was hoping you could help me actually build it."

His eyebrows pinched together. "Right. Your famous video game. I've heard you and Megan talking about it. So you really want to build it?"

Bailey's face split into a wide grin. "Yeah, I love video games. It's like *Assassin's Creed*, *Call of Duty*, *Halo*, and *Dance Party Central* all combined into one. I have character histories, settings, rules of engagement, levels—all of it."

"Um, *Dance Party*?" Chase repeated. "Um…it sounds, uh…great."

Bailey rolled her eyes. "Yes, controller-less play. I want a gesture interface."

Chase's eyebrows leaped into his hairline, and she beamed. When his mouth fell open, she laughed. "I want to tell you what I have so far. Wanna grab a burger?" Bailey knew a lot about gaming but only a little about computer programming. She just liked playing video games and figured designing one couldn't be much harder than writing down all the outcomes and handing it all off to a programmer to code. Chase was a member of the computer club at school. Who better to take her baby from idea to reality?

Chase's teeth snapped shut, and she was sure he'd rolled those emerald eyes of his behind their lids. She shrugged. He wasn't saying no, so Bailey counted it as a win.

"The McDonald's next to the theater okay with you?" he asked.

Bailey's lips twitched. That was right where Meg worked. This couldn't be more perfect. She wanted Meg to see her with Chase. It was time Meg realized that Chase Gallagher was a total hottie and wasn't going to wait forever for her to get her head out of her butt.

Ten minutes later, they were eating burgers and fries at a table near the window. Meg would be sure to see them if she was working the ticket counter. Bailey told him all about her game, but Chase was brooding.

"Chase?"

He shook his head once like he was knocking loose a blockage. "Uh, sorry, Bay. What were you saying?"

"Okay. It's based on our history class from last year. I was having trouble passing, so Meg helped me come up with a way to remember all those facts and places and dates and people and stuff and so—" she said and splayed out her hands with a flourish, "video game!"

"Uh-huh." Chase just looked more confused, so Bailey started over.

"Okay, it's pretty simple actually." She bit into her burger and talked with her mouth full. "Players move from level to level by figuring out what really led to the major historical incidents of a particular time period, like the Renaissance or the Crusades or World War I."

Chase's eyebrows rose as he sipped his Coke. "What do you mean...what really happened?"

Bailey bounced in her seat. "Well, it started when Meg told me that there isn't just one thing that led to the major incidents throughout history. Usually, it was a combination of things, a buildup, a chain reaction. Our history books just scratch the surface. There are dozens of things that never make it into the books, like the Civil War wasn't only about slavery and World War I wasn't only about Archduke Ferdinand's assassination."

"What was it about?"

"Well, the Civil War was also about money."

"Money?"

"Yeah." She emptied her fries into a pool of ketchup. "Slave labor was free except for...you know, buying the slaves and having to feed them and take care of them and stuff. But that was still cheaper than running a big Southern cotton plantation with paid labor. And then there was the imbalance between the heavily industrialized North and plantation South."

"Imbalance?"

"In the electoral college."

Chase blinked at her. "Right. The electoral college."

Bailey rubbed her lips. No ketchup. She angled her head at Chase, but he just kept looking at her. "Um, yeah...so the country was already pretty much divided politically before the slavery issue heated up."

She paused to pop a French fry in her mouth. Chase scratched his head and narrowed his eyes.

"So what caused World War I?"

"World War I was really caused by the sinking of the *Lusitania*, but even that was a conspiracy designed by—what?" Bailey grabbed a napkin and rubbed her forehead when Chase looked at her funny again.

Chase shook his head. "Um...nothing. I'm just impressed."

Bailey's face split into a wide grin. "Really? You are?"

"Yeah, but there's one problem. The Crusades? Renaissance? *Assassin's Creed* already did that."

Bailey shook her head. "Yeah, I know. That's why there's more."

"More?"

"Yeah. Time travel, you know, like *Halo's* slipspace or maybe campaigns like in *Call of Duty*. I'm not really sure yet. But players are chasing these bad guys who are really aliens through time—kind of like Lavos in *Chrono Trigger*, only a lot more—before they can change history.

"Um. Aliens. Right."

"No, seriously. It starts off with a mission, you know, like a 'Should you choose to accept it' thing." Bailey made air quotes. "You travel back in time to figure out what set off that moment in history and discover it's nothing like what the textbooks told you. It's an alien invasion. You battle the aliens and then rewrite the history books so that the truth is hidden."

"Why do you have to hide the truth?"

"Because the MIBs work without glory, without fame."

"MIB? Like the movie?" Chase blinked at her and finally smiled. "Okay. What the hell? Tell me more."

Bailey squealed. "Yay! Okay. It's called *Lost Time*." Bailey told him how she envisioned playing the game, describing the various levels and achievements as well as characters and their backstories.

"How long have you been working on this?"

"Since sophomore year."

"What about wire frames for the landscapes or maps of the time periods?"

Bailey frowned and shook her head. "I...well, I'm not a great programmer."

"Can you program at all?" He finished his burger and licked ketchup from his fingers.

She shrugged. "I mess around in Java, but I suck." She slurped the bottom of her Coke. Simon had promised to buy her the software she needed to build her video game. They'd spent hours talking about it, arguing over the points system and leveling up, how the environment would look. He'd said he was impressed too. Her eyes misted and she blinked the tears away.

"It's not hard if you know the basics. I can get you a game library. Know what that is?"

Bailey nodded. That was the software Simon had promised her. "Sure. It lets you use precoded objects for common functions."

"Right. I'll get you one and you can—"

Bailey stopped him with a raised hand. "Yeah, I know what it is, but I don't know what to do with it."

"Oh, okay. I've got a few game engines we can try out."

That term was new. "What's that?"

"It's software that helps you rapidly develop video games. It does the heavy lifting, like rendering graphics—"

Bailey held up a hand again. "Yeah, and that's when you lose me."

Chase grinned. "Sorry."

"No, no, I have to learn all this." She didn't mention that learning how to use all this software would help her stop obsessing over Simon.

"So what do you have so far?"

"Nothing digital. I have notebooks filled with sketches Meg did and notes I've been making on the rules, the maps, and stuff."

Chase's face tightened when she mentioned Meg. Bailey squeezed his hand. "I know it doesn't feel like it, but trust me, she likes you too."

His eyes slipped shut. "I wish."

"I know her, Chase. Better than she knows herself. She's nuts about you. She paints you."

Chase's face lit up like a five-year-old's at a playground. "Me? She paints *me?*"

"Yep. Like every day. And she'd *kill* me if she knew I told you that, so that stays between us, okay?" She stood up and piled their trash on the tray.

Chase stood and grabbed her in a hug.

"Oh! Um…it's okay, Chase. She'll come around."

"Thanks, Bay." He grinned and took the tray.

Bailey glanced toward the theater and smiled. *Please tell me Meg saw that!* She prayed.

Chapter 5
Meg

Meg sat at the ticket counter gleaming brightly under the harsh lights. She'd cleaned it about six times so far. And refilled the machines with paper. And reorganized the gift card supply. And even brought her homework to do during her break. She stared out the window, her fingers itching for a paintbrush, a sketchbook, something—anything that would occupy her mind for more than a minute.

Stupid, stupid, stupid! Losing her cool over a stupid picture…in front of Chase. She shut her eyes and groaned. He'd looked at her with horror. But he hadn't run. He never judged. Well, okay, he *was* shocked, but still, the only thing she saw in those potent eyes was worry, and that made her feel kind of warm and fuzzy. She scrubbed at another spot on the counter and felt sick. He shouldn't worry about her. She shouldn't like that he did. They weren't dating. They weren't even friends—at least not like she and Bailey were. How had this happened? Despite all her efforts, despite The Plan, Chase was sneaking under her carefully drawn lines, and damn it, she wanted more.

The research project they'd been partnered up on last semester had been a lesson in more ways than one. She wasn't sure how it had happened. They'd visited the Museum of Modern Art on their own because Bailey had some family commitment and couldn't make it. Chase wasn't the least bit saddened by that news. He'd bought her train ticket, pulled her out of the path of a taxi that jumped the light, and let her push him from floor to floor to stare at exhibits. At some point during all that, the echoes of her dad's voice died away. She never protested when he dragged her to Rockefeller Center, pointed to a spot, and said, "This is where the tree goes every year. Close your eyes and imagine it's Christmas." She did, and he kissed her, and it was like all the colors in the world exploded.

They'd had a great day and finished all the research they'd had to do. On the train ride home, she'd even let Chase make plans—movies, the school dance. He even said something about taking her to his prom. They'd "worked" for hours after they'd gotten home, talking, laughing, sharing, and eventually typing up their paper. Long after the sky had darkened, Chase stood up, said he was going on a food run, came back, and served her.

Her cold little heart thawed and then melted for him and then refroze when they'd gotten their grades.

C-.

She'd never gotten such a low grade before. She hadn't really talked to him about it. She'd just…stayed away. It hurt. But it got easier every day. She was over it. Mostly.

The next movie would start in less than an hour. She would soon be busy again. She tossed the rag on the shelf under the counter and looked out through the glass doors and—*bam!* Her gaze locked on him like a guided missile. Her belly did that slow roll it always did when she saw him, and she *knew* she had that stupid smile on her face.

And then he grabbed Bailey in a hug.

The earth tilted on its axis. Her stomach pitched. Her smile burned—oh, how it burned. Her fingers curled with the need to tear Bailey's highlighted curls out by their roots. When she found herself at the door with no memory of giving her legs the command to walk, she forced air into her paralyzed lungs.

In.

Out.

Damn it. It wasn't supposed to be like this. She'd taken every precaution—stayed distant, apart, aloof. It wasn't supposed to hurt. It wasn't supposed to *matter*.

No. Fight it. She forced herself to see through the green mist of jealousy. Green Envy, she'd call this color if she were painting this scene. Or maybe Jade Avarice. Calmer, she recited her list of reasons. She had to focus on school. She had to graduate. She had to find scholarship money and get a degree. It didn't matter what field. Any degree. Something that would help her find a good job. A job with benefits. A future. The Future. *Her* future. She *had* to be able to take care of herself. She'd promised her dad she would not waver. This hurt would stop soon as long as she was smart and stayed on course.

The other hurt never would.

Chapter 6
Bailey

Bailey figured that ordering burgers for two parents and four brothers would take a long time, so she decided to visit Meg while Chase fed the Gallagher army.

"Hey!" She skipped through the doors and waved with her whole arm.

Meg lifted her head, and Bailey gasped. "What's wrong?" Meg's face was pale and her eyes were just…flat. "Are you still mad at Chase?"

Meg grunted once. Bailey couldn't tell if that was a yes or a no or a laugh or a sob. "Hey…so Chase said he'll help me with the game. Isn't that great?" Bailey bounced on her toes.

Flat dark eyes snapped to hers. "Great. Sure."

Bailey bit her lip and blinked back tears. Meg was—*oh!* Of course, she saw the hug! *Achievement: Unlocked.* Bailey swallowed her smile and glanced over her shoulder. "Chase should be here in a minute. He's picking up burgers for his entire family. He was supposed to pick up Dylan and forgot, so Dylan walked all the way home by himself, and his parents are totally pissed about it, and then Ethan and Evan cried because Dylan and Chase were fighting, and then Connor got mad because Dylan yelled at him, and all that made his parents even angrier," she said before she paused for a breath. "So Chase promised to buy everyone Happy Meals to make them feel better."

Meg only stared at her, so Bailey thought she should tighten the screws—nothing too cruel, just a little twist. "Oh, I almost forgot why I came in. I just wanted to tell you not to come by after work. Chase and I will be working on the game. I mean, you can come over if you want to, but Chase will be there and I know you don't like leading him on and stuff, so—"

"So."

Meg said nothing more. Bailey shivered. She'd always heard about people acting cold, but she'd never actually been on the receiving end of such frost before, and she didn't like it. But it was for the best of reasons, and Meg would forgive her.

Eventually.

She hoped.

She glanced over her shoulder again, saw Chase carrying two huge bags of food, and decided it would be best if she helped him instead of waiting in here. "Bye!" She spread the word over two syllables, waved, and hurried out of the theater before Meg said a word, biting back her smiles all the way home.

When Chase dropped her in front of her grandparents' house, she figured she'd find Gramps in the family room with his newspapers and coffee. Gran would probably be doing the laundry or making up some delicious treat in the kitchen. She walked up the porch steps, fished for her key, and heard a car pull into the drive. She turned, watched her mother climb from a hot sports car, a BMW coupe by the looks of the front end. Bailey had dated a boy who had driven one—well, it must have been his parents' car—but it was still pretty cool. He'd taken her to the movies and to dinner and dropped her off. What was his name? With a mental shrug, she decided it didn't matter. He'd never asked her to go out with him again. Stupid jerk.

Nicole climbed out of the passenger seat, her curly blond hair ruthlessly straightened by a Brazilian blowout. She didn't shoot Bailey the warning look, the one that warned her time and again she was to pretend to be Nicole's kid sister, not her daughter. Bailey froze in place. Should she run down and meet her or stay where she was? Her entire routine was now out of step. Nicole smiled brightly and waved, and Bailey instantly knew her mother planned to introduce her to the latest guy.

This was serious. Like big. Deal. Serious.

Okay, I can do this. She shot back her own bright grin and a waved. "How was your trip?" she asked, slipping into a new routine—that of the loving daughter.

"Bailey, this is John. John, this is my daughter, Bailey." Nicole's smile was pretty realistic, and she even slipped an arm around Bailey's waist, pulling her close. Bailey only just managed to keep her face from registering shock at this major playbook revision.

John never got out of the car to meet her. That cost him some points in Bailey's opinion. He leaned over the floor-mounted shifter and shook her hand. He was hot, she supposed, in that soft corporate way she knew her mother found attractive. He gripped her hand longer than necessary, and his eyes did a careful head-to-toe inspection. One look at the gleam in his dark eyes, and she knew exactly what thoughts were circling his brain.

Perv.

She tugged her hand out of his grasp and subtly wiped it down her pants.

After a moment or two of small talk, John reversed out of the driveway and headed down the street. Nicole stared after the car, her expression unreadable.

"So?" Bailey dropped the act. "How was it really?"

Nicole dropped her arm from Bailey's waist. "I don't know yet. When he found out I live with my parents, he freaked and actually asked me if I was in debt." They unlocked the front door, called out greetings to Gramps, and walked into the kitchen. "Then he had the nerve to suggest I was only interested in his money."

Maybe it wasn't the only thing that interested her, but money *was* a big factor in who Nicole dated, though Bailey knew better than to point that out.

"So I told him about you. He handled *unwed teen mom* better than *gold digger*." Nicole poured coffee into a cup and sat at the kitchen table. "We have another date lined up." Nicole saw Bailey's frown. "What's wrong? I thought you'd be happy to not have to pretend to be my sister anymore."

"Mom, do you love this guy even a little?"

Nicole looked at her over the rim of her coffee cup, her blue eyes serious. "Love?" She laughed once. "Bay, love is—oh, hell. I was in love once. Real, gut-twisting, toe-curling love." She stared into the bottom of her cup and shook her head. "It wasn't enough." When she lifted her eyes, Bailey gasped at the heartbreak in them. "I wasn't enough." Nicole blurted in an uncharacteristic moment of total honesty. "John's good for me, Bailey. As long as we like each other, the rest will come." Nicole stood, drained her cup, and put it in the sink. "See you later. I need to shower." She waved and went upstairs.

Ewwww.

Bailey washed the cup her mother left in Gran's sparkling sink, her mouth in a tight line. She hated when Nicole performed her act. This was the guy she hoped to spend her life with! Wasn't love supposed to be exciting and passionate and romantic and fun? Bailey knew that was her fault. Nicole often told her that most of her boyfriends freaked out and took off as soon as they set eyes on Bailey. They didn't want a kid any more than Nicole did. A pang of guilt halted Bailey's thoughts, and she reminded herself that at least Nicole tried. Her dad hadn't even stuck around long enough for that. He'd bailed the second the stick turned blue...or the plus sign appeared...or whatever the tests did seventeen years ago.

She set the coffee cup in the dish drain to dry and trudged upstairs to her room. Nicole's off-key shower singing made her smile. Her date must have been more fun than she'd shared. That was something at least. But then Bailey's smile faded. She didn't have a teen daughter of her own, and yet guys didn't stick with her very long either. Maybe it was a Grant curse. Maybe she should just accept reality and stop dreaming about love and happily-ever-afters and be more like Meg. Practical, realistic, determined Meg, who wasn't going to let any guy sway her from her plans, including the guy next door who was madly, passionately, and pointlessly in love with her.

Bailey clicked through channels for five solid minutes before she huffed out a heavy sigh and tossed the remote to her comfy full-sized bed and wondered why she even bothered to try watching TV because there was never anything good on unless it was Thursday night when *The Vampire Diaries* aired. She thought about playing Xbox, but what fun would it be without Simon? She logged into Facebook and read the status updates her friends had posted. No, it wasn't true that she'd bloodied Simon's nose. No, it wasn't true that she'd caught Simon with Caitlyn's pom-poms and—*gasp*—of course it wasn't true that she was pregnant.

God! She rolled her eyes. People should get a life. She abandoned Facebook and decided to update her blog. She typed her name and password and waited for the site to appear. Her blog had been a work in progress, as Meg always said, since the day she'd started it. At one point, she'd called it "Grant's Random Ramblings"—that had been when she was in her heavy metal rock phase and had a mad crush on a satellite radio DJ named Grant Random. She'd written a three-part series on stamp collecting—that's when the site had seen its lowest dip in visitors ever—and then switched to reviewing her favorite TV show episodes. Those were always fun. But lately, the blog had become a place where she could just muse and vent and wonder and dream, which is why she now called it "Take It for Granted."

It's been a hard day. I guess days are always hard after a breakup, especially a breakup you don't really want. But when the guy you're seeing, the guy you think could be "The One," suddenly starts looking at you like he's bothered and would rather get cavities filled instead of be with you, don't you have to ask yourself which is harder—breaking up or staying together? I'm lucky to have a friend like Meg who forces me to call it what it is—total crap! When you do that, when you have that, even the hard stuff is a little bit easier.

Bailey twirled her hair and bit her thumbnail while she considered how to respond to the various rumors posted on Facebook. She finally decided that complete denial was the best idea. She wrote a paragraph on the rumors and then switched to tips on removing red Gatorade from expensive jeans—you know, just in case Caitlyn decided to try it on anybody else. Her thoughts turned to her absent dad and she added one last thought before she posted the update.

> Times like this are when I miss having a dad the most. I wonder if he'd be like Bella's dad, you know—all I'm-a-cop-so-I-know-how-to-use-a-gun. Or would he come up to my room with a bowl of ice cream and a movie and tell me the guy's a total loser for not seeing the girl he sees and keep handing me tissues while I cried away my broken heart? Or maybe he'd slam his hand on the table and shout, "I never liked that boy anyway."

Bailey thought about talking to Gramps about Simon, but the one time she'd talked to him about a boy, he turned sheet white and fled, tossing something that sounded like "Go ask your mother!" over his shoulder on the way out.

She published the new blog update and trolled her favorite social networks for a little while. Simon's relationship status was single, but Caitlyn's was "in a relationship." She tried not let that bother her.

Failed miserably.

She switched over to email and saw her new blog post had already gotten a comment.

> Sorry about your breakup. Why'd you end things if you didn't want to? I'm a guy. I wouldn't look at you the way I look at my dentist.

Aww, that was so sweet. It was from someone signing his name as WyldRyd11. She clicked his profile link, but there was no photo. Only a one-sentence bio: *Gamer, athlete, lover. Serious girls, inquire within.*

She thought about it and decided to reply.

> Thanks for your comment, WyldRyd11. I broke up with him because I
> don't think he wants to be with me, and I deserve to be with someone
> who does.

That sounded exactly like something Meg would say. She was right, wasn't she?
Why be with someone if that someone wants someone else? Bailey crossed her
arms over her chest and wondered when the ache in her heart would go away,
when the urge to keep checking for messages from him would stop.

Chapter 7
Meg

"Megan, a word with you please."

The manager on duty did not look happy, but Meg followed him to the employee lounge, where the scent of stale popcorn and pizza hung so thick in the air that she could taste them. He scraped out a chair from under the table, where an empty soda can sat in a pool of condensation.

"Have a seat. How ya doin'?"

"I'm fine." She knew what he was going to say but sat anyway. Best to just rip off the bandage instead of prolonging the pain.

Mr. Reese pulled an envelope from his suit jacket's pocket. "This is your last paycheck, Megan. I'm sorry. The theater's closing in three weeks. I can't afford to keep you on the whole time." Bushy eyebrows climbed over the rims of his glasses when he gave a helpless shrug.

She took the envelope and nodded. She'd known it was coming. This tiny two-screen theater just couldn't compete with the multiplex that had opened a year before, with its eighteen screens and restaurant food brought right to your seat.

"You're a hard worker, Megan. Never gave me a minute of trouble. So I tucked a letter of recommendation in there too. Maybe that googleplex can use you," Mr. Reese said with a sad smile.

Meg laughed once, wondering if Mr. Reese made the lame joke on purpose, and shook her head. She wouldn't apply there. It…well, it wouldn't feel right.

"Thanks, Mr. Reese." She stood, took the soda can, and tossed it in the recycle can on her way out.

"Megan?"

She turned at the door, surprised to see Mr. Reese's eyes wet. "Grab some boxes of candy on your way out. I know how much you like those things."

She grinned through the bright stab of pain. "Parting gifts?"

Mr. Reese shrugged. "A token of appreciation."

"Thanks. Um, bye. Oh…here." She took off her name tag and put it on the table.

Outside in the cold night air, she felt nothing. Absolutely nothing. No anger, no fear, no regret. Just a numbness that was kind of a pleasant change of pace. She walked home, the bag holding two boxes of the Junior Mints for Bailey and two boxes of M&M's for herself. The boxes banged her thigh with each step. It was early. She thought about heading over to Bailey's place, but she didn't want to see any more of her wrapped in Chase's strong arms.

The pain stabbed her again, putting a hitch in her step, but she didn't falter. Tomorrow, she'd visit the stores within walking distance and find another job. She would have to buy canvas soon and—

"Hey."

Megan froze, one foot still in the air. Her lips instantly twitched up, and she tried her hardest not to smile, knowing she'd fail miserably but trying anyway.

"What are you doing here?" She put her foot down, forced herself to walk up the porch steps to the front door, where Chase sat looking like a poor, abandoned puppy.

"Uh...waiting for you."

"Why?"

"I...I had a fight with my parents after dinner and had to get out for a while."

"You've been sitting here that long?"

Chase shrugged. "I don't know. Maybe. Well, first, I hid in the garage for an hour and pounded nails. Then I came here. That was long enough ago to freeze my ass off."

"Pounded nails?"

He gave her half a laugh. "Yeah, I do that to channel my 'excess rage.'" He quoted the psychobabble with an exaggerated eye-roll.

"Does it work?"

He blinked. "Um...yeah, it kinda does." He climbed slowly to his feet, wincing as he stretched.

Jesus, he must be frostbitten by now. She dug her keys out of her pocket. "Why didn't you go to Bailey's?" She would not look at him. She would not let him see how much it hurt her to see him with Bailey.

Chase frowned. "I...I didn't think about it. I just...wanted to come here. Can I come in?"

Didn't think about it. She whipped her head up at that. And then the rest of his question penetrated her Green Envy brain. He wanted to come in? *Red alert!* She swallowed hard and nodded. "I guess. For a few minutes."

She unlocked the door, shoved it open, and flipped on a light in the living room. The clock on the wall said it was 10:00 p.m. Her mother wouldn't be back for hours yet.

Not good.

She tossed the bag of candy on the garage sale coffee table that she'd covered in red paint and peeled off her hoodie. "Um, you can sit down." She sat on the chair well away from the sofa.

Chase sat with a loud sigh, angling his body to face her chair. He filled damn near half the couch that way, his long legs stretched in front of him. He rubbed his hands together to warm them. She should make him hot cocoa or something. If she did, he'd want to stay.

She remained in her chair.

"Um…so how was work tonight?"

"Um—" Meg looked at her hands and tried to force words out of a throat that had suddenly formed a lump. "Not so good, I guess, since it was my last night." She gulped.

Chase shifted in a blur, leaned forward, his hands hanging through the gap between his knees. The expression in his eyes went from weary to worried in a microsecond. "They let you go? So soon? That sucks. I mean, I figured they'd keep you on until the end, you know?"

"Yeah." She folded into herself, tried to stay positive. "I'm sure I'll find something else."

"Well, yeah, duh. You're a good worker."

Her lips twisted into a sneer. "And how do you know that?"

"I know you."

Her amusement disappeared.

He waited a moment and then made a sound of frustration. "Megan, why do you always do that?" He flung himself back against the cushions.

"What?"

"That." He retorted, waving a hand in the air between them. "Look uncomfortable whenever I say something nice."

"I'm not uncomfortable." She straightened her spine.

"Yeah, right. You don't even want me in here. You're so uncomfortable you had to sit across the room from me. God! It's like you actually think I'm gonna attack you or something."

Meg's mouth hung open for a moment. "Um...I'm sorry. I didn't mean to make you uncomfortable." Jeez, how did her life get to be this soap opera?

Chase flung his head back and shut his eyes. "Megan, I came here because I needed a friend to talk to." He lifted his head and met her confused gaze. "You're the only person I feel comfortable talking with. I just wish you felt that way about me." He finished with a shrug, his eyes a storm of emotion.

Meg stared for a minute, her steel resolve now a puddle of molten indecision. "I'm sorry," she repeated, meaning it this time. "So...what happened today to cause this fight?"

He shut his eyes again, and Meg wanted to protest. Even in the low light of the lamp on the table where she sat, his eyes drew her in, and she wanted to see them. She waited, not patiently, while he collected his thoughts.

"It's not a pretty story. It ends with no college. No lacrosse. No life—except for watching my brothers and helping at the store."

She gasped. No college meant no degree. No degree meant no career. No career meant no financial independence. He'd be—

"Trapped," he whispered, and she blinked at his uncanny ability to know exactly what she'd been thinking. "I don't know if I can stand it." He let his head fall into his hands. "I can hardly stand it now."

She ached to move closer to him, to put her hand on his back and rub small circles to comfort him. So she slid her hands under her legs and forced herself to remain in her chair.

"In September, I planned to go to community college. My parents won't let me go away to school and I didn't get any scholarships, so that was the only option left. But today, there was a coach from Manhattan College at practice. He had a bunch of kids change their minds and decide to go to other schools. He's got spots to fill and decided to give us a chance."

He slouched lower on the old lumpy secondhand sofa. "My mom triple-booked herself today, and somehow, that was *my* problem. She texts me in school, tells me I have to pick up Dylan at some birthday party because Connor's got music lessons and she had to take Ethan and Evan to the doctor. I don't have the car, and she wants me to take the bus all the way home to get it, come back to pick up Dyl, and then go to practice. I'm annoyed, but I say okay because...well, it's not really a choice, you know?"

Frustration rolled off his shoulders in waves, but she let him vent.

"Then I find out about the coach, and there's no way I can miss practice now. So I text her back, tell her I can't pick up Dylan. Only she never got that text. Dylan walked home by himself, and I—"

He didn't need to finish the sentence. Meg could see the what-ifs play out on his face and knew every one of those scenarios ended horribly.

"Anyway, my dad shows up at practice. We fight all the way home. Then I get the cold shoulder from my mom and then Dylan won't talk to me and Ethan and Evan are up my ass about old Micro-Machines they found in my room, which they're not supposed to be in and—" Chase flung up his arms in a huge shrug and then let them fall. "Sorry. I guess I didn't use enough nails."

She shook her head but said nothing. Sighing, Chase shut his eyes and scrubbed both hands over his face.

He lifted his head and turned Technicolor eyes burning with pride on her. "The point is, the coach liked me, Megan. Me."

The feeble bulb in the lamp next to her flickered once. Her stomach flipped and she squirmed in her seat. Yeah, even lightbulbs reacted to Chase's power.

"He told me to get the application in right away—there's still money left. I have no idea how much or even if they'll give me any, but I have to try."

She nodded. Of course he did.

His phone buzzed. He dug it out of his pocket, frowned, and ignored it, tossing it on the bright red coffee table.

"They must need someone to run an errand." He sneered at the phone. "Probably didn't even notice I was gone until now."

Meg knew that wasn't true. His family adored Chase. Whenever she saw them all together, Chase's mom and dad always wore smiles so full of pride. The thought gave her pangs in her chest.

"I don't know what to do, Megan. Can I stay here? I can sleep on the couch. Please?"

Yes, God, yes! Her stomach pitched and fell. *Crap.* "No, Chase. My mom would have a fit. Don't you have any…any, like, *guy* friends who can help, friends whose relationship statuses aren't lies?"

He snapped his mouth shut and stood up. "I'm outta here."

He was leaving. Good. That's what she wanted. So why did she suddenly blurt out, "You're already eighteen. You don't need their permission anymore."

His eyes widened as they snapped to hers. "You mean, just…just defy them?" He sank back down to the sofa.

Slowly, she nodded. "Yes, they can't stop you from doing what you want now."

He rolled his eyes. "Oh, yes, they can. They can kick me out."

"You have money. You can get your own place."

"Megan, my money is their money. I work in the store whenever they need me. The credit card and the allowance are all theirs. I have nothing that's mine. Not really."

That was the entire problem, she knew. She suffered from the same problem—a deep need to do something that she could take pride in. Something that was hers.

"Chase, what do you want to do?"

He groaned. "That's the problem! I have no idea. I only know I really don't want to work in a bakery until I die." He angled his head at her. "What about you? What do you want?"

She swallowed thickly. Her plan, her future, and everything in it faded to green when she looked in his eyes. Her heart raced and her throat tightened. What did she want? Or maybe the right question was who did she really want?

She shook her head. Who, what. It didn't matter.

It was the one thing she could never have.

Chapter 8
Bailey

Bailey sat alone in her room, steadily exploring Facebook for signs of Simon. He hadn't posted an update all day.

He was probably over at Caitlyn's house. She kicked the pile of clothes on the floor. She checked her email too. Still nothing. Oh, this was stupid and pointless and maddening, so she turned to her game system. Maybe spilling some blood and guts in *Call of Duty* would get her mind off Simon. She signed in, loaded up the game, and noticed someone had messaged her. She really hoped it wasn't another of those annoying Tenth Prestige Lobby invites.

Like she needed to cheat.

From: WyldRyd11
To: Goldilx

Hey, I got your gamertag off a *Call of Duty* forum and I thought maybe we could play a match together—I totally want you on my team. I'll be online Monday from three until about seven. If you're online, I'll invite you.

WyldRyd11. Wow, what are the odds? He probably didn't even know that her Goldilx gamertag and "Take It for Granted" blog were her. He didn't say what forum, not that it mattered since she was in about eight of them. With a shrug, she figured it couldn't do any harm, so she decided to accept the invitation if and when it came through. She'd just made her first kill when the invite flashed. She accepted it and started a new game.

"Hi, this is Goldilx." She spoke into her headset, but no one answered, which was weird since she could plainly see WyldRyd11's avatar on the screen, leaping from an abandoned truck. She pressed the Guide button on her controller and found another message.

From: WyldRyd11
To: Goldilx

Sorry! Headset's broke. I can hear you but can't talk back. My name's Ryder. What's yours?

Bailey smiled. "Oh…hi, Ryder! My name's Bailey. I'll check for messages once in a while, so if you have something to say, just do something to get my attention, like shoot the ground near me or something, and I'll go read it." She ran up a flight of stairs in some abandoned apartment building and shot at a target on the street.

"Ryder, behind you!" She pressed down on the right stick of her controller to access her knife and stabbed his attacker before he could react. "Ha! Got him. No need to thank me."

A spray of bullets hit the ground nearby and she laughed. "Okay, hold on."

From: WyldRyd11
To: Goldilx

Holy crap, girl! You have some mad assassin skills. We should play *Assassin's Creed* after this.

"Sure! I love that game too."

They played for twenty minutes or so, prowling through streets and abandoned buildings, shooting at enemies. When he took a knife in the back, she checked his next message.

> **From:** WyldRyd11
> **To:** Goldilx
>
> Mistakes were made.

She laughed out loud into the headset.

His next message showed awe.

> **From:** WyldRyd11
> **To:** Goldilx
>
> You got the *Call of Duty* joke? Impressive. Want to chat on Instant Messenger? I'm WyldRyd11 on IM too. Send me your ID. Or you could friend me on Facebook if you want. My name is Ryder West.

Bailey nibbled a fingernail and thought about that for a moment. Meg would totally have a cow. She smiled, imagining Meg's perfectly logical and smart and safe and boring reply to Ryder's suggestion. First, she'd remind her of all her past mistakes. And then she'd try to scare her with things like "What if he's a pervert?" or "What if he's an ax murderer?" But really, what could possibly happen? It's not like he knew where she lived or anything.

"Okay."

She switched screens to her computer, turned on Instant Messenger, and found WyldRyd11.

> **Goldilx:** I'm glad you invited me to play.

WyldRyd11: Yeah, I'm glad too.

Goldilx: Most people hate playing with me.

WyldRyd11: Why?

Goldilx: I'm freakishly good at video games, and guys hate that.

WyldRyd11: No. Guys LOVE gamer girls.

Goldilx: Guys love gamer girls but hate when gamer girls kick their ass.

WyldRyd11: U are a girl, right? Not some 60 year old dude in a prison cell?

Bailey giggled.

Goldilx: I was thinking the same thing about you. I am definitely a real girl.

WyldRyd11: And I'm a real boy. I'm 17, not 60. :) And I won't mind if you kick my ass.

Goldilx: Cool! I'm 17 too. And I promise not to kick your ass that much. Or bug you for help designing my video game.

WyldRyd11: UR designing a video game? Cool.

Okay, he didn't actually ask for the details, but she'd give them to him anyway.

Goldilx: It's called *Lost Time*. My BFF and I thought it up during world history class last year. You have to examine major stories in history to find the stories behind the stories, the ones that are like never in our textbooks, you know?

WyldRyd11: Wow. Sounds complicated. How would u play?

Goldilx: I have a bunch of character outlines. Players could choose one or create their own.

WyldRyd11: Single or multiplayer?

Goldilx: Single player. The whole idea was to be able to play it by myself, but I did add a subplot about art so Meg would play.

WyldRyd11: Who's Meg?

Goldilx: My BFF.

WyldRyd11: Is there a BF?

Goldilx: No. Not anymore. I just broke up with my last BF.

WyldRyd11: Sucks for him. UR awesome!

Goldilx: Aw :)

WyldRyd11: Did u break up w/ him or did he break up with u?

Goldilx: I broke up with him.

WyldRyd11: Good. :) U need APIs and game engine software. I can get that for u if u want.

Good? Why was it good? Oh, my God, he was flirting with her. She almost clapped until she remembered she should be cool. Low key. She'd ignore the flirting and comment on the APIs—whatever they were. Simon had once tried to explain game engines to her. And Noah before him. And Chase the other night.

Goldilx: No, it's ok. I don't know much about programming.

WyldRyd11: u have to learn!!!!! u have to build this game so I can play it!!!

Could he be any sweeter? Bailey's face split into a wide grin.

Goldilx: I'm not good at programming and stuff. I just like games.

WyldRyd11: I can help! I'm really good at programming. What's ur email?

Again, Bailey heard Meg's disapproving voice in her head. With a frown, she refused to believe Ryder West was bad. He was sweet and kind and helpful and really smart. Oh, she bet he was cute too. Bailey logged onto Facebook and did a search for Ryder West. She found a bunch. Virginia, Oregon, two in California, and a few in New York, but when she found one on Long Island whose avatar was Ezio Auditore from *Assassin's Creed*, she knew she'd found the right Ryder and sent him a friend request.

Just as she clicked "Add Friend," her cell buzzed with a message from Meg.

Meg: Leaving work. Want me to bring u candy?

Aww. That is so sweet. Bailey grinned. She opened the phone, ready to tell Meg all about Ryder and how awesome he was and how he was totally into gaming and—

She tossed the phone to her bed and crossed her arms over her chest. What Meg didn't know wouldn't get Bailey another long, boring lecture on The Future. Another message from Ryder showed up.

WyldRyd11: I'll play u anytime :)

She did a little chair dance, happy he didn't mind getting his ass kicked by a girl.

Goldilx: I want to see pictures of you. You have none on your Wall.
WyldRyd11: Sorry. I don't have any pictures to post. They're all home.
Goldilx: Home?
WyldRyd11: Yeah. Montana. I just moved here.
Goldilx: Where's here?
WyldRyd11: I can't tell you. UR a stranger. LOL.

Goldilx: OMG, seriously? You think I'm a psycho stalker?

WyldRyd11: I don't know what u r yet.

Fair point, Bailey decided.

Goldilx: OK, fine. So tell me about Montana.

WyldRyd11: I grew up on a ranch.

Goldilx: A ranch? Like with horses and stuff?

WyldRyd11: Horses, cattle, poultry, hogs.

Goldilx: I love horses.

WyldRyd11: Can u ride?

Goldilx: Yep. I took lessons when I was little. Classical dressage.

WyldRyd11: LOL. U are such a girl.

Goldilx: What's wrong with dressage?

WyldRyd11: Dressage won't help u wrangle a lost calf, Goldilx.

Goldilx: I never planned to wrangle lost cows. I just wanted to ride horses, and those were the lessons they signed me up for.

WyldRyd11: OK, OK, I was just kidding. I think it's great u can ride. Are there any stables around your town?

Goldilx: There's a place in Hempstead I go to.

WyldRyd11: OMG. There's a town called Hempstead not far from where I live.

Goldilx: Do you live on Long Island?

WyldRyd11: Yes! So cool. Maybe we can ride one day.

Goldilx: Are you asking me out?

WyldRyd11: If I say yes, will u say yes?

Goldilx: That's cheating. I can't say yes unless you ask first.

WyldRyd11: OK! OK! I'm asking.

Goldilx: Then I'm saying yes.

WyldRyd11: Really? Cool.

Goldilx: Does this mean you want to meet me in person?

WyldRyd11: Yep.

Goldilx: Great!

WyldRyd11: It would be kinda hard to go riding online. LOL

Goldilx: Shut up! I was just making sure.

WyldRyd11: UR hot. Which is good, since I'm hot too.

Goldilx: Thanks :) Will you send me a picture of you?

WyldRyd11: U don't believe me?

Goldilx: I don't know you yet.

WyldRyd11: I like u.

Bailey smiled. He liked her. Whoa.

WyldRyd11: I gotta go. I'll text you later, pretty Bailey. Send me ur email and cell #.

Bailey sent him her contact information and flung herself on her bed. Pretty. He thought she was pretty. She did another happy dance that messed up her comforter and pillows. Maybe he'd text her a picture of himself. She really hoped so. And then her mood shifted when Simon popped back into her head. She got up, stood in front of the mirror over the white dresser she'd had since she was a baby, and stared at her reflection. Ryder said she was pretty. Simon Kane could just run away with his little alley cat sidekick for all she cared. Who needed him?

Not her. Not anymore.

She had sent Ryder West her email address, cell number, and the house phone number. Just to be thorough. She was about to turn off her phone when she saw the clock display. It was after ten and she hadn't heard from Chase. He was supposed to come over tonight to help with the game. Bailey tapped out a text message.

> **Bailey:** Hey, you didn't show, so I'm guessing the happy meals didn't work? Hope things are better tomorrow and we can sync up when you finish practice. Also, stop worrying about Meg. She gets angry a lot, but she's not depressed or anything serious. TTYL.

Bailey plugged the phone into its charger while the words she'd just typed brought her back to that look in Meg's eyes. She'd assured Chase Meg wasn't depressed, but was she right? How would she even know? It's not like she was an expert on emotions. She twirled a curl around her finger, counting the number of times Meg fell into dark holes and brooded her way out of them. She didn't smile often except when she saw Chase and almost never laughed. But that was just Meg on her normal setting. Whenever Meg thought about her dad, Bailey knew she'd be in her dark broody hole for days at a time, painting and…and, well, brooding. And when that stopped working, which was typical, a patented Meg Farrell Blurt could strike. It was kind of like a perfect storm where a bunch of conditions all had to be just right. Bailey had seen a blurt only a handful of times since she and Meg had become friends, and the last one had been about a year ago when Meg learned the movie theater where she worked would soon close its doors for good.

She shivered. It wasn't pretty.

Meg had spiraled down into the closest thing to a panic Bailey had ever seen. Money was tight for the Farrells, Bailey knew. But until that night, she had no idea how tight. Creditors were threatening them. There was often no food in the kitchen. The cable TV had been canceled. Bailey always assumed Meg didn't like TV—except for *The Vampire Diaries*, of course. She had no idea how much Pauline's books for her night classes cost or that they'd lived upstairs last winter because they just couldn't afford to heat the entire house. She'd never suspected that Meg's aversion to shopping wasn't because she didn't like designer clothes. It was because she had to help pay the bills and couldn't splurge on an expensive pair of jeans.

Meg's blurts were like hurricanes—they formed slowly, blew in, wreaked havoc on everyone and everything around them, and then faded away.

Bailey's jaw clenched when she thought about the way Meg had worshipped her dad. He was the cause of their problems! His death left them poor. Meg should be mad and resentful and throw tantrums and definitely not live out the stupid plan he'd taught her, but she couldn't let it go. Even when she skipped meals, she never ever blamed—

Wait.

Chase asked her what Meg's dad had done to her and said that he'd seen her stabbing a picture.

That was it. After all these years, she'd finally cracked. Yes! Bailey pumped a fist in the air. Maybe now Meg would relax those impossibly high standards of hers and act normal. With a wry grin, Bailey figured she'd need lots of help with that. Meg didn't know anything about acting normal.

Her enthusiasm faded while she considered that. *God, it must be awful to be angry at someone you can't talk to anymore.*

It *was* awful to be angry at someone you couldn't talk to.

Bailey hated her own dad too. Maybe not stab-his-picture mad, but close, and the only reason for that was because she'd never seen a picture of her dad. She didn't even know his name. Nicole had gotten pregnant with her while in her third year of high school. She was an accident.

A mistake.

She'd asked over and over, but Nicole refused to talk about her dad. Even Gran and Gramps wouldn't tell her anything about him. When she was little, Bailey used to have imaginary dads. She used to make them up—younger versions of Gramps. She saw Tim Allen in some movie and pretended he was her dad until she saw Rick Moranis shrinking his kids in a different movie. She'd tried to get Meg to play her game, but Meg said they were entirely too old for wishes that couldn't come true. Eventually, Bailey realized wishing for a dad hurt more than having than no dad, so she stopped playing too.

She left her bed and roamed around the room her grandparents had decorated with pink ruffles and stuffed animals when she was born, a room they then had redone in sunny yellow when she was in elementary school and again in a soothing green when she was fourteen. The soft green walls were still there, the stuffed animals that used to line her bed now replaced with lots of fluffy pillows, and the pink ruffles had long since been put away. The corner where her Barbie town house once stood was now home to a laptop on a sleek desk, which now showed more unread mail.

She leaned over, clicked the touch pad, and saw a notice from her favorite shoe store that new summer sandals were in and—

The next one had her sinking into the chair to read closely.

"Oh, my God." She pressed both hands to her mouth to muffle her squeal.

Maybe she wasn't too old for pretend after all.

Chapter 9
Meg

At the bus stop the next morning, Meg wore a hoodie because the weather was warm and she kind of hoped Bailey would threaten to take her shopping for something more fashion-forward. A few kids tossed a ball around. Right. Baseball practice had started. She heard the buzz of a leaf blower, smelled freshly cut grass. Spring had officially reached Long Island.

She shifted her weight from one foot to the other and tried not to look at Chase. He was twenty feet away, laughing with some friends. She hung back, hoping he wouldn't notice her or ask her about the cell phone he'd left on her coffee table. It was a long time before she was able to sleep after he left her last night. *What do you want? What do you want?* His words played on an infinite loop because she never answered the question. If she was brutally honest with herself, it was because she couldn't answer his question.

She didn't know.

Not anymore.

A year ago, even a few months ago, it would have been easy to tell him. She wanted a degree. She wanted a good, steady job with a decent salary. She wanted—needed—to be able to take care of herself. For years, that's all she'd ever wanted. Until they'd been assigned to that stupid research project. Ever since then, ever since he'd looked at her like she was the most beautiful work of art ever sculpted, she'd wanted more and couldn't have it. His magic eyes, the words heavy with promise that he murmured to her, the way his strong hands trembled when he touched her, the scent of sugar that always clung to him, though you had to be really close to notice it—all of it, all of *him* was a test she couldn't afford to fail. *Look but don't touch. Wish but don't hold your breath.*

Because always—always—her father's words hunted down Chase's.

She'd finally told him to leave when she imagined his lips touching hers the way they had the night before their project was due. His eyes swirled green with hurt, but she refused to cave in. She would not risk her future again. He shook his head once and left without a word.

She thought about calling Bailey, but she didn't want to hear all the pro-Chase rhetoric she was sure Bailey would spew. Her mom got home at midnight. Meg heard her key in the door and sat up in her bed. But Pauline's steps were slow and heavy, so Meg let her go straight to the small room beside hers, where two minutes after the thud of shoes hitting the floor reached her ears, there wasn't a sound.

Meg hitched her backpack up and shoved her hands into the pockets of her jeans. She looked back up the street and still saw no sign of Bailey. When she turned back, she felt Chase's gaze burning through her. She wanted to turn and run, but he held her there with nothing but his eyes. Her lips lifted in that smile, that damn smile like he was the one who controlled them, controlled her. Maybe he did. With a last word to his friends, he strode over with a cautious grin.

"Hey."

"Hi."

"You okay? You don't look so good."

"Thanks a lot."

Chase's eyes popped. "No! I didn't mean you don't look good. You always look good. I just mean you don't look like you're having a good day—"

She shot up a hand to stop him before he backpedaled off a cliff. "Relax. I get it. I'm not mad."

"Good. That's…um, good." He looked at his feet. "I'm sorry if what I said upset you. That's not what I was trying to do."

"It's okay. Forget it." Please, dear God, please just let it drop. She looked at his shoes, at her shoes, down the street, anywhere but at him and his irresistible eyes. "Here's your phone." She shoved a hand in her pocket and then pulled out the phone he'd left at her place.

"Oh…right. Thanks."

She watched him scroll through the messages, including the one from Bailey, which she'd read and then changed back to Unread and would pretend to know nothing about. He shot her a worried look, but luckily, Bailey headed down the street.

"Hey, Bailey!"

Bailey stopped short, narrowed her eyes. "Um…hi, Meg. What's up?"

"Nothing's up."

Chase gave half a laugh. "She's happy you're here to save her from big bad me. She's afraid of me. Isn't that right, Megan?"

She stiffened. "I am not afraid."

"Liar," Chase said without smiling. He turned and headed back to his friends as the bus turned the corner.

"Meg, did you guys have a fight or something?"

"Or something." When Bailey's mouth opened, Meg quickly changed the subject. "Why are you so late? You almost missed the bus."

Bailey bounced on her toes. "I was doing research."

Meg's jaw dropped.

The bus stopped with a squeal of brakes and a belch of exhaust. The group still gathered on the corner shoved their way on board. "Meg? You coming?"

She followed Bailey to a pair of empty seats and slid beside her. "You were doing 'research'?" she asked with air quotes. "On what?"

Bailey frowned. "On yearbooks. And what's with the quotey fingers?"

Meg let out her breath and slouched lower in her seat. She should have known. Bailey never willingly did anything resembling schoolwork without lots of whining and eye-rolling. "Yearbooks. Is this for your game?"

"No." Bailey lowered her voice. "My dad."

"What?" Meg straightened with a snap.

"I was reading my spam last night, and I got an email from that classmates site and signed up as my mom. And then I found her yearbook."

Just under Meg's skin in the middle of her gut, there was the faintest crawl of envy. "You found him."

"No, not yet. But I found her class. I'm going to find him, Meg. I'm going to find my dad."

Meg shook her head. "Bailey, don't get your hopes up."

Bailey turned to watch the houses go by—one minute and then two. "I thought you'd be happy."

"I don't want you hurt, Bay."

She turned, blue eyes arctic. "Megan, how could it possibly hurt me to find my father?"

"There's a reason your mom doesn't talk about him, Bailey. What if finding *him* makes you lose *her*?"

Bailey returned to watching scenery. "I honestly don't think she'd mind all that much. She's got John now."

Meg sighed. "After school, come over. We'll look together."

Bailey turned, smiled for a second. "Thanks. I'm kinda scared."

"Scared." That stunned Meg. "Why? I thought you wanted this."

"I do. But I'm still scared. I mean…what if he hates me or already has kids and doesn't want me?"

Friendship demanded Meg lie. Her personal code of ethics insisted on the truth. "Um…okay. Look. You're smart to be scared. You don't know why Nicole kept you apart all these years. Maybe he's married with a minivan and soccer practices and golf buddies or whatever. But I do know this—it's not possible for anyone to meet you and hate you, Bay. It's just not."

Bailey's lips quivered and she laid her head against Meg's arm. A few seconds later, she took her phone from her pocket, glanced at the screen, and hid a smile.

"Who's that?"

But Bailey merely shook her head, tucked the phone back in her pocket, and stood up. Meg let her by, frowning after her as they left the bus, feeling Chase's eyes burning through her back.

Chapter 10
Bailey

Ryder texted her!

Bailey hadn't heard a word the teachers in her first five classes had said. She'd spent the entire morning bouncing over Ryder's message.

She'd nearly caved when Meg had asked who'd texted her. But Ryder was special. Okay, true, she hadn't known him very long or…well, even met him in person, but Bailey could tell he was sweet and kind and smart and—and damn it—too special to risk sharing with Meg.

There. She'd said it. Or *thought* it at least.

She bit her lip, wondering how she was going to keep a whole boyfriend a total secret from her best friend.

No, no, no! He wasn't her boyfriend. They hadn't even met in person. He was just a boy. That's all. She would take things slow and not mess up this time. Maybe Meg would like him.

Meg hadn't liked a single one of Bailey's boyfriends. Ever. It was so ironic—Bailey wanted to catch boys, while Meg kept tossing hers back. Sometimes she wondered if Meg expected her to live her life alone so that they could live alone together, even though that wasn't really being alone.

She rolled her eyes at the silliness of it all and then skidded to a stop when she spotted her best friend twenty feet down the corridor. Meg would take one look at her and just *know*. It was like a freakish superpower. She couldn't be near Meg right now and keep a secret this big. She searched the corridor for a handy escape route when her cell phone buzzed.

Ryder: Hey, pretty Bailey. RU at lunch? Am free for the next .5 hour. Can we chat?

Oh, my God, yes—absolutely! Bailey grinned and ducked into the closest girls' restroom to spend the lunch period with her guy.

Bailey: Hi! What's up?

Ryder: Miss u. *COD* tonight?

Bailey enjoyed *Call of Duty* but had planned to work on her game. Oh! She smacked her forehead. She was supposed to meet Meg and go through her mom's high school yearbook.

Bailey: I can't. Meg's coming over to help me do research.

Ryder: I can help u. What RU researching?

Should she tell him? It couldn't hurt.

Bailey: I'm trying to find my dad. Long story. Found mom's yearbook. Plan to look for pictures of her with guys.

Ryder: Never met him?

Bailey: Don't even know his name.

Ryder: That really sucks. xo

Bailey: I know.

Ryder: I'll help. Send me info l8r. Then we play :)

Bailey: Sure! We'll kick some enemy ass.

Ryder: Looked at game ideas u sent me the other night. Think it may work, but gestures??

Bailey: I know. Would B cool to play without controllers, but too hard.

Ryder: Right. Try controller play first. U can design gesture interface later. Don't worry about coding. Just storyboard for now.

Bailey: Good idea.

Ryder: Hey, check UR email later. Sent you some more level ideas.

When the bell rang, Bailey hurried to class but did her best to avoid Meg. She didn't know how much longer she could keep a secret as big as Ryder. As soon as she got home, she checked her email and discovered Ryder had not only sent her tons of ideas for game levels but had also included his rules for achievements and respawning new lives.

Oh. These were good ideas. Bailey's fingers blurred as she added notes to her "Ideas" file. The game began as a classic puzzle design—simple rules, really, with a small battle capability. Ryder's ideas for achievements and spawning new lives—oh, that really took it up a few notches to a true adventure game. She read the rest of Ryder's list. Whoa, using military ranks for game levels was a really cool idea and maybe that could provide the foundation for the entire game universe—some sort of covert government branch whose mission is to change history. No, their mission can be to rewrite it so that certain facts are obliterated. She sent him a text message to pitch the idea. He replied with a lot of exclamation points and the :) emoticon.

She clapped and did a happy chair dance. This was going to be the coolest thing ever.

With her Ideas file open, Bailey grabbed blank sheets of paper from her printer, sharpened a brand new pencil, and started sketching her vision of The Foundation. She nibbled the eraser for a moment and sent another text.

Bailey: What do you think of The Foundation as name for secret gov org?

Ryder replied with a single word:

Ryder: Meh.

She frowned. Maybe it should be an abbreviation like CIA or something. Or a one-word mythological creature, like Pegasus or Cyclops. She could spend hours on the name alone. Okay, The Foundation wasn't the best name, but it would do for now. She drew corridors and cells and laboratories, and she leaned back to assess her work. Squinting at a shape that looked like a turbo engine on the south wall, Bailey had to face facts. Art was definitely out as a career choice. Unless—she leaned closer, used the eraser to smudge a few lines, and smiled. What if that shape *was* an engine? What if The Foundation were a ship? Yeah. Oh, yeah, a ship run by The Admiral. She could picture him—tall, stern, dressed in a white uniform, recruiting the lost. No, The Lost. Characters that time forgot.

Oh, wow, this was epic. She texted Ryder, sketched and erased and labeled and typed notes into the idea document until her eyes burned.

She never did call Meg.

Chapter 11
Meg

Meg was going nuts one brain cell at a time.

It had been a week. Seven whole days.

At first, it was little stuff, things she could easily dismiss as crankiness, forgetfulness…or even PMS. For about five minutes, she thought Bailey might have been organizing a birthday party for her, even though she'd told her—repeatedly—that she didn't want one. But then Bailey hadn't been on the bus…or at their usual lunch table. Meg was forced to face facts—Bailey was avoiding her. Even Chase had been MIA, which is exactly what she wanted, but still, it hurt.

Why? What had she done? Okay, sure, she wasn't exactly overjoyed at the idea of poring over old yearbooks, but she'd promised. Bailey would know that giving her word meant something to Meg. Or at least she should. So what reason would Bailey have to avoid her?

Not even after that time back in seventh grade when she'd accidentally blurted out the news that Bailey had gotten her period in front of a bus stop full of boys had Bailey actually *avoided* her. Sure, she'd pulled her hair and screeched that she'd hated her and would never speak to her again but didn't go a whole week without speaking to her. In fact, by the end of that day, it had been forgiven and forgotten. Why? Why, damn it? What had she done? They hadn't argued; they hadn't even disagreed except for the way Meg treated—

Oh.

It was Chase. It had to be. Megan came to a screeching halt in the middle of the main corridor, forcing a freshman to skirt around her with a squeak of shoes on the waxed floor. Students hurried to class. Others rifled through lockers. Announcements blared over the PA system, but Meg didn't notice. Bailey wanted Chase but didn't know how to tell her. Meg had said no to Chase repeatedly. It was none of her business if he wanted to hook up with Bailey. She would let Bailey off the hook and give them her blessing.

No matter how much it killed her.

Meg blinked the Green Envy from her eyes and waited at Bailey's locker Thursday morning, trying not to flinch when Bailey slowed at the sight of her. "Hey."

"Hey!" Bailey managed a smile with tight lips that showed no teeth, and Meg's face burned.

Swallowing hard, Meg hoped her voice would sound casual. "Missed you."

Bailey frowned. "Right. I was supposed to call you. Sorry about that. I had some other stuff to take care of. What about *TVD* tonight? Can you come by after work?" She fished her cell out of her bag, not looking Meg in the face.

Meg went still. "Bailey, I was let go, remember?"

Bailey clicked some buttons on her phone before she slid it into her bag. "Oh, yeah…right. I forgot."

Meg shook her head slowly from side to side. Bailey would forget things like homework assignments and due dates for term paper, but plans with friends, things like lost jobs? No. Deep in Meg's heart, a battle went on. Part of it just wanted to shrivel up in a ball. But another part kept insisting there was no way Bailey would be—could *possibly* be—cruel. Maybe it had nothing to do with Chase. Was Simon still harassing her? The thought gave her hope, and she laid a hand on Bailey's arm, gave a little squeeze.

"Bay, are you okay?"

She gave Meg a stunned smile. "I'm great. Gotta go!"

Meg stared after her, jaw dangling.

She tried again at lunch, even though Bailey hadn't been sitting at their usual spot. Meg caught up to her by her locker again, trying hard not to say anything when Bailey stuffed all her textbooks inside, even though she'd need two of them for her after-lunch classes. "Bailey, you want to hit the mall tomorrow?"

"Um…can I get back to you on that? I may have other plans."

Hope withered. "Plans with Chase?" Green Envy tinted Meg's vision again.

Bailey looked puzzled for a second and then nodded. "Chase. Right. I need to call him."

"Yeah. No problem. You should call him. You and Chase would be great together." Meg hurried to her next class.

The next day, Meg ended up going to the mall alone. Bailey never replied to her texts. The weekend was long and lonely. Megan spent most of it painting, studying, and painting some more. She didn't bother trying to text Bailey again. Nor did she bother looking for Bailey at lunch on

Monday. She sat in the cafeteria, picking apart a sandwich when the chair beside her squeaked. Meg grinned and looked up. "Oh." The grin faded. "It's you."

Chase pouted. "Jeez, Megan. I haven't seen you in a week. That wasn't long enough for you?" He cracked open a soft drink.

Her face heated up. "No, um, sorry, I mean, I was hoping you were Bailey."

Chase's eyebrows went up. "You two fighting or something?"

"Like you don't know," Meg countered.

"Know what?"

"Aren't you two—" The word got stuck in Meg's throat. "You know... together?"

Chase's eyes went round.

"No! I don't know where you got that from, but I haven't see her all week. I was sick." He looked down at the table, picked at a scratch in the surface. "You...you didn't notice I wasn't in any of our classes?"

Meg shrugged. "I figured it was an Easter thing." The holidays were always busy in the Gallaghers' bakery. "Extra shifts and stuff."

"No, I had the flu. And now I have a ton of work to make up, which reminds me, I need your notes."

She slid a three-subject notebook from her pile of books and handed it to him.

"Thanks."

Meg studied her tray, wishing he'd leave, hoping he wouldn't.

Chase blew out a gusty breath and pulled his tray closer. "Any ideas what's up with her?"

She spread out her hands and let them fall. "God, like a dozen. I thought she was fighting with her mom, or maybe Simon was harassing her, and I even thought—" She pressed her lips together and shifted in her seat.

"What? Tell me."

"Um…okay. Don't laugh, okay? But I thought maybe she was planning something for my birthday."

"Oh, right. It's like a couple of days from now, right?"

She nodded, her eyes on the tray between them.

"Okay, well, did you try to talk to her?"

Her shoulders lifted but not her spirits. "I tried. She either blows me off or just says everything's fine."

"Maybe she's just got, you know, stuff on her mind. SATs and college and crap like that."

Meg laughed once. "I'm not sure she'd even have taken the SATs if I hadn't nagged her."

His green eyes went sharp. "Why do you do that?"

Meg blinked. "Do what?"

"Talk like she's some dumb blond."

Meg's hand tightened around her water bottle. "I *don't*."

He smirked and nodded. "Oh, right. My mistake." He tipped his bottle in a mock toast. "Maybe she'd tell you what's going on with her if you weren't so judgmental."

Meg slammed her half-eaten sandwich back to her tray and shoved back the chair. "I'm out of here."

Chase shot out an arm to hold her. "Wait…here she comes now."

Glaring at each other, they said nothing until Bailey sat down.

"Hi, Bay," Chase said.

"Hey."

It was obvious she was distracted. Obvious to her, so Meg shot Chase a look that said, *See?* Chase kicked her under the table, and Meg narrowed her eyes. He wanted her to talk? Fine.

"Bailey, can I talk to you a minute?" Meg asked before she could talk herself out of it.

She looked worried. "Um…I guess. What's up?"

Meg's heart twisted. *I guess?* A friend asks if you can talk and you say *I guess?* "Are you mad at me about anything?"

Her eyes popped. "No! I'm not mad. Why would you think that?"

Oh, God, did she really need to give her the list? "*The Vampire Diaries*. The mall. The movie. The yearbook."

"Oh, right!" She winced and slapped her forehead. "I am so sorry. I just…forgot."

"You forgot?"

"Yeah, I know that's really lame, but it's true. I'm…well—" She hesitated a moment and drew in a deep breath. "There's this guy I really like, and I've sort of been hanging out with him a lot and—"

"Right. You and Chase are working on the game," Meg interrupted, trying to ignore the burn in her gut. Red Bloom. Or maybe Crimson Gush.

"Not me. I told you I was sick all week." Chase put up his hands.

Bailey said something under her breath that sounded suspiciously like *Oops*. "Um…it's not Chase, Meg. His name's Ryder."

Not Chase. Meg's stomach flipped a somersault at those words. Relief spread to every cell in her body.

"How'd you meet him?"

She wouldn't meet her eyes. "Playing *Call of Duty* on Xbox Live. He's—"

A pedophile. "How old is he?" Meg demanded.

Bailey rolled her eyes. "Jesus, Meg, are you my mother now?"

Chase arched an eyebrow in her direction.

Meg drew in a deep breath. Okay. Maybe she was being a little overprotective.

"We just want to know if he's our age—that's all," Chase said.

"He's seventeen and he's homeschooled and grew up on a ranch in Montana." Bailey's face lit up like it was Christmas morning.

Meg pressed her lips together.

"We play video games all the time."

Great.

"Meg, are you gonna say something?"

Meg looked to Chase, but he just shrugged and challenged her with a smile. She sighed. "Um…yeah. When do I get to talk to him?"

Bailey's face froze for a second. "Talk to him?"

"Well, yeah. Maybe we could all play a match online or something."

Bailey twisted a blond curl. "Um…yeah. Maybe."

Meg narrowed her eyes at her. "Bailey."

She wouldn't look at her.

"Bailey, you have no idea if this boy is seventeen or seventy or even a boy, do you?"

"Of course I do!" She rolled her eyes. "We talk every day."

The lightbulb went on. "How long?"

"Um…like a week."

Bailey's words hung in the air for a few seconds, circled her brain, and then slammed into her heart with maximum impact. "You…so…you've been blowing me off to talk to some guy? Only you've never even met him?" Meg heard enough. She crumbled up her napkin, grabbed her tray, and slung the bag on her shoulder.

"Meg! I'm sorry! Meg—"

Meg fled before Bailey finished the sentence, tossing her trash and hiding in the privacy of the girls' bathroom. Locked into a stall, she cried through the next two periods and didn't even try to name the colors she felt.

Chapter 12
Bailey

"What the hell just happened here?" Chase glared and Bailey spread her palms apart, her face burning under all the curious eyes that watched Meg's abrupt departure and then swung back to her to accuse her.

"Oh, my God. I didn't mean to hurt her feelings. I have to go after her. I have to—"

"Bailey, going by the look on her face, you're the last person she wants to see right now. Let her settle and then apologize."

Bailey bit her lip. What had she done? She only wanted to keep Ryder's existence a secret just for a while—a little while—before she had to be responsible and mature and logical and practical. What was so wrong with that? Okay, so she'd been ducking Meg all week. And ignored a few texts. And ditched her for lunch. It's not like she *wanted* to hurt her feelings. She'd just wanted to enjoy feeling special again. She hadn't felt that way since Simon. Bailey's eyes narrowed. Meg had reacted exactly as Bailey had expected, which was why she'd been keeping Ryder a secret in the first place, so really, Meg should be apologizing to her, shouldn't she?

"What?" Chase folded his arms.

"What exactly do I need to apologize for?"

Chase sighed. "You want the list? Okay. You've been blowing her off. You made her think we hooked up. You forgot about her birthday and you kept an entire boyfriend a secret from her. Jeez, Bailey, I thought you guys were best friends."

"We are, but—"

"Really? This is what best friends do?" He shook his head and rolled his eyes. "Girls."

Bailey's lip quivered. She hadn't forgotten Meg's birthday. Not exactly. She just…well, hadn't actually planned anything for it because she wanted to hang out with Ryder. She pressed both hands to her face and did her best to hold back the tears. Beside her, she heard Chase sigh again.

"Who is this guy, Bay?"

Chase's voice no longer sounded harsh, and she was bursting to tell. "Oh, he's so awesome, Chase! We met during a *Call of Duty* match. We've been talking video games, texting, and chatting. He's really into programming and sent me some ideas for new levels and said he'd show me how to use a game engine. Oh, and he grew up on a ranch—like a real ranch with horses and cattle and stuff."

"He sounds too good to be true."

Bailey's spine straightened. "You too, huh? I should have seen that coming. I mean, obviously, you'd take Meg's side." She shook her head and pressed her mouth into a tight line.

"Bailey, I'm not taking sides here. I'm just stating facts. You didn't go meet this guy, did you?"

She avoided Chase's gaze and merely shrugged.

"Bailey? Oh, tell me you're smarter than that."

"I tried, okay? He's busy with other things."

Chase brought both hands up to his hair, raked it back, and stared at her like it was the first time they'd met. "I can't believe this."

"Oh, my God, you sound just like Meg!" Bailey flung her hands up. "I'm a big girl, Chase. I don't need you or her looking down on me because I finally found a guy who really likes me."

"You hope."

Bailey wrinkled her brow. "Hope what?"

"You hope he's actually a guy. Megan's right. He could be some perv."

She shot him a long look and then merely nodded. "So I'm just some stupid little girl who can't see a con unless her friend draws her a picture? Thanks. Thanks a lot." She shoved back her chair and stalked off, ignoring Chase's pleas to wait.

She thought about hiding in the girls' bathroom again but then decided that she had no reason to hide. *She* hadn't done anything wrong. She spun the combination on her locker and flung open the door, swallowing a frustrated scream. Okay! So she wasn't as smart as Meg or as athletic as Chase, but she had skills, skills that other people admired, people like Ryder. Just because they'd met online didn't automatically mean he was a perverted ax murderer, and it didn't mean she was a brainless airhead. She grabbed books without even looking at them and slammed the locker door. It *wasn't* stupid to be Ryder's friend. She stomped to her next class, ignoring the looks and whispers. What was stupid was everybody treating her like she still wore training pants.

She was seventeen years old! Old enough to know who she shouldn't trust, old enough to know who her dad was, and old enough to know why her mother had kept him a secret all these years. She ground her teeth together and made a promise. She'd not only keep talking to Ryder, but she'd meet him in person and track down her dad too. She didn't care if that pissed off Meg and Chase and her mom.

The only apologizing that would be done today would be *to* her.

Chapter 13
Meg

The day finally ended. Meg boarded the bus without waiting for Bailey for the first time in years and folded herself into a seat all the way in the back. She drew her hood up and tried not to sob when the tears came. Someone took the seat beside her and she sighed. *I'm always alone except when I need to be alone.*

"Here." A cafeteria napkin appeared in front of her face, clutched in Chase's hand. His eyes sparkled like gems in her blurry vision. "It's clean, I swear."

"Chase, I—"

"Don't talk, Megan. For once, just don't talk and let me help, okay?"

Jeez, if I want to talk, I'm damn well going to talk. Besides, she was only going to say—oh, hell. When all the color bled out of her anger, Meg nodded and slid further down her seat, propping her feet on the seat in front of her.

"Aw, what's the matter, Meg? Lose your best friend?" Somebody mocked from across the aisle, and the rear of the bus exploded in laughter.

Chase stood up and the laughter abruptly stopped. When he sat down again, Meg squeezed his hand briefly. He sucked in a sharp breath of air, so she tried to move her hand, but he only tightened his grip. For a moment, Meg looked at their clasped hands and finally looked up at him. "Chase—"

"Megan." He smiled.

"Why are you on the bus? Don't you have practice?"

He shook his head. "Canceled. The coach is sick. Probably has what I had last week. Besides, I thought you could use a friend."

A friend. She bit her lip. "Why do you keep doing this? You know how I feel." She almost rolled her eyes. Expecting him to know how she felt when she wasn't sure was pretty damn ludicrous. She felt like throwing herself into his arms and running away at the same time. But she didn't have to spell it out for him. Didn't have to elaborate. Because he didn't bother to deny it.

"You're right. I *do* know how you feel." He leaned over with a grin that was almost wicked and whispered in her ear. "Because I feel the same way."

No. Meg tugged her hand back, and again, he tightened his grip, still grinning wide.

"Megan, I won't hurt you. I swear. Not the way your dad hurt you and your mom." He was completely serious now.

Her entire body clenched and she snatched her hand away. Meg never talked about her father. Ever. No one knew what had really happened. She'd never told anybody about her parents, except—

"Bailey. She—oh, God. She told you." *Damn it.* No. No, it wasn't possible. She swore she'd never tell.

Chase frowned. "Told me what? It doesn't take a genius to see you're pissed at your dad."

Meg turned her head away and breathed a sigh of relief. Her anger was a weird thing. It was like someone had poured mad over her entire field of vision, tinting it a murky red. It was like trying to see through Alizarin Crimson. She should have known better. Bailey would never tell.

Then again, she didn't think Bailey would stand her up for some guy either.

"I never understood why you guys are friends," he murmured.

Meg whipped her head back, eyebrows raised in question.

"You're both such different people. Bailey's all fun, and you're—"

"Not."

He rolled his vibrant eyes. "I was gonna say serious. She's all fashionable, and you're—"

"Not."

This time, he blew out a frustrated sigh. "Will you stop that? I was gonna say you always look great, even though you're not all tied up in knots trying to look that way. I guess I just wonder what you guys talk about."

Meg blinked. "We talk about anything. Everything. I don't have to be special for *her*."

His eyebrows shot up. "You don't have to be special for me either, but you won't let us be friends like that. I just wish I understood why."

Meg looked down at her feet and tried to find a good excuse. "Too scary."

He laughed. "You really are afraid of me?"

Meg burrowed deeper into her hoodie. "Not *of* you, just…uh, afraid in general."

He frowned and shook his head. "Okay, that cleared it up."

The bus reached Meg's stop. "Bye. Oh, um…thanks for…you know, just thanks."

Chase stood up to let her by. She walked down the steps, jumped to the curb, and drew in a breath of the cool spring air, wondering if she'd ever feel warm again.

"Chase, this isn't your street." Meg reminded him when he fell into step beside her. Chase's house was around the block. Meg could see his bedroom window from hers and often lay in bed at night, refusing to shut her eyes until his window went dark.

"I know where I live, Megan."

They walked beside the freshly cut lawns, the crocuses, and tulips bursting from sleep and around the corner to Meg's tiny house.

"So why aren't you going there?" she finally asked him.

"I'm walking you home. And then you're going to invite me inside so I can make you hot cocoa."

Meg arched an eyebrow, tried not to let her galloping heart escape from her chest. "Again, why?"

"Because you're upset. Because you need to know Bailey's not the only friend you have."

Bailey. Just the sound of her name had Meg's vision going Alizarin crimson again. She shouldn't do this, not with Chase, but damn it, better he was with her than with Bailey. Besides, she knew more tears waited behind her eyes, and as soon as she was alone, they'd drown her. "Faience Blue," she murmured.

"What?" he asked on a laugh.

"Never mind," she said and sighed. "Come on then."

They sat in the kitchen, an open bag of stale marshmallows between them on the old oak table with the scarred top. Meg sat with her legs curled under her, looking around the room her mom loved so much. It was big and sunny. Pauline had an herb garden growing in one window and one of Meg's early paintings hung on the wall over the table.

"Your mom's not here?"

Meg shook her head. "No, she won't get home until after six." And then she'd head right back out.

"What do you do all by yourself until then?"

Meg's eyes tracked the gentle rise of vapor from her cup. "I'm not usually alone. Usually, I have Bailey to keep me company."

"So what would you and Bailey be doing right now?"

"Homework. Giving each other advice on stuff."

The corner of Chase's mouth twitched.

"Maybe we'd make a few snacks or watch a movie. We'd shop. Read. And we'd talk. We talked a lot. I've been trying to convince Bailey to get a computer science degree."

Chase nodded. "Yeah, she told me about the video game. She never showed me any of it though. We just talked. It sounds really complicated."

Meg's mouth tightened. The night Bailey had told Chase about the video game had been the night he'd hugged her. She squirmed in her chair.

"You okay?"

"Um…yeah." She felt her face flame.

Inspiration struck. Maybe there was a way to beat Bailey at her own game. Ha.

Meg tugged Chase's hand, leading him upstairs. "Come on. You have to check this out."

She led him into her room, cluttered with half-finished sketches, brushes and paints, canvases, and clothes that didn't look good on her, but she didn't care about the mess.

"You gonna show me your sketches, Megan?" Chase waggled his eyebrows.

Meg rolled her eyes. "Shut up and come over here." She searched the bookcase over her desk for the binder she and Bailey had filled with ideas, outlines, character sketches, and plot threads. "Here. Look at this. I sketch these out for her when I have time." Meg handed the pad to Chase, who was busy looking around the canvases hung or propped on every wall like he'd fallen into another dimension.

Meg's heart dropped a few inches when his gaze settled on her easel, which she'd forgotten to cover.

"Chase?"

"Oh. Sorry." He came back to his senses and leafed through the binder for what felt like hours. "These are good. I mean, like, *really* good."

"I know, right?" Meg took the binder back and leafed to a page she knew by heart. "This all started with a bad grade on a history test. I told her she should think of history like a video game with various levels, and next thing I know, she's got all these worlds designed around our history lessons."

"I like this." Chase pointed to one of the plot arcs circled in the margin. "It's like a *Da Vinci Code* thing."

Meg smiled and shook her head. "No, it's more than that. She knew the only way I'd ever play the game was if it had something to do with art. I told her she should use famous works from each period and add in the artists as backstory, but she said no. That was too much like *Assassin's Creed*. So we kept adding stuff, tweaking ideas until it covered all of tenth-grade history. She has the whole thing worked out in her head."

"I know. She told me." He laughed. "When she said it was a little like *Dance Party Central*, I nearly lost it."

Meg's excitement faded. Every time she remembered their hug that night, that flare of envy tinted her vision. "Right. I forgot. Now *you're* building it for her."

He looked at Meg sharply and his voice dropped a few degrees. "'For her?' You don't think she can do it herself, do you?"

Meg gasped, insulted. "No, *she* doesn't think she can, so she doesn't bother. Her biggest goal right now is to marry rich so she can afford to pay somebody to code this for her." Abruptly mad, Meg tossed the book back on her desk. "That's what got the whole Simon thing started in the first place. She figured he'd build it for her." Meg ran fingers through her hair, the tug on her scalp easing the pain in her heart when she thought about Bailey. When Chase didn't reply, she glanced at him and saw his fairy eyes cloud with annoyance.

"What?"

Chase shook his head and waved a hand. "I'm sorry."

Meg's eyebrows shot up. "For what?"

"For what I was just thinking about you." He shrugged. "You look out for her." He smiled. "It's…um, cool. It really is."

Cool. Meg blew out a loud breath and carefully tucked the binder back on her shelf. "I try. She doesn't make it easy."

"Well, maybe you could cut her a small break—you know, forgive her because she wasn't ready to share this guy with you yet?"

Meg's brows drew together and her face got hot. Chase hit a nerve, but she wasn't quite ready to admit that yet, so she quickly changed the subject. "Let me ask you something. Do you think she's pretty?"

Chase stared at Meg, agape. "Um...yeah," he finally admitted. "Why?"

She ignored the knot in her belly, the little flare of jealousy. "She...well, she's really insecure, Chase. Every time she meets a new guy, she...she just loses herself in him. Everything she's ever been into, it's because she wanted to impress a guy. Rock climbing. Heavy metal. Acting. Working out." She ticked the hobbies off on her fingers. "I can't even remember who got her started on gaming."

"Yeah, well, she's still into it, so that's got to mean something," he pointed out.

"True." Meg lifted a shoulder. "But it's more than just picking up a guy's hobbies. She believes anything they tell her, Chase. Whatever they say, she believes it, and it really annoys me."

He frowned. "Why?"

"Because." Meg flung out her hands in frustration. "She doesn't see herself! For every guy that gives her the time of day, she falls hard and then totally changes herself for him. Simon thought she was sexy, so she started talking about getting a boob job."

He snorted, and when Meg turned to face him, he was looking at her sideways. "That's a girl thing. You all do that."

"I have never and will never consider a boob job."

His eyes flicked down and immediately back to hers. "Um...good. That's good. But that's not what I meant. I mean, girls are always trying to change themselves. Even you."

"I do not!" Before he could argue, Meg stated her case. "I would never change myself for some guy. That's exactly why I—" Abruptly, she snapped her teeth together.

Chase angled his head, an unspoken acknowledgment of what she didn't say. "No. You're right about that. But I was talking about not being happy with your looks."

"I know exactly what I look like." She waved a hand at the mirror over her dresser. "I'll never get any modeling contracts, but I'm not hideous. I have nice eyes, even though they're brown, and my skin looks good. I'm too skinny and my hair needs an intervention. None of that matters all that much to me or I'd do something about it."

"Wow, do you even hear yourself?" He crossed the room to stand next to her, took her shoulders, and spun her around to face the mirror. "What exactly is wrong with having brown eyes?"

Meg met his gaze in their reflection, wondering how the hell he could even ask that question. His hands tightened on her shoulders, and then he trailed one hand slowly down her body, stopping at her hip.

Meg's heart skidded to a thought-scattering, life-shattering stop.

"I like what I see. Why don't you?"

She opened her mouth to retort but realized that with his hand on her body, she had no answer to give, even if she could form words.

"Maybe you do care?" He filled the silence.

Holy Moses, she was going to faint. Chase Gallagher touched her. Chase Gallagher was still touching her.

And she liked it.

Unable to tear her gaze away, Meg watched his impossible-colored eyes darken and drift to her mouth. Her entire body tensed, and her mind screamed "Run!" but she didn't.

She couldn't.

He turned her to face him.

He bent his head lower.

When had he grown so tall? When had his jaw formed those contours that just begged for her fingers to trace?

And then he touched his mouth to hers, the lightest of touches. Sweet. Friendly even. She'd replayed this moment a dozen, a hundred, a hundred dozen times since the first time he'd kissed her, and each time—every single one of them—she'd imagine coolly stopping him, reminding him they'd never be more than just friends.

But that's not what happened.

She exploded. There was a split second of hesitation, and then Chase went wild. The hand gripping her hip tightened and his fingers pressed into her flesh. The hand on her shoulder snaked around her back, reached into her hair, and pulled. Her head came up. Her mouth opened in a gasp, and he swallowed the sound, touched his tongue to hers. She held on, held tight while he poured a year's, a decade's, a lifetime's worth of love into his kiss, and she cried at the beauty of it, cried that she'd denied them this for so long.

Reality came skipping back home at that moment, dragging with it every memory of every time she'd heard her mother sob late at night when she was supposed to be asleep, and she froze.

Chase was suddenly across the room. "I should go. You gonna be okay?" His voice was a deep rasp.

Meg blinked, nodded, and leaned back against her desk, suddenly too dizzy to trust her legs. "Um…yeah, sure." Her voice was just as raspy.

"You mind if I borrow that?" He jerked his chin to the binder. "I can do some basic flat files for you guys."

Her mind clutched at that single sane thought. "Oh, sure. That…that would be awesome." What the hell was a flat file?

In two steps, he had the binder, and in two more, he was at the door again.

Suddenly, Meg didn't want him to go. "Thanks for the…um…company."

"No problem." He turned at the door. "By the way—and I know this doesn't matter much to you—but I think you're pretty too."

He grinned his toothpaste commercial smile, and Meg struggled to breathe.

Chapter 14
Bailey

Bailey's will had remained brick-solid right up until the final bell rang and she saw Meg, shoulders slumped and face long, drag herself onto the bus.

She elected to walk home, even though the sky was overcast and the humidity was doing terrible things to her hair. She headed out of the school parking lot, her bag already too heavy for her shoulder, and tried to remind herself that Meg never looked happy, even when she smiled—and that only happened when Chase was around. All she wanted was time, just a little bit of time to enjoy the sparkle and tingle of a brand new friendship that hinted at more to come. The weight on her shoulder felt like it had gotten inside her. Her steps slowed, and she raised a hand to rub at her chest.

Okay. Okay, she admitted it. She shouldn't have ditched the movie or the mall trip or not texted. It wasn't nice to be forgotten or abandoned. Hadn't she been mad at her mom for forcing her dad to do just that to her? But it wasn't intentional. Or…well, not entirely intentional. She got caught up in all that sparkling and tingling, and she would explain that to Meg, apologize for that much at least. Meg would understand.

That put a hitch in her stride.

Meg would *not* understand, not one bit.

Meg didn't allow herself to sparkle and tingle and sink into that soul-soaring feeling you got when a boy looked at you like you were the sun itself. Meg didn't let herself get caught up in anything except school and painting, and even when she was up to her eyebrows in a project, she'd never forgotten plans with Bailey.

Bailey slowed to a stop, found herself in front of a coffee shop, and went inside. She sat in a corner booth, far away from the laughter and teasing from the other students squeezed around a table for six. A horrible conclusion struck her hard, and she covered her face. She was a terrible friend. But yet, thinking it, accepting it churned up all this outrage deep inside her that kept trying to rebel against it. Bailey needed Gran and took out her cell, made the call, and then settled back to wait for Gran to rescue her, wallowing in pity.

"Bailey."

She looked up, saw Simon frowning down at her, and hunched lower in the booth.

"You okay?"

She turned away. "Sure. Perfect."

"You…ah…need a ride or something?"

At the other end of the shop, Bailey noticed Caitlyn trying to draw blood with her glare. "I'm good. You should get back to her before her face freezes that way."

Simon took a quick look over his shoulder and snorted. "Yeah…okay." He waited a second and then walked away.

Bailey refused to look at their table. She sat with her face turned to the window. Time floated around her, but she was outside it. She registered the arrival and departures of various customers, smelled the French fries on trays going by, and sipped the coffee in front of her that she didn't remember asking for. A hand reached across the table and squeezed hers.

"What's wrong, sweet girl?" a soft voice asked.

Bailey looked up into her grandmother's familiar face. There were lines there now, a little gray around her temples, but she always looked so beautiful and always spoke so softly—even when she was mad.

There was no annoyance reflected on her grandmother's face, only concern.

Tears burned behind her eyes. "Oh, Gran! I...I really hurt Meg." The story tumbled from her lips and the tears fell, her earlier stubborn willpower nothing but rubble now.

Gran listened, sipped her own coffee—where had that come from?—and made little sounds of commiseration. When Bailey was finally done spilling her guts, Gran asked one question: "What will you do now?"

Bailey stared at her. It was a simple question but still wrapped her in a blanket of love. She could have asked, "What do you think you should do?" Or, as Nicole might have asked, "Why did you do that?" On the surface, the questions were the same. But deep down, where it counted, only Gran's held no hint of accusation or blame or disappointment or even disapproval. After all, she'd just admitted to befriending a boy she'd met online.

Bailey smiled through her tears and squeezed Gran's hand. "I know I have to apologize for ditching her, but that's all, Gran. I'm not sorry I'm friends with Ryder, and I'm not sorry I want to find someone to love, even if Meg won't. I shouldn't have to apologize for that."

Gran angled her head and tucked her stylish blond hair behind an ear. "Why do you think you have to?"

"Um—" Bailey wasn't sure how to answer that. "I always get this feeling that Meg expects me to stay single for the rest of my life so she won't be alone. But that's not me! I want to get married and have kids someday. Don't get me wrong—that's not *all* I want. But Meg has no room for that in her plan. She doesn't get that I have my own plan."

"Do you?"

She lifted her shoulders. "Sort of. I know I want an exciting career, but I don't know what that is yet. I know I want a family who loves me—husband and kids someday, a lot of them. I don't know who he is yet. I'm not going to skip any opportunity for finding him and I shouldn't have to, right?"

Gran held up her hands, palms up. "This is your life we're talking about, not mine. It's not my job to tell you if you're right or wrong here. That's up to you to discover and decide."

Bailey smiled. "See? This is why I called you. Mom would have lectured me on what's right. And Meg would have lectured me on what's right for her. Nobody seems to get that I have my own ideas. Except you. Thank you." Bailey leaped up and kissed Gran on her nose.

"Um, well, thank you." Gran wrinkled her nose and laughed. She angled her head with a sparkle in her eye and grabbed a menu from the holder on the edge of the table. "Now how about we split a really big and fattening dessert before we head home?"

"Deal." Bailey wiped her eyes and pointed to the triple-scoop chocolate sundae with a sparkle of her own. They ordered and dug in, and in minutes, the large dessert had been reduced to nothing but a dirty dish.

Gran sat back on her side of the booth and patted her belly. "Well, I don't know about you, but I sure feel better."

Bailey laughed. "I do too. Thanks, Gran."

"Anytime, sweet girl. Have you figured out what to do?"

"Yeah, I have a few ideas. But first, I'll apologize." Bailey uncrossed her legs, recrossed them, and finally tucked them both under her butt. "I made her sad, Gran. She upsets me and annoys me and maybe she doesn't always understand me, but I made her sad. I hate that part the most. So that's the part I'll fix first."

Gran stood up, put some cash on the table, and put both hands on Bailey's shoulders. "That's exactly what a good friend would do."

A good friend. Bailey shook her head. Sure messed that up, hadn't she? But she reached out and hugged her grandmother when an idea for fixing things struck. Thirty minutes later, after making a few phone calls and begging people for various favors, Bailey opened her blog and started a new post.

> You know what totally sucks? Admitting to yourself that you messed up big time, that you hurt someone you really love. No, not a boy. A different kind of love. Best friend love.

She smiled at the thought, even though guilt was burning a hole in her heart. Meg would forgive her. She knew that without a doubt.

> Best friends are honest and loyal, and I forgot that for a moment, but now I remember. Best friends know where all the bodies are buried, you know? And yet love you anyway. It's the kind of love that doesn't

> need to impress anybody the way you do when you're trying to get a new guy to notice you. My best friend knows what I look like without makeup and doesn't care if I didn't wash my hair or get out of my pajamas. She sticks with me no matter what happens—even when I'm a jerk.
>
> I was a jerk.

That was still hard to admit even after the triple-chocolate sundae she'd shared with Gran. But it was true. She'd kept Ryder a secret from the person who meant the most to her. It was selfish.

> I hate that about me—hate that I not only can make my best friend cry but that I did. I am so sorry and hope she'll forgive me. To make it up to her, I'm buying her the biggest bag of M&M's I can find. They're her favorite.

That was an understatement—M&M's were like Meg catnip. Bailey smiled and hit the Publish button that sent her latest post public. Sometimes it was easier to blog about the mushy stuff than it was to say it out loud. But she had to. She owed Meg that. She unlocked her phone and held her breath until Meg answered.

"Hey, it's me."

Chapter 15
Meg

Meg's pulse continued to skip beats long after Chase had left. He'd kissed her…or she'd kissed him. It was all a bit of a blur now. She ran a finger over her lips. They still tingled.

No. No, this wasn't what she wanted. She wanted school and a degree and a career, not kisses that tingled. So she grabbed a canvas and started prepping. Work always centered her. It would take her mind off tingling lips and aching hearts. She glanced outside and decided to recreate the last snowstorm when Chase and his little brothers had tried to save their snowman. She mixed shades. She needed to contour, to highlight. She dabbed white over green, layered snow over bits of green lawn with—

Her phone buzzed and she cursed out loud. She didn't want to talk about it, analyze it, dissect it. They were just feelings and they would go away if she could take her mind off stuff. But the caller ID showed it was Bailey, and now Meg wavered. Every cell in her body screamed *Ignore it!* She even thought about smashing the phone against the wall of her room, but she needed her phone with its ancient flip-out keyboard. Cursing her own weakness, she dropped her brush and finally answered.

"I'm so sorry, Meg!" Bailey's voice, thick with tears, wailed in her ear. "Meg?"

"Yeah, I'm here. I'm listening." Meg's own voice was just as thick. She'd never expected Bailey to apologize. She'd forgive Bailey. Of course she would. Hell, she already had.

"I'm really sorry. I didn't mean to hurt you. I just wanted to—"

"Not share him. I get that." Chase's words replayed in Meg's mind, and suddenly, it all made perfect sense.

"You do?"

"Yeah, I'm sorry too. I know I can come on really strong sometimes, but I hate knowing something I did made you keep a boyfriend a secret from me."

Bailey was quiet for so long, Meg had to look at her phone to be sure the call hadn't dropped. "Bay? You still there?"

"Yeah…sorry. Oh, Meg, really, I'm so sorry. I never wanted you to feel bad. I just wanted—"

"It's okay, Bailey."

"Yay!" she squealed.

Meg twisted a paint rag into a knot. Apologies were a huge first step. Now came the true test—acceptance. "Tell me about him."

Bailey told her everything, and Meg bit her lip, hoping she wouldn't say anything to upset her all over again. "Meg, I think—well, I *thought* I made a mistake breaking up with Simon. Until I met Ryder."

But you didn't actually meet him, did you? Meg bit her lip harder.

"I really miss Simon. I know he wasn't always nice to me, but I still miss him. Or I did. But with Ryder, the whole Simon thing doesn't hurt so much. He's just—well, he's sweet. He treats me the way you always said I should be treated."

Meg's shoulders dropped. Hard to argue with your own words. .She squeezed her eyes shut and hoped this worked out for Bailey. "He sounds great, Bailey. Really great."

"Oh, he is. Trust me."

Trust me. Bailey's words were like a hammer to the head. That was the whole problem, wasn't it? She hadn't trusted Bailey. Chase said she was judgmental. Meg sank to her bed, squeaked an apology of her own. "I'm so sorry, Bay. I don't want you to hide guys from me."

"Okay, let's not do this anymore. Can you come over?"

"What? Like now?"

"Yeah, right now."

"Okay, I guess so."

"Great! Bye!" Bailey always said *hi* and *bye* in two syllables.

Meg closed her phone, cleaned her brushes, and changed her clothes. Fifteen minutes later, she was standing on the porch in front of Bailey's front door, her eyes still wet.

"You're here!" Bailey flung open the door, wrapped her in a hug, and tilted her from side to side, and Meg laughed.

They were okay again.

"Come inside."

Meg followed Bailey through the living room and into the dining room. "Surprise!"

She froze half in the room, half out. Bailey's grandparents, Bailey, Chase, even her mom clapped.

"Mom! What are you doing here? I thought you had a class—" Her face burned and her cheeks hurt from the damn smile she couldn't stop.

"Oh, honey, I can miss one or two. It's not every day when my baby girl turns seventeen. Here. Happy birthday." Her mom pressed a card into her hand.

Meg opened it to find a gift certificate to her favorite art supply store. "Mom," she gasped. "This is too much. We can't—"

"We can. Go buy yourself a rainbow."

Meg flung her arms around her and squeezed.

"Megan. Happy birthday." Chase smiled and jerked his chin at the huge cake on the Grants' dining room table and Meg's eyes went wide.

"You...no way. You made this?" It was decorated like an old-fashioned art palette, complete with a brush and paint wells. "This is amazing. Thank you." When did he have time to do all this?

Bailey rushed over and guided Meg into a chair, where she was forced to endure the worst version of "Happy Birthday" ever sung.

"Oh, my God, you guys, that was so...so terrible," she groaned. Chase tossed a balled-up napkin at her with a laugh.

Mrs. Grant passed slices of cake around the table and Bailey poured coffee. Meg took a bite and felt something crunch under her teeth. "What—*oh*. Oh, God, I don't believe it."

Chase grinned. "There's a layer of M&M's under the icing."

"Okay. Why?" Mr. Grant frowned at his plate.

"Gramps, they're Meg's absolute favorite thing." Bailey nudged Meg with a shoulder. "Right, Meg?"

"Mmmmm."

"Nice touch, Chase." Pauline clapped.

When everyone had cake, coffee, or milk, Bailey slipped into the chair next to Meg and took her hand. "I'm so glad we're okay again. Just so you know, Chase has been working on your cake all week."

Something in Meg's chest expanded and warmed, and she tried to stomp on it, to will it to be something simple like indigestion or maybe a minor heart attack, fearing it was something much, much worse.

A few hours later, her mother headed off to class and Chase walked her home, carrying the leftover cake under a sheet of aluminum foil. "You reminded her it was my birthday, didn't you?"

Chase's stride faltered for a second. "Um…no. Not really. The thing is—"

"Relax. It's okay. She was mad at me. I get that. But you made her stop being mad. So…thank you. And thanks for the cake. It was totally amazing."

He waited while she unlocked the door and then handed her the cake box. "Happy birthday, Megan." Before she could move away, he pulled her toward him and lowered his head, his lips just a breath from hers. All she had to do was lift her head and…and…

She leaped back and into the house, closing the door in his face.

On Saturday morning, Meg thought about not showing up, about sulking and getting back at Bailey for forgetting her, for making her feel like Fallow Brown—in other words, like crap. But not only had Bailey organized a tiny little birthday party, but she'd blogged about it, bought her M&M's, and somehow managed to get a whole bunch of people who read her blog to also buy her M&M's.

Staying mad and trying to get even after all that just felt petty.

So on Saturday morning, Meg steadied her nerves and walked up Bailey's porch steps to ring the bell, ready to accompany her friend to I-CON. The thought of strolling past booth after booth to hear the merits of another dumb game and watching Bailey squeal over costume characters had Meg's teeth clenching.

But she'd *promised*.

It was going to be a long day.

Chase was there, she noted with a gulp when Bailey flung open the door. Meg hadn't stopped thinking about their disastrous near-kiss when she practically turned into an ice cube. She told herself he had finally gotten the message. She wasn't interested in him and never would be. She told herself she was happier without him.

Both were lies.

She nodded stiffly to him while Bailey grabbed her in a hello clutch that rocked her from side to side and ended with a bounce. Chase looked like a guy struggling hard not to laugh at Bailey's excitement. When his eyes met Meg's, he didn't say a word and only nodded. She breathed a bit easier.

On the train east to Stony Brook, Bailey seemed oblivious to the strained silence between Meg and Chase. She seemed happier, perkier than usual, Meg noted with passing interest. That was a good thing. It meant she wasn't holding a grudge. So Meg wouldn't hold one either. She hung back while Bailey skipped from one booth to the next. Chase had gone off on his own, for which Meg was profoundly grateful. It was kind of sweet watching Bailey go all gooey over costume characters. She'd collected a bag full of action figures, autographs, card decks, comic books, video games, and…a bunch of phone numbers.

"She's like a queen holding court," Chase said when he found her in the midafternoon at the concession area.

Meg snorted.

"Hey, it's not every day a guy meets a girl who looks like Bailey *and* who loves video games. These guys are toast," he added when he saw Meg's eyes roll.

Meg tried to ignore the stab of pain. Everybody loved Bailey. Except Bailey, she reminded herself. Well, at least Chase wasn't acting weird around her. "Not you too."

"Come on, Megan. Do you know how seriously cool it is for a girl to be into gaming? I'm surprised no one's proposed to her yet." He waved a hand toward the long autograph line where Bailey waited, chatting excitedly to the guys behind her.

"Wait. That blond dude looks ready to drop to one knee." He laughed. "So what about you?"

Meg swallowed the last of her hot dog and swilled some water. "What about me?"

"What's your favorite game?"

Meg shrugged. "I don't have one."

"Okay, what about a character?"

Meg shrugged again.

"Oh, come on!" Chase nudged her with his shoulder and Meg pretended she never felt the tingle. "There's gotta be something here that interests you."

Meg dropped her gaze to her water bottle. That she was interested, even a little bit, was a secret she had to protect at any cost. But Chase wouldn't let it go. He moved closer, nudged her again, green eyes teasing. The tingle was impossible to hide.

"The only thing I'm interested in is the exit," she lied.

"I've been watching you, the way your eyes track all this bright color... all this animated action. I *know* you, Megan. Tell me you're not itching to get your fingers on a sketch pad right now." He raised his hand, tucked a strand of hair behind her ear, and her knees jolted, smacking the bottom of the table.

She tried to ignore the way her belly flipped when he admitted he'd been watching her...or the way her heart took that extra beat when he'd said, "I know you, Meg." Distance! She needed distance. She strode to the trash can, crumbled the paper liner into a wad, and pitched it. Damn it, why did he have to be so freakin' observant? She turned, only to find Chase blocking her way, all proud of himself, his prismatic eyes crinkling with suppressed laughter. Meg huffed and whirled around, but he caught her around the waist and she nearly combusted.

"Seriously, Megan. Is it that hard to admit I might know you better than you think?"

Oh, Chase, you have no idea. "Chase, just because you live a few houses behind me doesn't mean you know me." She wriggled out of his arms before her heart exploded.

"Yeah, it does. And you didn't answer my question."

It was all she could do just to remain upright and he expected her to answer questions? She sighed. "What question?"

"Do you wish you could sketch all this?"

"Fine. Yes. Are you happy now? Maybe I should go get my napkins out of the trash and draw that guy in the cape over there." She folded her arms while his grin stretched wider.

"Or…you could use this." He held out a plastic bag. "Happy birthday."

He'd…he'd bought her a gift. Meg's heart gave a squeeze. "You gave me a gift. A cake. A pretty awesome cake."

"Cake is required at birthdays. So are presents. This is a present."

"Chase, I can't—"

"Oh, come on, Meg. Just look." He dipped into one of the bags he carried and pulled out a notebook and some colored pencils. It was exactly what she'd have bought herself if she could have afforded to.

No, damn it. *No!*

Meg stared at them for a long moment and felt her resolve crumbling like a stale cookie. She wanted to grab them and curl up in the corner over there and sketch Chase's eyes. No. *No!* She should shred the notebook and grind the pencils to stubs.

Wrong! This was so wrong. Meg inhaled a breath for courage but made the mistake of looking at Chase's smile and she couldn't do it, couldn't say the no she should have said and instead took his gifts with a mumbled thanks. She moved to the bistro table a couple had just vacated, leaving behind a wad of napkins and straw wrappers. Impatient, she swiped them to the floor and peeled the cellophane from the notebook.

It wasn't a notebook. It was a comic book pad. Every page had blank panels for artwork plus ruled lines for bubble text. Meg dumped the pencils on the table and grabbed one, fury guiding her hand while the image in her mind clashed with the one in her heart.

Bold splashes of color.

Thick black lines.

Meg drew like she was possessed. Maybe she was.

"Wow. This is cool." Bailey startled her and Meg jolted, scattering pencils all over the floor.

They bent to collect them while Chase grabbed the pad and stared at Meg's sketch, his forehead creased.

"Is this what you see?" he asked quietly.

Meg crossed her arms and angled her head, considering him. "Yeah, that's how I see you."

She'd wanted to piss him off, so she'd drawn him with an exaggerated squareness to his jaw, jagged edges to the soft hair that always hung just right and his eyes—Meg didn't bother getting the colors right. She just tossed them all into the mix, wedges of radiant color emphasized by dark downward slashes of eyebrow—all fierce and ready to leap off the page.

"Not me." He tossed the pad on the table and pointed to the blob in the lower corner. "You."

He stared at her, waiting for an answer Meg refused to give. Finally, he sat back down with the pad and the pencils and sketched, looking up at her every few moments.

Meg's jaw dropped.

"I didn't know you liked to draw, Chase," Bailey said, pulling up a chair and dropping her swag bags to the floor under the table.

"I'm a man of many talents," he murmured, and she giggled.

Meg didn't know Chase could draw either.

"Sit down, Megan."

Meg shifted her weight to one leg and made a sound of impatience. *How could I not know this about him?*

"Sit. Down," he glared.

Fine. With a heavy sigh, Meg sat, arms folded. She refused to look at him and watched the crowd mill about the cavernous conference center. She should have known this. He knew all about her artistic aspirations. It…it's something that should have come up in a hundred conversations. It should have come up when they worked on their research project.

But he never told her. Meg dug her nails into her palms.

"Oh, Chase, this is *so* good," Bailey gushed. "Don't you want to see it, Meg?"

"No."

Bailey opened her mouth to push the issue and then paled at something over Meg's shoulder. Meg spun, saw Simon stroll by, his arm slung over Caitlyn's shoulders. He spotted Bailey, tensed, but then turned away.

"Come on, Bay. Let's leave." Meg put her arm around Bailey.

The train ride home was tense and quiet. Meg stared out the window at the neighborhoods blurring past, wishing she had the colored pencils and the pad in her hands. Bailey texted on her cell and Chase sat opposite her, one leg propped on Meg's seat, his eyes shut.

He looked so different with his eyes closed.

Flat.

Impassive.

Ordinary.

Those motley eyes of his opened, caught her checking him out, and suddenly, it was like God breathed life onto the canvas. Meg flushed hotly and turned back to the window.

Chase chuckled once.

Bailey texted.

The scenery blurred.

A few hours later, Meg dumped the conference swag on her bed and collapsed next to it, feet screaming. Her eyelids slipped closed, and just when she was about to surrender to a much-needed nap, Meg remembered Chase's sketch pad. She stared at it for a moment. Oh, hell. She flipped it open to her angry rendering and gasped.

Chase had reshaped the faceless blob she'd carelessly scribbled for herself. He'd added in defiantly crossed arms under an overly generous chest that made her snicker. He'd drawn the mousy brown hair that fell in front of serious eyes. But he'd angled the eyes so that they stared up at his from under spiky lashes.

To the image she'd sketched of him, he'd reshaped the face so that instead of the grimace she'd drawn, he now smiled warmly at the blob that used to be Meg, one arm extended, as if in invitation.

He'd drawn *them*.

Meg ripped the page out of the notebook with every intention of crumbling it into a little ball she could pitch into the wastebasket. Instead, she carefully folded it and tucked it under her pillow with a rueful laugh. *Look at me, wishing for impossible things.*

Foolish and futile.

Chapter 16
Bailey

Bailey dumped bags of conference swag all over her bed and wondered where Chase had found that comic panel pad. That would have been cool to buy. She could have used it for game design. Speaking of Chase, she twirled a curl and thought about the way he and Meg had acted today. Meg was mad. No, that's not right. She was off-center. She'd been hyperaware of Chase, her eyes tracking him throughout the venue. Bailey doubted Meg was even aware of that. Something was different—it was like their connection had gotten stronger somehow. When had that happened? She should have paid closer attention, but she'd been so caught up with Ryder and keeping him a secret that she'd neglected Meg.

Bailey hoped that hugging Chase at McDonald's that night was what—finally—opened Meg's eyes. She rubbed her hands together. Now all she had to do was get Meg to admit her feelings for Chase.

It wouldn't be easy. Bailey laughed, amused by her understatement.

She paused in her swag-sorting and then grabbed her phone when inspiration struck. She didn't even bother to text. She just called Chase.

"Hey, what's up?"

She had to play this just right. "I wanted to thank you."

"Oh, no sweat. I had fun—"

"No, not I-CON. I wanted to thank you for taking care of Meg and for baking that incredible cake."

Chase's voice got a little deeper. "She was pretty upset with you."

There it was. "I know. I'm glad you were there for her when she needed you. So…thanks."

"I didn't do it for you."

Bailey didn't doubt that for a second. "I know. I got a little dazed. It's hard not to," she admitted.

Chase groaned. "Okay, spare me the details. Just, you know, don't leave her out, okay? She worries about you and that really bugs her."

Oh, does it? Bailey grinned and did her best to sound solemn. "I promise."

She ended the call, tossed the phone to her bed, and paced, wondering just how many ways there were to make Meg mad enough at *her* that she'd turn to Chase for comfort. It had worked once and it could work again, especially now that the door had been opened. All she needed was a way—

She froze when an excellent idea hit her. Oh, this would seriously fry Meg's bacon. Could she be this devious? Bailey picked up her phone and texted Ryder.

Bailey: Hi!

Ryder: So how did u like I-CON?

Bailey: Awesome! Met the *Zelda* team.

Ryder: NO WAY!

Bailey: Hand to God! Got autographs, got some samples. It was cool. Wish you could have come with us.

Ryder: Yeah, me 2. Woulda been perfect 1st date.

Bailey pressed both hands to her mouth. First date? Oh, God, could he be any cuter?

Bailey: Why perfect?

Ryder: 'cuz u luv gaming

Bailey: Yeah, but what about you?

Ryder: 1st dates R 4 impressing the girl

Bailey: LOL. Tell that to my 10th grade BF. He rented a movie.

Ryder: Lame!

Bailey frowned. It wasn't lame, not really. Andrew, the tenth-grade love of her life, heard her say how much she'd wanted to see that movie about the guy who travels in time, so he'd rented it and invited her over.

Bailey: No, it was pretty great. Until it wasn't. Just like last BF.

Ryder: Wasn't?

Bailey: Yeah, stopped being great. Stopped trying to impress me. Stopped caring.

Ryder: Then he's a loser

Bailey: No, he's really not. Things just didn't work out.

Ryder: U miss him

Bailey: No, I'm over it.

Ryder: I won't stop trying 2 impress u

Bailey: You know what would impress me? Meeting you IRL.

Ryder: I know. I'm trying. Meg still pissed at you?

Bailey: She doesn't trust you, but she's trying.

Ryder: I swear, I'm a good guy. Want me to tell her?

Bailey: You'd do that?

Ryder: I'd do anything for u :)

Bailey: Yes! Xoxo

Ryder: Txt her nmbr. Xoxo back :)

Bailey sent Ryder Meg's number and wondered how long it would take Meg to erupt all over Chase. Maybe she should give Chase a heads-up. She bit her nail, weighing the options, and finally decided not to get his hopes up in case Meg didn't vent on him. She happily turned her attention to sorting through the rest of her conference swag, reliving the day. It was perfect—except for seeing Simon and Caitlyn. And why was Caitlyn even there? It was so pathetically obvious that she didn't know anything about gaming, but there she was, hanging off Simon's arm like a cheap accessory. She pulled in a deep breath, forced herself to stop thinking about them. She'd gotten all this free stuff like autographs and had even met the *Zelda* developers—who cared about Simon? She thought about the tall blond guy she'd met in the autograph line.

He was there with his dad.

The dad was outrageously excited to be there. He knew every game and character name. The guy wasn't that excited—she could tell—but he was there, hanging out and busting his dad's chops. A sad little smile formed on her lips. Would her father have gone to I-CON with her? He would have, she believed. He would have geeked out and tugged her from booth to booth, introducing her to people he knew because he was a bigger gamer than she was. She'd have inherited her mad skills from him. She was sure of it.

The computer beckoned her. She logged on to the classmates website where she'd registered as her mother and checked for notifications. A few messages awaited—long-lost pals looking to reconnect, a plea for donations from the alumni group, and a form letter welcoming her to the site. She'd hoped that the guys her mother had let go might see her name, reach out, and say hi.

That would be a good starting point to locate her dad.

At the sound of her bedroom door opening, Bailey spun in her chair, barely managing to hide the window and look nonchalant.

"Mom, hey. Um, you look nice."

Nicole frowned at a sheet of paper in her hands. "Bailey, what's this?" She thrust the paper under Bailey's face.

Crap. It was this month's credit card statement. She hadn't expected the fee for the classmates website to show up so quickly. But there it was. "Oh, that's nothing. I just wanted to stay in touch with some of the seniors leaving this year. You know, like Chase?" She twirled a lock of hair and smiled.

Nicole folded her arms and angled her head. "Try again."

"Mom—"

"Bailey, I got calls this week from two different people I haven't thought of in seventeen years and both mentioned how happy they were to find me after all this time."

Bailey scrunched up her shoulders. "Oh."

"That's it? 'Oh'? Why don't you tell me what's really going on?"

Fine. She would do just that. She forced her shoulders to relax and dove in. "Okay. I'm looking for my father."

Nicole's lips thinned and she sucked in a sharp breath. "You're *what?*"

"I want to find my dad."

"You can't. I forbid it." Nicole took two steps away and turned her back.

Bailey rolled her eyes. "Mom, I'm not four years old anymore. I want to find my father, get to know him."

"What for? You're already too much like him."

Bailey's mind went blank. It was just for a second. One brief second of numbness before her mother's comment slashed at her heart and she gasped at the shock of pain. "I bet you hate that, don't you? That's why you won't tell me anything about him. Because you're punishing both of us!"

Nicole spun around. "Oh, honey, I'm sorry. I didn't mean that."

That was the reason. It had to be. "Then why won't you tell me who he is?"

"God, Bailey, it's not that simple." Nicole moved to her bed, sat down, stared at her hands. "I didn't want him to hurt you the way he hurt me."

"Hurt you? Like hit you?"

Nicole put up a hand. "No. No, it wasn't like that."

Her mother hiked up the skirt on her designer suit and tucked her legs beneath her on the bed. It made Bailey's breath hitch. She looked like a little girl. A sad, brokenhearted little girl.

With a jolt, she remembered Nicole wasn't all that much older than she was.

"Okay, I'm sorry. I'm not trying to hurt you. I just…need to know."

Nicole said nothing for a moment. "Okay," she said finally, holding up her hands only to let them fall back to her lap. "We met when I was fourteen. He was older. He wasn't like any of the boys in my school. He was…fun. Nothing ever bothered him, ever made him stop smiling." Nicole raised her head, managed a brief smile. "Just like you. I loved that about him." She stood, walked back to the window, and stared down at the street. "I did. I really loved him, Bailey. I loved him with every atom in my body. But he never took anything seriously. Everything was a game! School. Work. Life. Just one big party. Even when I told him I was pregnant, he laughed."

Bailey listened. But honestly, she wasn't seeing the problem here. Her dad sounded great.

"I knew I'd never be able to count on him for anything more than just fun. I was sixteen years old and pregnant, and I needed more than that. I needed to know he'd be there for us, that he'd support us." Nicole turned back and shrugged. "He wasn't."

"What did he do?"

"He left town. I never saw him again."

No. Damn it, no. Bailey's eyes filled. "That was years ago! Maybe he grew up and changed, you know? Matured. What does it hurt to just—"

"No!" Nicole's sharp retort had Bailey backing up a step. "I made my decision. If he wanted to find me, he could have...easily! I'm exactly where he left me." Nicole stopped and took a deep breath when Bailey's lip trembled. "Bailey, I'm sorry. I can't. If you're determined to know him, I guess you're right. I can't stop you. But I'm not going to help you either."

Nicole spun, left the bedroom, and closed the door with a soft click behind her. Bailey waited until she heard mom shut the door to her room and let the tears take her.

Chapter 17
Meg

As the evening slowly ticked down, Meg wondered what to do with herself. Her mother had already been home and left for her second job waiting tables. She nuked a frozen meal for dinner and threw a few hours into studying that wasn't so bad because she had leftover cake. Around 9:30, she grabbed a paintbrush. She clipped a piece of Bristol paper to her easel. Its smooth surface was great for testing colors. She got out some acrylics and starting layering colors—olive green, khaki, mustard, golden rod, chocolate, moss, ochre, and ivory. Meg mixed and blended and scraped but still couldn't get the eyes right.

Thank God Chase never asked about the easel. She'd have cracked like dried-out paint and never been able to face him again. If he'd noticed, he pretended he hadn't. She thought of his hands on her shoulder and her hip, and her eyes slipped shut. She relived his lips, his tongue on hers, and sighed at the way her body reacted to just the thought of his hands on her. If he'd pressed her for more, she wasn't sure she'd have said no. When the stab of pain came, as it always did, she carefully draped a cover over the easel and started cleaning brushes.

That's when her cell buzzed.

Meg glanced at the screen, but it was a text message from a number that wasn't in her contacts list.

Ryder: Hey. I hear u been asking a lot of questions about me.

Meg frowned at the screen and quickly typed a reply.

Meg: Here's a question. Who is this?

The phone pinged with a reply.

Ryder: Sorry. My name's Ryder. Ryder West. I'm Bailey's friend.

Her eyes narrowed. Bailey's friend? She'd be pretty pissed to find out he was just a friend and not a boyfriend. Meg texted back.

Meg: Well, Ryder West, I'm Bailey's friend, and you're right. I do have questions about you.

Ryder: Fine. Ask.

Oh, she planned to.

Meg: How did you meet?

They hadn't met, not officially, as far as Meg knew.

Ryder: We both like Xbox games.

Meg knew that much.

Meg: So you played a few games and thought you'd pick up the other player?

Ryder: U know it's not like that. Stop wasting time and get to the point.

Meg shook her head in disgust. Ryder wasn't quite the gentleman Bailey thought.

Meg: Fine. What's your deal?

Ryder: No deal. Just like hanging out with her.

Oh, she wasn't letting him off the hook that easily.

Meg: So what are you texting me for?

Ryder: I just wanted to show u I'm not jerking Bailey around. Can u ease up on her? I don't like hearing her so upset.

Upset? Bailey was upset? This was news.

Meg: Why is she upset?

Ryder: Testing me again? Fine. She told me UR mad at her because she forgot about plans she made with u.

Meg wished she could believe that. The truth stung a bit, and she tapped out a reply.

Meg: She didn't forget. She just wants to talk to you more than me.

Oh, God, could she be any more pathetic?

Ryder: I feel the same way about her. If u were really her friend, u wld be happy 4 her.

Oh, hell no. Meg stabbed at the buttons with extra fury.

Meg: I really am her friend, and that's why I'm making sure you're really who she thinks, so why don't you prove to me you're not some 50 year old pervert getting off by the sound of her voice?

Ryder: UR really sick. Why can't u just be happy for us?

Meg rolled her eyes. He's the creep hiding behind a keyboard and she's the sick one?

Meg: Is English not your first language? I'm not backing off until I know you're for real.

Meg waited, but no further texts arrived.

Chapter 18
Bailey

Bailey stared at her phone, willing it to buzz or vibrate or do something other than look cute in its glitter skin. She'd given Ryder Meg's phone number ages ago and neither one of them had contacted her. What were they talking about all this time? She nibbled a fingernail and obsessed. Meg was probably doing her TV lawyer routine, citing all the statistics and facts and reasons why Ryder was a liar and Bailey was a ditz for trusting him. Ryder was probably being his usual adorable self and doing his best to calm Meg down.

Unless—what if Meg was right and Ryder really was a guy in jail for murdering some poor teenager he'd met in person and then hiding her body in a creepy corn field? What if Meg totally scared Ryder away and she never heard from him again? She'd never know what he was really like…or what he looked like. She didn't even know where he lived.

She stared at her computer screen and opened the last email he'd sent. It held a link to a new game engine he'd mentioned—one that was geared toward newbies like herself and much easier to use than the one Chase had told her about. She clicked the link and did her best to concentrate on roughing-in the game's bones instead of on what Ryder and Meg were talking about.

Meg must have been furious with her all over again. It was the only explanation Bailey had to explain her silence. With luck, Meg was even now turning to Chase for comfort. This was a lot harder than she'd expected. What if Meg hated her for doing this? Could she live with that? What if even after all this scheming, Meg and Chase still didn't hook up?

Bailey couldn't stand it another second. She picked up the phone and texted Ryder.

> **Bailey:** Did you text Meg?
>
> **Ryder:** Wow, she's a total B. Don't know Y UR friends.
>
> **Bailey:** What happened? What did she say?
>
> **Ryder:** She demanded I stop lying to u. Said I'm a perv, a liar, and a freak. Even blamed me for the fight u had.

Bailey's eyes went round. Wow. That was over the top, even for Meg. What happened to the promise she'd made to give Ryder a chance?

> **Bailey:** OMG, I'm sorry. She overreacts.
>
> **Ryder:** Whatever. I gotta go. U should call her, hang out.

Wait…what? She sent him one more text to say she was sorry, but he didn't reply. She plugged the phone in to charge and stared at it for a long moment. This hadn't gone exactly as planned. She had wanted *Meg* to worry, not Ryder. Oh, hell, this was all just so messed up. Tomorrow, she'd straighten it all out and just confess.

Meanwhile, she had a new idea for a blog update.

> Somewhere in the BFF Code, there should be rules for when your best friend hates the guy you like. Rules like don't tell him he's a pervert and

a liar and a freak. Maybe BFFs shouldn't meet boyfriends at all—like they can never occupy the same space around you at the same time. That could work. Girls should be issued those Aperture Science hand-held devices like in the *Portal* game. That way, whenever a BFF and a BF are within a few years of each other, we can open a portal to send them somewhere else and avoid all this competition and drama.

She considered that for a moment. It really was a competition, wasn't it? Chase had said it to her face. Meg was really upset that Bailey had ditched her. But that wasn't all of it. No, she knew Meg. She knew that Meg took a lot of pride in her grades and her intelligence. It was more like she couldn't stand that Bailey wasn't listening to her advice. She was a big girl and certainly able to make her own decisions.

When you really tear it down to the wire frame, it's about respect, right? You like him, and you like her, and you want them both to like each other so things are easy. They should both get that. BFFs know your luck hasn't been that great with boys and should try to put in some extra effort. And boyfriends should know that BFFs have been around a lot longer than them. They should be trying to make the best possible impression.

They should never make you choose. And you should never choose one or the other.

Would Meg expect her to drop Ryder because she didn't trust him? Was that why she was so ticked off? Well, she wasn't going to do that. Meg would either get over it or not.

Her choice.

Bailey published the post.

Chapter 19
Meg

At school on Monday, Meg headed to her locker with her head down and her steps heavy. She hadn't talked to Bailey since Saturday. She thought about calling her...until she saw Bailey's latest blog. She hadn't asked Bailey to choose anybody! She was only looking out for her. Isn't that what friends did for each other? If Bailey thought Meg would allow her to get hacked up by some ax-murdering freak, she had another thing coming.

"Um...hey, Meg."

She jerked and found Bailey standing beside her. Meg opened her mouth but couldn't squeeze any sound out. She fiddled with the lock, her fingers cold and stiff, and finally managed to get it open.

"I shouldn't have asked Ryder to text you."

Tears stung the back of her eyes and Meg only stared. "You *asked* him?"

"I'm really sorry."

"It's okay," she replied automatically. And then wondered why. It *wasn't* okay. It wasn't the least bit okay. They were friends. Friends were supposed to talk to each other, not hide and avoid and forget and abandon. Meg stuffed her jacket inside her locker and grabbed a textbook without even looking at the title. She slammed the locker and Bailey jumped.

"If it's not okay, you should say so." Bailey shifted her weight to one side. "I just thought if you guys talked, you'd believe me."

Meg fell back against the locker, let her eyes slip shut. "Bailey, I do believe you. I just want to know he's the real deal."

"Oh, Meg, he is. He really is." She smiled and wrapped her arms around her middle.

"Bay," Meg started and then looked around to make sure no one could hear. "What about Simon? I mean, one day you're all hung up over him, and the next, it's Ryder. This isn't a video game where you get to keep pressing reset."

Bailey jerked, and Meg knew she'd hit a nerve.

"I know that, Meg. I still miss Simon. But Ryder's so smart. And we have a lot in common."

"Besides your video games?"

Her smile froze and then brightened. "He grew up on a ranch. We spent hours talking about horses."

Bailey loved horses and had wanted one for as long as Meg could remember. She'd taken Meg to a public stable to ride, but it hadn't gone well. Bailey's horse was a gentle mare. Meg's was Satan. So Bailey rode alone and Meg watched from the safety of the bleachers that circled the ring.

"Um…Bay?" Alarm bells pealed in her head. "Does he know where you ride?"

"Sure. I told him."

"So he could have been there, watching you, but you wouldn't even know it, would you?"

"Meg, he—"

Why didn't this frighten her? "He could have been there, Bay. Watching you."

"Oh, my God, Meg!" she shouted. "Just stop it. I haven't been to the stable since I met him. He didn't follow me. He didn't stalk me. This is exactly why I hid him."

"Bailey, I know how you get with guys. I'm trying to make sure—"

"God, do you even hear yourself? The only thing you're making sure of is that I never find love like you." Her eyes got hard. "I don't want to be like you! Why don't you get that?"

Bailey's words tore through Meg's gut like bullets. Meg flinched and gasped, unable to catch her breath. She pressed her hands to her stomach, unable to remember grabbing the textbook clutched in them, and sucked in air. She forced her feet to move. She couldn't see anything...anything except the furious disapproval in Bailey's eyes.

Away. Meg had to just move away. It was all that mattered. One step. Two. Stumbling into lockers, Meg walked and then ran to the exit and shoved the door open, gasping in great gulps of the chill that clung to the spring air.

She ran until her legs felt like they'd left her body. Finally, she fell to her knees and sat on the cold ground for ages, replaying Bailey's words, the look in her eyes. Cars drove past, but no one stopped for the broken girl on the side of a road.

A buzzing sound interrupted her self-punishment. Meg dug her cell out of the pocket of her jeans and glanced at the screen.

Chase.

With a sigh, Meg hit the button that sent him straight to voice mail. For a long moment, she stared at the phone clutched in numb fingers.

And then Meg got mad.

She flipped through the call history and found Ryder's last text message. She pressed Reply.

Meg: We need to talk. It's about Bailey.

Several minutes ticked by until the phone buzzed.

Ryder: Is this Meg again? Busy now. Email if u want. Ryder909@mail.com.

Oh, Meg wanted to all right.

She picked herself up and headed home to an empty house. Mom was at her day job and probably had already gotten the phone call letting her know she'd skipped class today. She didn't have much time and hurried up to her room, powered on the computer, and started composing a long email to Ryder.

To: Ryder909@mail.com
Subject: Who are you?

Ryder,

I don't know you and you don't know me. But I do know Bailey. You may think you know her too, but you don't. Not the way I do. You don't know the things she's been through. You don't know what hurts her.

I do.

I know everything about her. I need to make sure you won't hurt her. If you really care about her, you'll help me. I need proof that you're real and not some psycho stalker pedophile. Text messages and emails are not the way to handle this.

What do you say, Ryder? Are you willing to meet us in person some place public?

Meg sent the message, and while she waited impatiently for his response, she changed into comfortable sweats and tied her hair back. Despite the run, she was wired and jittery. She needed something to burn off energy, something that would soothe. She tugged the tarp off the easel and started mixing color combinations. With a filbert brush, she dropped gray over the Bristol paper, shaping it into an oval. The whites of eyes are never truly white, so maybe starting with a layer of light gray might tell her what she kept missing. She switched to a round brush and outlined the folds of an eye. Upper lid. Lower lid. Creases. Soon, Meg was captured by the work, lost in a world of color and lines until the phone buzzed.

She flexed her hand and answered.

"Meg, why aren't you in school?"

Meg winced. "Oh…hey, Mom."

"Don't 'Hey, Mom' me. I want to know why you aren't in school."

"Sick."

"Don't lie to me, Meg."

Meg didn't have the energy to come up with anything clever and decided to go with the truth. "Mom, It's Bailey. We…well, we had a horrible fight and I just couldn't—" she trailed off.

She heard a sigh. A loud squeak from her office chair. Mom was fidgeting. She always fidgeted when she didn't know what to say.

"A fight, huh? What was it about?"

More squeaking.

"She's been talking to this guy online. She hasn't even met him and she thinks she's in love." Meg thought she was empty. But fresh tears fell. "I'm worried, Mom. I don't trust this guy. But she does. And now she's taking his side against mine. She said I don't care about her...that I only care about myself...and making sure she has no friends...just like me."

Squeak. "Okay, Meg. Okay." *Squeak.* "I'll be home at lunch and we'll talk then. You hang in there, okay? I'm sure she didn't mean any of this, and once you talk, everything will be fine again."

Meg ended the call, tossed the phone on her bed, and flung herself on the mattress after it, crying until the computer let out a soft ping.

An email from Ryder West.

From: Ryder909@mail.com
Subject: re: Who are you?

Meg, I know you and Bailey are best friends. She talks about you all the time. I think it's pretty great that you look out for her. She told me how you help her with her video game designs. They're sick! I know you're really worried about Bailey, but I won't hurt her. I swear. Things here are totally messed up. I have to use this ancient computer, no printer, no web cam. As soon as I can, I'll take you and Bailey out. We can go to the museum. Bailey says you really like art. My mom used to take me to the museum when I was little. I really liked the Impressionists. Renoir's my favorite. Mom liked all those Italian renaissance artists, but those paintings are all pretty much of chubby people. LOL. I have to go to work now. I promise I won't hurt Bailey. Could you just maybe ease up a little on her. I hate seeing her upset and I feel like we're tearing her apart. —R.

Meg read it again.

And again.

Meg read it until her mother knocked on the bedroom door.

Over lunch in the sunny kitchen, her mother shook her head. "Meg, you're right to be concerned. But maybe you could dial it down a little? Bailey's a big girl now. She knows enough not to run off and meet some Internet guy by herself. Trust her."

Meg stared at her mother across the kitchen table, at the lines under her eyes, the fatigue visible around her mouth, and guilt attacked. Mom worked at an office during the day. At night, she took college courses toward a degree in accounting when she wasn't waiting tables. Sunlight reflected off all the gold appliances and the room felt warm and cozy, but Meg was cold inside, and Mom…well, she just looked beat.

"Maybe this boy really is on the level."

Meg pressed her lips together and let her head fall back against the chair. "There's that word again," she murmured.

"What word?"

"Maybe," Meg replied.

"You have to give Bailey space, honey. You have to let her grow. All she's doing is talking. That's it. Just talking to a boy online. If she starts talking about sending money or running away, then you should worry."

"But Mom—"

"Meg, I'm not saying you're wrong. You're being smart and that's really good. But you're pushing Bailey away. In fact, you're pushing her directly into the arms of the boy you're afraid of." She stood up, took her plate. "Why don't you try being more supportive...you know, show Bailey you're here for her?" She put the plates in the sink, washed her hands, and ripped off a paper towel. "I have to get back to work. Are you better?"

Meg nodded and smiled tightly. "Yeah, I guess so."

"Since you're taking the day off, you can straighten up the kitchen." She handed Meg the paper towel. "See you later, honey."

And she was gone.

Meg heard the door close and the car start. She washed their dishes and wiped down the table. Upstairs in her room, she thought about everything Pauline had said. And some of the things Chase had said.

That *judgmental* thing still stung.

She loved Bailey and only wanted to protect her. Bailey was so trusting, almost to the point of—

Meg gave herself a mental kick in the rear. She was doing it again.

Eventually, she settled on a course of action, grabbed her phone, and sent a quick reply to Ryder's email.

To: Ryder909@mail.com
Subject: Backing off

OK. You win. I'll back off. I want to see Bailey happy, not hurt, so I'll stop giving you a hard time if you promise to make meeting us in person in a safe public place your top priority. Also, I attached an image I thought you'd like. You said you like the Impressionists. –Meg

Meg sent the message, powered down the computer, and then grabbed her keys, her phone, and her jacket. Bailey should be getting off the bus in a minute or two.

Chapter 20
Bailey

The weather was crisp but unseasonably mild for early spring. Bailey drew up her hood and headed toward home, trying to avoid looking at Meg's house across the street. Looking at Gran and Gramp's house always made her feel warm inside. It was a cute two-story house that looked like it belonged in a Mother Goose story. Gingerbread trim adorned the porch. Flower boxes currently empty would be overflowing with cheery blooms in a few weeks. Meg always said she should bring an easel with her and set it up right there beside the path to the porch steps. She would paint it in watercolors.

Bailey eyebrows drew together. This whole thing with Meg was snowballing and—

"Meg?"

There she was, sitting at the foot of the porch steps, staring at her with a furrowed brow. "Hey."

"What are you doing here?"

"Um…well, I came to apologize."

Bailey shook her head when every last ounce of anger evaporated. "I'm the one who should apologize. I didn't mean what I said today."

Meg waved a hand. "Bay, listen. For what it's worth, I liked Ryder. I even emailed him again today. I think you're right. He really likes you."

The frown disappeared and her smile exploded. "What did he say? Tell me everything!" She ran up the steps and curled beside Meg on the top one.

"He…well, he said I should back off. That we're tearing you apart." Her voice cracked and she had to stop before she embarrassed herself.

"I want you guys to be friends," Bailey said after a moment. "But it's hard since we can't hang out."

"See, that's the part I don't get. Why can't you hang out?"

Bailey stared down the street, her face long. "Ryder's whole life is a mess. Remember when I told you he just moved here?"

Meg nodded.

"He's living with an aunt he hasn't seen since he was little. His mom is dead."

"Oh, Bay!" Meg gasped. "What about his dad?"

She shook her head. "His dad's out of the picture. His mother was killed—"

"Killed? Like…murdered?"

Bailey nodded. "Yeah, Ryder was the one who found her body. Because he's underage, they won't let him stay in Montana, so he had to come here. He's living with relatives, but they're strangers. He was homeschooled, but his aunt wants him to go to real school. They argue all the time. He says he feels trapped. He has no car. No friends. The only cool thing there is to do is play Xbox."

Meg stared at her feet. "You…um…already know a lot about him."

A bright smile spread over her face and she hugged her legs to her chest. "Oh, Meg, I do! I feel like I know him almost as much as I know you."

Bailey stood while Meg's eyes roamed up and down her face, searching for proof that she was lying. Finally, she nodded once. "I'll back off, Bay. But please…could you do me two favors?"

With her eyes narrowed, Bailey nodded slowly, hoping these favors were easy.

"Don't meet him alone. When he's able to handle all the stuff in his life and make a date with you, don't go alone. Call me. Call Chase. Call us both. Just don't go alone, okay?"

Bailey's lips tightened. Ryder wasn't—aw, hell. Meg was right. She had to be careful. "Okay."

Meg grinned. "Thanks. And could you maybe not forget about me? I know it's immature, but I was here first. I look forward to the plans we have and it's not cool to dump me for some guy."

Bailey lowered her head. "You're right. Ryder said the same thing. Thursday night, *TVD*?"

Meg managed a smile for a second or two. "Oh, I am so there. Do you think Damon is going to kiss Elena this week?"

They spent the next half hour talking about *The Vampire Diaries*.

And then Bailey's cell phone buzzed. Bailey's worried eyes shot to Meg's.

"Is that him?"

Bailey nodded.

"Go ahead. Reply. It's okay."

With a touch of her finger, Bailey unlocked her phone, a tiny smile dancing on her lips as she read the text. "He says he's sorry for the other day." She turned the phone sideways and tapped out a response. "I told him it's okay. We're okay."

Another message arrived and Bailey twirled her hair. "Oh, this is good. What do you think?" She handed Meg her phone. Ryder's latest text was about the video game.

> **Ryder:** Was thinking about the point of UR game. Have to switch motive. Foundation should stop missions, not assign them.

Meg blinked and then shrugged. "I don't get it."

"Oh…um," Bailey shifted. "We thought it would be cool to have this shadowy government organization oversee missions and send players out on assignments. But Ryder's right. The game's called *Lost Time*, not *Changed Time*. All the missions *have* to fail. Otherwise history is rewritten. Have to invert the Foundation's purpose, which isn't a big deal since nothing's done yet. I can't believe I didn't notice that before."

Bailey's thumbs flew over her phone and her brow wrinkled.

"Go build levels." Meg gave Bailey a hug.

"Wait…are you sure?"

"Yeah, you're doing it, Bay. You're making your game." She smiled and then turned to go.

That's what Meg always wanted for her, Bailey reminded herself after Meg left. The confidence to stick to something. Meg was always telling her she needed more confidence, needed a boy who'd build her up, not tear her down. Someone who wouldn't build the game for her but encourage her to build it herself. True, Meg would have blocked Ryder immediately if he'd tried contacting her the way he had Bailey, but Meg was all about playing things safe. Bailey needed this, needed the connection. Ryder was not only

Chapter 21
Meg

The days went by and the weather slowly grew warmer and wetter. Bailey had kept her promise. She'd invited Meg over on Thursday night for their weekly vampire viewing. And she'd stopped shutting Meg out.

Meg was doing her best to stop being judgmental and overbearing. Everything was going so well. Ryder had even given her a great tip on a college she'd never considered—New York City's Cooper Union. If—and this was a big if—if she could get in, the tuition was covered for all students. Meg could hardly wrap her brain around the concept—a full ride. All she'd have to cover would be living expenses. Of course, she had to submit a home test and art portfolio too, but thankfully, there was still over a year left to work on those requirements.

She hadn't been able to find a new job though. That had her worried. She'd asked Pauline for money, but her mom lectured her on better saving habits between paydays. Her mother didn't know the theater was closed and Meg decided not to add to her worries. She'd find work somewhere. In the meantime, she'd squandered what money she had left—and that included what she found between the sofa cushions—for her train ticket to the city the following Saturday morning.

She stood on the sixth floor of the Museum of Modern Art in New York City, Bailey and Chase at her side, awed by the hundreds of pieces in the Print/Out exhibit. Print/Out was this year's homage to the evolution of commercial art. She'd been looking forward to it for weeks, and now that she knew about the Cooper Union, she hoped she'd get ideas for something she could do with an art degree—something she'd never seriously entertained because it didn't meet her Plan requirements. Meg turned to grin at Bailey.

She was texting.

Meg rolled her eyes and turned to grin at Chase.

He stared at the display, confusion muddying his vibrant eyes.

Meg turned back to the display with a sigh. She had her two best friends with her, and yet, she was here alone. She noticed the name of the artist. "Hey." Meg nudged him with her elbow. "All of this was done by an artist named Ellen Gallagher."

He smirked. "Probably a distant relative."

"So?" Meg spread her arms. "What do you think?"

"Um…she really likes yellow."

With a snort, Meg nodded. "Bay." Meg waved a hand under her face. "Bailey! I told you cell phones aren't allowed in the building. Put it away before you get caught."

"Oh…right." She slipped the phone back in her pocket like it was the last drop of water on a hike through the desert.

Meg caved. "Okay. Okay, I give up. Come on, you guys."

"We're done?" Chase brightened considerably.

"With this floor. I want to go down to the next floor and look at some of my favorites before we leave."

Meg turned to the escalators, Chase sighing heavily beside her. She swallowed a grin and dragged them to Van Gogh's *The Starry Night*. "Well? What do you think?"

"This is your favorite?" Chase looked dubious.

Meg nodded. "One of them." They hadn't stopped to view it when they were here for their research project.

Bailey and Chase exchanged glances.

"Okay, look." Meg grabbed Chase by his shoulders and oriented him in front of the oil. "Look at the colors. Van Gogh's famous for rendering the dark with these bold streaks of light. And the clouds! God, I love the movement. And the way he painted the stars—they look like tiny galaxies. People say Van Gogh painted this from a vision, and I can almost believe that, you know?"

Meg caught Chase's eye and was surprised to find he was looking at her instead of the artwork.

"What?"

He smiled for a fraction of a second and looked at the floor. "Nothing. I… it's nice seeing you so excited."

Her face burst into flames, and Meg was certain it bore the same shade of red as the jacket she wore. Pyrrole Red, she decided. She cleared her throat and led them to Dali's *The Persistence of Memory*.

"I love this."

"Um…why are all the clocks melting?" Bailey asked.

Meg smiled, staring at the canvas. "This is Salvador Dali. You look at some artists' work and say to yourself, 'Wow. Pretty.' Maybe you wish you can do something so good. But that's not what Dali did."

Chase shifted his weight to one side. "Okay, so what did Dali do?"

"He painted ideas. Concepts."

Bailey and Chase exchanged another look. "You lost me," she said. "What concept?"

Meg peered at the painting. "Confusion, I guess."

"If it confuses you, why is it art?" Chase frowned.

She thought about that for a moment. "The Impressionists painted things you could recognize, like landscapes, city scenes, moments captured in time. Dali didn't paint those things. He painted abstractions. Questions. There's something kind of cool in painting stuff that still makes people wonder eighty years later, you know?"

"Like is time even real?" Chase murmured.

Meg glanced at him, but he was still staring at the work.

"What?" He caught her eye and frowned.

"That's…that's a good one." Meg turned back to the painting. "Every time I come here, I stare at this painting, but that question never occurred to me. I figured it was more like we can't understand time or we rely too much on time. But you—I think you nailed it."

His face broke into a beautiful and maybe relieved grin. A surge of want rose up in her so strong, it felt like it had its own pulse. It would be so easy. *Tilt your head*, it whispered. *Touch his hand. Just smile,* it murmured. Oh, she wanted to. Her hand came up all by itself. Slowly, it moved closer to Chase. She felt him tense. She heard his quick little gasp of breath. Their hands were a breath apart, and that's when her mind decided to replay all its stored images of her mother crying over which bills to pay.

Meg forced her hand back down. "We should go find Bailey."

"Yeah, okay," Chase said on a sigh. He seemed surprised she was gone.

They roamed the galleries and finally found her in "Shop Modern," the gift shop, thumbs blurring over her cell phone's keyboard, a private smile ghosting on her face.

"Bay?"

She jerked. "Oh! Sorry, guys."

"Are you texting *him*?" Meg demanded.

Her body stiffened. "Yes, I am."

Okay, this was a *moment*. Meg could pout and demand that she be with her like Bailey had promised. Like she'd done for her. Like Meg always did for her without ever—

Meg took a deep breath.

Or she could be supportive and trust Bailey's judgment, even though her batting average was pretty much a 1.000 when it came to picking losers. Even though—

Meg took another deep breath. She could do this.

"Why doesn't he meet us so we can all hang out?"

Bailey's lips pressed into a tight line and her shoulders fell an inch. "I asked him. He has to work."

"Aren't you afraid you'll get him into trouble texting him so much?"

Bailey's eyes snapped to hers before she lowered them, shrugging sheepishly. "I won't."

Chase's hand squeezed Meg's in warning. She bit back the rest of her argument and just nodded. She wandered around the gift shop, not ready to go home yet but unable to afford anything worth buying. The glossy cover of a book of Impressionist prints caught her attention and she ran a hand over it. Then she lusted after the acrylic paint kits and felt the paper quality in the sketch pads. It must be incredible to be able to paint without worrying about conserving materials.

"I guess we saw everything," Meg said when she'd tortured herself long enough.

Chase and Bailey fell into step, and they headed for the exit. Outside on Fifty-Third Street, Chase halted, patted his pockets, and cursed. "Hey, I think I left my phone in the men's room. You guys stay here. I'll be back." He took off at a jog.

Bailey was still texting.

The aroma of street vendor pretzels made Meg's stomach growl.

"Wanna split one?" Bailey asked.

"Um…sure." Meg half-smiled. She was hungry but didn't have enough money to splurge. When Bailey headed to the push cart, Meg promised herself just one bite. Meg sat on the steps and waited, watching people walk by. A few moments later, Bailey was back, tearing a hunk of hot pretzel off and popping it into her mouth.

"Mmm. That's good. Here." She handed Meg the rest.

Meg hesitated. Instead of taking it all, Meg tore off a piece and returned the remainder to Bailey. She'd bought it. She should get most of it. She ate another piece and offered Meg some, but Meg shook her head. She'd had her one bite. Bailey sat next to Meg and pulled out her phone. A secret smile played on her lips while she read a text.

"Ryder?" Meg asked, even though she knew it was, but she was trying to be understanding. Supportive.

The smile grew. "Yeah."

"Is he still at work?"

She nodded. "For about two more hours."

Chase jogged over. "Sorry about that."

"Find your phone?"

"Uh, yeah." He held it up. Then he jerked his chin toward Bailey. "Ryder again?"

Bailey grinned and kept texting. She never noticed Meg's mouth tighten into a line, but Chase did. He took her elbow and pulled her away.

"I thought you talked to this guy and changed your mind about him after he went all art school for you." Chase waved a hand around.

"I did. I—Look, I still don't want her to get hurt, okay?"

"Megan, you have to stop running her life."

Meg rolled her eyes. Why did everyone keep telling her that? She started walking toward Penn Station, mentally justifying her actions. She had good reasons for not trusting Ryder. Very good reasons. Several of them. But Meg couldn't tell Chase. They were Bailey's secrets, and Meg kept her secrets just like Bailey kept hers.

Chapter 22
Bailey

They shuffled off the train with sore legs and rumbling stomachs. Bailey's grandfather waited at the train station.

"Hello, sweet girl!" Mr. Grant opened the car door and held out his arms. Bailey ran into his hug.

"Gramps." She pecked his cheek.

"We ordered pizza. Plenty for all."

Meg shifted her weight from one leg to the other. "Um…are you sure?"

"Megan, there's always enough for you. You too, Chase." Gramps waved their objections away.

Bailey relaxed when she saw Meg exchange grins with Chase and figured she'd stop worrying about imposing because it was obviously a group thing now. Bailey called shotgun, forcing Meg and Chase to share the backseat of the car.

"Thanks, Mr. Grant," Chase said.

"How was the museum?"

"Excellent!" Meg said, and then she launched into a floor-by-floor account of all they'd seen.

Chase watched her with a funny little smile, but Meg didn't notice. The ride from the train station to the house didn't take that long with Meg chattering away. It was nice to see. Chase was totally charmed, hanging on every word. When Gramps pulled into their driveway, Bailey grinned at Chase.

"What?"

She shrugged. "It's good to see her excited, right?"

But Chase frowned and looked away.

"Where's Mom?" Bailey asked Gran when they were seated around the old dining room table Gran and Gramps bought when they'd gotten married.

"Upstairs in her room. She said she's not hungry," Gran raised her eyebrows at Bailey. "She's upset about something."

Bailey's posture snapped rod straight. She bit into her pizza, saying nothing.

They finished the meal, with Meg still talking about the amazing art, the color, the texture, the juxtaposition—whatever that meant. Bailey just smiled and nodded and said little until Gran started clearing the table and Gramps went back to his favorite chair.

"Bay," Meg said and nudged her with her elbow. "What's the matter?"

Bailey lifted a shoulder. "My mom's mad at me." And because that wasn't news, she quickly added, "I mean *super* mad at me." When Meg merely raised her eyebrows, she sighed. "She found out about the yearbook site."

Meg gasped, and Chase's eyes swung from one to the other. "What? What happened?" he asked.

"I'm trying to find my dad. I registered as my mom for that classmates site, the one where all the yearbooks are posted. I figured I could find him myself. But she found out."

Meg reached over, squeezed her hand. "Bay, I'm so sorry. Did she cut you off?"

Bailey shifted, traced a finger over the pattern on the tablecloth. "No," she admitted.

Chase angled his head. "Does that mean she's letting you keep the account?"

"Definitely not." Bailey rolled her eyes. "She was really mad. She tried to forbid me to look for him, but I told her I wasn't four anymore."

Meg breathed out a loud sigh. "Bailey, maybe you should give this a rest if it upsets her that much."

She'd thought about it. She'd thought about it for hours after her mother left her room. She dropped her head, scooped both hands through her hair, and finally lifted misty eyes to Meg's. "I can't. I'm so close, Megan. I just have to find him. Ryder's helping too."

Meg opened her mouth but then closed it, and Bailey let out a sigh of relief.

"But why?" Chase asked. "What do you think's gonna change if you do?"

Maybe nothing. Maybe everything. Wasn't that the point? To find out? Frowning, she lifted her hands, tried to find the right words. "It's like trying to play a game without knowing the rules. I have all these questions and—" She gave up. She just had to know—that's all. "She said I was just like him."

Meg propped an elbow on the table, cupped her chin. "How?"

"She said he was always laughing, always trying to have fun. Just like me. It's what she loved most about him." She smiled. It now made her happy, even though her mother had fired it out like an insult.

"Bay, that's great. That's something you never knew and she told you. Why don't you meet her halfway and just maybe give it some more time?"

"I don't know. Maybe," she hedged. It was so hard to talk about, hard to find the words. Even though Meg's dad died, at least Meg and Chase knew their fathers. All she had was a great big black hole. How does anybody ever figure out who they're going to be when they don't know who they came from?

"Bailey," Meg began and then swallowed. "God, this is hard." She took a deep breath. "I wish I never knew. He was my dad, and I loved him. I miss him every day, but Bailey, I swear to you...I wish I never knew."

Bailey's hand fell to the table with a loud smack. "Then why the hell are you so determined to be just like him?"

Meg flinched, stared at her with huge wounded eyes, and finally shoved back from the table.

"Meg, I'm sorry. I didn't mean it."

But Meg was already at the door.

Chase sighed and patted Bailey's shoulder. "I'll talk to her. Thanks for the pizza."

She managed a sad smile when he trailed after Meg and put her head in her hands.

Chapter 23
Meg

Meg hurried out of the house before her tears drowned her. She hadn't touched the last step off the porch before Chase called her.

"Megan, wait!"

Meg huddled deeper into her hoodie and kept walking, frustration adding a strut to her stride. *Why, why did Bailey say that?*

"Leave me alone, Chase."

"No! What the hell happened back there?"

Meg pressed her lips together and Chase cursed.

"Okay, I get that you and Bailey have secrets, but what she said hit you hard. I can see it. Tell me why."

Meg whipped around. "I *can't*. Don't you get that?"

But of course, he didn't.

"Well, explain it to me then!" He grabbed her by the arms, held her in place to glare at her with glittering eyes.

The breath stuck in her chest while Meg stared up at him. The Want, oh, God, it was back. It whispered in her ear that one kiss hadn't killed her, so why not take another? The last time he'd been this close to her, she wondered when he'd gotten so tall…so strong. His hands on her pulled her closer, his grip tightening almost painfully. His eyes lowered to her mouth and darkened as he pulled her even closer. Meg didn't want to stop him.

But she would.

She had to.

She took a step back. Stopped looking into his charmed eyes. That was the key—never look him in the eyes. Chase-charmed. She might have laughed if her heart didn't hurt so much.

"Stop it, Megan!" Chase raked his hands through his hair and then closed the gap between them to get in her face. "Just stop. You want me. I know you do. So why the hell aren't you with me?"

She stepped around him, strode to the opposite side of the street. "It's not that simple, Chase."

"Oh, it's *exactly* that simple." He sprinted and caught her by the elbow, spun her around to grab her shoulders. "Just tell me why. Why am I not good enough for you?" He shouted, gave her a little shake. "Do you want Simon's millions?" His face changed into something else—something mean and foul. "Or maybe you want Ryder. You like Bailey's guy, don't you? All that concern and worry, that was just a show, right? You want *him* so you can talk art."

Shock dropped her jaw. Anger reddened her vision. But it was pure fury that brought her hands up to shove him.

They stood on the street glaring at each other. He tugged down his hoodie and drew himself up to his full height. He raised wounded green eyes to hers and shook his head.

"Here." He tossed a brochure at her. She fumbled and it fell to the ground.

"I saw this at the museum and grabbed it for you because I thought—" Abruptly, he snapped his teeth together. "Forget it. It doesn't matter what I thought. I'm done, Megan." He shook his head again. "I'm…I've given you time and space and…and—all the patience I could squeeze out, but *shit!* It's not enough. It's never enough." He shoved his hands in his pockets. "You said you're scared, but you won't tell me why. You tell me you're worried about Bailey, but you won't tell me why. For God's sake, I see you stabbing a picture of your own father, but you still won't tell me why. I'm sick of it, Meg. Don't you understand? Don't you get it yet? I love you!"

A car went by. The beam from its headlights caught Chase straight on. "Fuck," he muttered and turned away.

Too stunned to say anything, Meg watched him take two steps before he spun back to shout in her face.

"Maybe you don't feel the same way, but I know you feel something. I know it! Call me when you can face it without freaking out." He turned and stalked away. This time, he did not look back.

Meg let him go.

It was what she wanted. She told herself that over and over, but watching him walk away cut a hole through her as big as the one her father had left. She bent to pick up the brochure he'd thrown at her.

The Cooper Union.

She ran down the street and up the path to her dark and empty house and then went up the stairs to her dark and empty room. She flung herself on her bed, the brochure gripped tightly in her hand, and let the tears drown her.

I love you, he'd said.

I love you. That was never supposed to happen.

I love you. She'd done everything possible to ensure her life had no room for love. She never wanted the mess. The pain. And yet—

Yet, her life was a painful mess. She'd stayed away, stayed uninvolved. But he loved her anyway, and damn if that didn't change everything. She folded up and sobbed, pounded a fist into the pillow. How had she so thoroughly screwed up everything? She grabbed the pillow, curled around it, and cried for what might have been. Her hand brushed the paper she kept under it—Chase's sketch.

Pain speared her, and she had her phone out, seconds away from calling him and begging his forgiveness when sanity managed to claw its way to the top of her tortured mind. It buzzed once—a text from Mom. She didn't bother to read it.

This was what she'd wanted. She hadn't wanted to hurt Chase. Never that. But she'd decided on her future and that included career goals and never having to answer to anyone or be responsible for anyone but herself. She would never be a burden on him as she'd been to her mother...and to her father before he'd checked out.

And Bailey knew all that. Knew it and still made her question why.

Chapter 24
Bailey

Bailey pouted in her room. She was so angry at Meg and her mom and even Ryder, and then she was sad for being angry and angry for being sad, and she didn't know what she felt anymore, and that just mad her madder. She typed a terse message and clicked Send.

Bailey: Hey, what's up?

She waited, not patiently, for Ryder to text back.

Ryder: I got into it with my aunt. It was like she was just waiting for me to screw up so she could attack. I can't stand living here.

Bailey nibbled a fingernail.

Bailey: Can I call you so we can talk? You're upset, and texting makes it hard to comfort you.

There was no delay for his next message.

Ryder: No! If she hears me on the phone, she'll take it away. UR already comforting me.

She sighed, wished she could be there with him, that they could go someplace together to be alone and thanked God Meg couldn't hear that thought because she'd never hear the end of it.

Bailey: What about Facebook? Can we chat? That's easier than texting.

She powered up her computer, opened an Internet browser window, and logged in. Ryder was already online, waiting.

Ryder West
• Hey.

Bailey Grant
• Seriously, how bad is it?

Ryder West
• It sucks, Bailey. Nothing I do is ever good enough. I work extra shifts just to get out of here.

Bailey Grant
• Where do you work? Maybe I can visit you there.

Ryder West
• The big warehouse store on Route 25. But I'd rather u didn't visit me. Some lady just got mugged in the parking lot. I'd worry about u.

Bailey's heart flipped over at that. Meg's wouldn't. Meg's heart would have rolled its beady little eyes and said "Yeah, right."

Bailey Grant
• You're very sweet. But I still want to see you. I need to see you.

> **Ryder West**
> • I know, Bailey. I need u too. I'm working on it. I swear. I have to work all weekend. But on Sunday, I'm done at 3. I'll meet u. Pick the place.

He needed her. Bailey swooned. Oh, God, he needed her. She quickly thought of a neutral meeting area because even though Meg was being way too prissy about this, even Chase had told her to be careful and she'd promised she would.

> **Bailey Grant**
> • What about the food court at the mall?
>
> **Ryder West**
> • Great. Be there at 3:30.

Before Bailey could type her next message, Ryder pinged again.

> **Ryder West**
> • O_O Were u supposed to hang out with Meg tonight?
>
> **Bailey Grant**
> • We had a fight. Why?
>
> **Ryder West**
> • She's texting me again. She's really pissed off.

Meg was texting Ryder? Bailey's eyes narrowed to slits.

> **Bailey Grant**
> • I thought it was just the one time.
>
> **Ryder West**
> • No, she keeps sending me art and stuff. Like I care.

Was that so?

> **Bailey Grant**
> • I'll call her right now and stop her.

Ryder did not reply. Bailey picked up her phone, but she didn't want to leave Ryder hanging.

> **Bailey Grant**
> • Ryder, you still there? Please don't worry about Meg.
>
> **Ryder West**
> • Hang on. She's ranting.

Bailey groaned. Of course Meg would be ranting.

> **Ryder West**
> • OMG, is it true that u puked on UR second-grade teacher? LOL

Bailey froze. Her blood went cold, and she wasn't sure but thought it was possible she'd passed out for a moment. She rubbed her eyes and read Ryder's last message again. There was no mistake. Meg had told him something she'd promised, something she'd *vowed* she'd never talk about. With hands that shook, she typed her reply.

> **Bailey Grant**
> • I'll take care of it. Meg's just mad. I'll see you tomorrow.
>
> **Ryder West**
> • No! Talk to me first. Is this true? That's pretty funny.

Her face flamed. How could she ever face Ryder after this? It's not like she purposely walked up to her teacher and threw up on her. She'd had the flu! She hadn't wanted to go to school, but Nicole made her go. And by the time she'd gotten there, she was shivery, achy, and her stomach was screaming. She'd tried, she'd really tried to be brave and strong, and when she couldn't stand the rumble in her belly another minute, she went to the teacher, intending only to ask permission to see the nurse. Instead, her last meal had come up the second she'd opened her mouth. Everybody laughed and pointed and made *eww* noises, and she'd wished she was dead. Unfortunately, she'd recovered and had gone back to school a few days later.

Annoyed and embarrassed all over again, Bailey grabbed her cell phone and tapped out a quick message to Meg.

> **Bailey:** WTF? I like this boy. I REALLY like him. Why would you tell him I threw up all over Miss Monroe? I'm sorry I keep forgetting our plans, but if you ruin this for me, I'll never speak to you again.

Bailey closed her phone with a snap and typed another message.

> **Bailey Grant**
> • You still there? I just told Meg to back off.
>
> **Ryder West**
> • Yeah, I'm here. But I don't think she got ur message. OMG, did u really write a love poem to somebody in 7th grade? That's really cute. Will u write me one too?

Bailey stood up so fast that she jostled her desk and everything on it. With her hands clenched into fists and her chest heaving, she tried to form a plan, but each of her ideas involved tearing out Meg's silky straight hair strand by strand.

What was *wrong* with her? She'd told her how much she liked Ryder. She'd even told her she'd never speak to her again.

A thought struck her with such clarity that Bailey stilled. All that pouting, all those times Meg pounced on Ryder's broken promises, their arguments—of course! She should have seen it. Meg was jealous.

But why? Why would she be jealous when she keeps warning her Ryder could be a serial pedophile? And Meg had backed off after she'd texted Ryder herself. Why? Oh, Bailey pressed both hands to her gaping mouth when the answer kicked her in the head. It was art. It had to be the art. Ryder knew a lot about art. Better, he even *liked* it. Meg said herself Chase thought *The Scream* guy was just a movie producer. Bailey never knew *Scream* had been anything but a movie either. But to Meg, it was like this huge deal.

The more she considered the possibility, the more likely it became. Her chest hurt. It was hard to breathe. She rubbed the ache, but it didn't help. All this time, she'd believed—really believed—that Meg was just worried about her safety. But that wasn't true.

Meg wanted Ryder.

Meg was trying to steal Ryder from her. Bailey wrapped her arms around her middle and tried not to throw up. It explained everything. And now she thought by telling him her most embarrassing moments, she was just going to hide? So not happening.

Bailey's mouth twisted. Meg wanted to tell stories? Awesome! Bailey had a bunch to tell.

"Ha!" Bailey laughed out loud and grabbed the mouse. She clicked the link to Ryder's Facebook Wall and then changed her mind. On her own Wall, she posted something she was certain would make Meg curl up and die.

> Hey, Meg! Remember that time in first grade when you wet your pants and had to wear a pair of underwear Mrs. Nichols kept in her desk? Too bad they were boys' underwear though. Do you still have them?

Laughing quietly, she added a link to a potty-training website and sat back while her Wall filled with comments. The computer pinged.

Ryder West
• OMG, Bailey, did that really happen? Meg's gonna be so pissed.

Bailey crossed her arms and nodded at Ryder's last message. Meg had gone too far this time, and Bailey wasn't taking it anymore.

Bailey Grant
• Just fighting fire with fire.

Ryder West
• Look, don't make a big deal out of this. Gotta go.

What? No! Bailey waited for another message, but no more came. She even texted Ryder an apology from her phone, but he never replied. Bailey flung herself to her bed with a curse. Damn it! It wasn't fair. Things had been going so well. Ryder was sweet and funny and really liked her, really understood her, and Meg had to go and ruin everything again.

Chapter 25
Meg

By Monday, Bailey's Facebook post had earned so many comments and Likes that Meg walked to school to escape facing the taunts on the bus. Huddled in her hoodie, she heard a car pull up beside her. She didn't bother to look. She knew it would be Chase. He'd had his license for a year now. Meg had her learner's permit but had never been behind the wheel. Her mother just didn't have time to teach her.

The car sped ahead with a sudden burst of acceleration, and Meg figured Chase was still mad.

Good.

As long as he was mad, he'd stay away. She adjusted her backpack and shoved her hands in her pockets. She would eventually have to face him. She knew this, didn't like it, but accepted it. She also knew she'd have to tell him why she kept turning him down and spare none of the gory details.

She owed him that much.

If, at the end of the tale, he still wanted to be friends, well, she'd have to turn down that request too.

It was too painful.

Kissing Chase was a mistake. It forced her to face the truth that she was in love with Chase too.

And that had to remain her little secret.

She reached the school with only seconds to spare before the final bell. She didn't bother with her locker, just headed to her first class, and slid behind her desk, aware of the hush that fell over the room when Bailey looked up, saw Meg, and quickly turned away.

Math was not one of Bailey's favorite subjects. Actually, Bailey had no favorite subjects. But Meg enjoyed it. She focused on the lesson, something involving polar coordinate equations, and soon lost herself in the work. She glanced next to her, saw Bailey struggling to understand the concepts, but did not swoop in with the answers today. Forgiveness, when she gave it, would be hard earned.

The bell rang and Meg scooped her work into her backpack, ready to flee before anyone could stop her. She'd just zipped her bag when a pair of Fruit of the Looms landed on it, accompanied by loud laughter. Her face blazed, but she did not make eye contact with anyone and instead fled, leaving the briefs behind.

In homeroom, the entire class lauded her with all manner of undergarments—from tiny thongs to granny panties. Mr. Allen asked her if she was taking up a collection and the class howled. Meg tossed them all in the wastebasket on her way out of class when the bell rang. In each class, someone asked her if her pants were wet. In the hall, somebody shot her with a squirt gun. In the stairwells, in the cafeteria, in the locker room, someone laughed. By the end of the day, Meg was certain she was immune to further embarrassment until Chase approached her at the bus stop, his face twisted in an expression of confusion.

"Hey," he greeted her. "Um…Bailey handed me this and said I had to give it to you right away—that it was an emergency." He handed her a paper bag. "Are you okay?"

"Yeah. Awesome." She poked inside the bag, flung the scarlet red lace panties at Chase, and turned dark, hurt eyes to his. "You too? I can't believe you'd do this!"

Chase looked at the underwear in his hand and cursed. "No, Meg, I—"

"Shut up, Chase."

She turned and went home on foot, slammed the door behind her, and sank to the floor against it. She hated crying, hated how weak it made her feel, how desperate. It took a long time, but she fought it, managed to come out on the top of the crushing urge to curl up and die. All it took was one thought.

Her dad.

Meg slowly rolled to her knees, pulled out her cell phone, and texted Ryder.

> **Meg:** I apologized. I even told you I'd back off. But that wasn't good enough. You had to get rid of me. Well, congratulations—it worked. I don't know what you told Bailey, but she's really pissed off. When you hurt her—and we both know you will—I will come after you. Yeah, that's a threat.

Since she'd spent lunch dodging more insults, Meg dragged herself to the kitchen for a snack. Again, there was little to choose from, so she snagged the last apple, grabbed a jar of peanut butter, and headed to her room, only to discover she'd forgotten a knife. With a loud sigh, she plucked an X-Acto blade from her brush jar and started slicing the apple into wedges.

"Damn it!" The knife clattered to her desk, leaving a long bloody gash in the webbing between the thumb and index finger of her left hand. She hurried to the bathroom and ran the wound under cool water, watched blood drip into the sink. It was a deep cut, but it didn't hurt much. She wrapped a towel around it, figured it would stop bleeding soon, and went back to her room to uncover her test project.

She mixed paints—acrylics this time. She stared at the test project for a long time and then tore it from the clips on her easel. She fastened her last canvas, grabbed a wide brush, and laid down a flesh-toned foundation and then switched to a smaller brush to put down the shadows and angles for a face. She moved with precision, certainty. Bold strokes and soft blended edges. Light and shadow. Lines, curves, shapes. Slowly, the image appeared. The image she couldn't get out of her mind, her dreams, her heart. Chase. Always Chase.

Perspective. That's what she needed. More perspective. She imagined the contours of his jaw under her hand the day she'd kissed him, the strength in his broad shoulders, the stubborn set of his mouth. She imagined those lips on hers, the scrape of stubble against her cheek. Her own lips parted. She switched brushes, painted hair. Oh, his hair. Her fingers itched to feel all that silk again. She imagined his nose—straight and perfect. He was beautiful. She could not deny that. But it was his eyes that always drew her in, made her wish she'd studied the Old Masters. She dabbed on color, stroked on contours, smoothed out rough edges with the tip of her finger.

She painted until the light faded, until her hands cramped and her head spun. When she finally put down her brushes and stepped back, she gasped.

She'd done it. She'd finally done it. She'd rendered Chase on canvas. Her eyes studied the play of color, the sepia-toned mood she'd managed to capture. There was blood on her palette, blood mixed with the paint and blood on the portrait, the portrait that perfectly captured his pain, his disappointment. Her betrayal. She lifted her hands, saw that her wound was still dripping. The towel was saturated.

Maybe that had been the key all along? To hurt like she'd hurt him.

Somehow, that felt entirely appropriate.

Meg capped her paints, cleaned her brushes, and wrapped a clean towel around her hand. She grabbed her keys and some money from the meager stash in her wallet and locked the front door.

It would be a long walk to the hospital.

Chapter 26
Bailey

The day had dragged on. When Bailey first posted Meg's little underwear problem, it felt right and just. It felt like payback. At first, she thought it was funny how the whole school lined up to attack Meg, pelting her with underwear and leak pads. But it got old fast.

Maybe she'd gone too far. Maybe that's why she hadn't heard anything from Ryder. Maybe she should apologize to Meg. She sent Meg a text, but there was no reply. She was probably painting. Meg often ignored the phone when she was caught up in a subject. Bailey would try again later.

Bailey went downstairs when Gran called her for dinner. When the dishes were cleared away, Gran handed her the plastic containers of leftovers and that made her think of Meg. And thinking of Meg made her feel guilty, so she went upstairs to find something else to occupy her time.

She tried Xbox, but WyldRyd11 wasn't logged on. She tried Facebook and saw no status updates from Ryder or Meg. But her little "wet pants" story had gotten a lot of airtime. Likes by people she didn't even know, comments by the screenful—and some of them were ridiculously funny, except for the one from Chase, who told them both to leave him out of their dumb fights from now on. She shrugged and then checked her email. Still nothing from Ryder, but she did find one from the classmates site.

They'd located her mother's yearbook.

Her mom still wasn't talking to her. She'd gone over it in her mind a dozen times. Should she forget the whole idea or keep going? And a dozen times, she'd arrived at different decisions. Now that her mother's yearbook was a click away, Bailey knew she had to keep going. She had to find him.

Bailey logged in, clicked the link, and flipped through the scanned pages. Nicole at seventeen looked a lot like Bailey at seventeen. They both had the same curly hair and similar body shapes, but Nicole's face looked older. Wiser. Tired. With a start, Bailey reminded herself most of these pictures were taken when she'd been just a few months old.

It must have been so hard to go back to school after she'd had a baby.

Bailey scrolled through page after page. Her mom was in a lot of pictures but never with any guys. So who was her father? Where was he?

"What's that?"

Bailey leaped and spun at the sound of Gran's voice behind her. "Oh, my God, you scared me half to death."

Gran didn't smile. "What are you looking at?"

Crap. "Mom's yearbook. It's online now." Bailey figured Gran already saw the screen, so there was no point in lying.

"I see that. Any particular reason why?"

Double crap. "I wanted to see who my dad is."

Gran came in, shut the door behind her, and sat on Bailey's bed. "Sweetie, there are some things way better off left unasked, unseen, unfound—this is one of them."

Bailey considered that for about three seconds and decided it was too bad. "For mom. Not for me. I need to know."

"No, you don't."

"Why?" She exploded with it—the years of secrecy and evasion. "Why can't I know who my own father is? Was he some evil rapist or something?"

Gran's mouth fell open, and she pressed a hand to cover it. "No! Why would you even say such a thing?"

"Why wouldn't I with the way everyone pretends I was hatched instead of conceived?"

"He broke your mother's heart. Can you not understand how painful it is for her, seeing you every day, a living, breathing reminder of that?"

Gran's words were like the crack of a palm on a bare cheek and she flinched. She sank to the bed beside her grandmother. "I guess so," she murmured. "But I still don't think it's fair. I'm not Mom! Why am I the one getting punished? He has rights too. Maybe he wanted me!"

"Do you see him here?"

Slowly, Bailey shook her head.

"Bailey, honey, listen to me. I know you're hurting. But so is your mom. It's been seventeen years and it still hurts her. Let your mom heal."

Long after she left the room, Bailey sat in the same spot, wondering if anyone cared that she needed to heal too. She turned back to her computer and logged into her blog page.

Girls love secrets. I think it's hard-coded into our DNA or something. We collect secrets, save secrets, even use them when it suits our needs. But we don't reveal them. That's against the BFF Code.

Girls have a code just like guys. Doesn't the guy code say never to hook up with your girlfriend's best friend? Well, girl code says never reveal your best friend's secret. Ever. Just don't, okay?

Secrets can be weapons and armor at the same time. They can be strengths and weaknesses at the same time. It all depends on who knows them. When it's your best friend, your secrets are protected. They're part of what holds you together. That's why there's no bigger pain than when a best friend spills one of your secrets. It's like she's chipping away at the foundation of your friendship and you wonder when the whole thing might collapse.

Bailey twirled a lock of hair and read her notes so far. It was almost ironic that she was upset with Meg for sharing a secret and just as pissed at her mother for keeping one.

Secrets aren't just for BFFs. Families keep secrets too. Is it worse for a relative to keep a secret from you or for your best friend to blurt one of yours? I don't know yet, but I know both totally suck. I wish I didn't have any secrets. Then I wouldn't be this sad.

Meg told Ryder one of her secrets. Bailey wondered how long before their friendship crumbled.

No.

No, she wasn't going to let that happen.

Chapter 27

Meg

Tired. It was the only thought that consciously formed in Meg's mind.

Her feet shuffled along the dark street, her eyes unfocused.

"Megan! What's wrong?"

She jerked and froze like she'd been zapped with a bolt of lightning. There was Chase in the car that had pulled up beside her, the car she'd hardly noticed.

"I'm fine." She started walking again. Chase jumped from the car with a curse.

"You're not fine. What the hell happened?" He blocked her path, gestured to the pocket of her hoodie, where she'd tucked her hand.

She followed his gaze, saw the dark wet stain, and inhaled sharply. Gently, he tugged her hand from the pocket. The towel she'd wrapped around it was drenched.

"Get in the car," he ordered, his mouth pressed in a tight line. When she didn't move, he pushed her toward the open door.

"The seats," she protested.

"Get in the damn car, Megan." He opened the back door, shoved her in, slammed the front door, and then climbed in the backseat with her.

"Megan, tell us what happened." Dave Gallagher demanded and pulled back into traffic with a squeal of tires.

"Megan?" Chase snapped his fingers when she didn't reply to his dad. "Talk to me. What happened?" He stripped out of his own hoodie and then his T-shirt and wrapped the shirt around her hand.

She blinked, and then her eyes traveled down his naked chest. Chase quickly pulled the hoodie over his head. "Um, I was slicing an apple and the knife slipped."

"When?" Dave asked.

"Uh, I don't—when I got home from school."

"Shit, Megan, that was four hours ago. Why didn't you call us immediately?" Dave increased speed.

"I...I didn't think it was that bad. I thought...I figured it would stop bleeding."

Chase increased the pressure on her hand and she hissed in a breath.

"Sorry, sorry. I know it hurts."

"It didn't. Not until now," she murmured, her words slurring.

They arrived at the emergency room entrance minutes later. Chase tugged her out, but as soon as she put one foot on the ground, she wobbled and her vision grayed. She felt Chase scoop her up under the knees and carry her through the ER entrance.

"I need help here!"

Was that his voice? It shook and sounded almost shrill.

Suddenly, a wheelchair held her. Chase was talking to someone, his voice still weird. "Her hand is pouring blood. She says the knife slipped while she was cutting up an apple, but that was hours ago. Maybe three o'clock. She didn't think it was that bad, so she started working on a painting." They unwrapped her hand, poked at the gaping sides of the wound.

"Get the vascular on call down here," the nurse said to his colleague. "What's your name?" a white blob asked her.

"Megan. Megan Farrell."

"You her boyfriend?" the white blob asked

And before Meg could think of a response, Chase replied, "Yeah, her mother's working. She doesn't know."

"We'll call her. Put her in bed seven!"

They pushed her chair behind a large room with lots of curtains.

"Megan. My name's John. We're gonna take care of you. Can you climb up here for me?"

She started to stand but wondered where *here* was. She didn't see anything. Leaning heavily on the arms of the chair that felt like it was now spinning, she reached out a hand, felt a bed to her right, and all but collapsed onto it.

"Megan, can you tell me your full name?"

Meg blinked and frowned. "Megan Elise Farrell."

"Good. How old are you?"

"Seventeen."

"Good, good. Tell me what day it is, Megan."

"Um…Monday?"

"That's good."

Meg felt a warm heavy blanket cover her.

"She's a little shocky. Start an IV."

They stuck a monitor on one of her fingers and she could hear cabinets and drawers opening and closing, the sound of metal meeting metal, footsteps rushing in.

"I called her mother."

"No! I'm fine. She doesn't need to come." Meg tried to sit up, but hands gently restrained her. A minute later, she felt a pinch in her good hand. Then tape was wrapped around it.

"You are not fine, Megan. You've lost a decent amount of blood and your body is starting to go into shock. If you hadn't gotten here when you did, we'd be transfusing. As it is, this is gonna need at least a dozen stitches, maybe more."

Someone—Chase?—gripped her arm and squeezed.

"I left a voice mail," Dave said.

"Thanks, Dad."

"Never been so happy my kid's a Peeping Tom—"

"Jesus, Dad, not now!"

Chase's voice sounded like him again. And her vision started to dial back in until another white-robed medic prodded and poked and tugged at her wound. Oh, God! The pain crossed her eyes and burned a track all the way to her brain, and she reached blindly for Chase's hand. He took it and squeezed. With his other hand, he smoothed her hair, and she shut her eyes, grateful for his presence.

Another spike of pain had her eyes flying open. The doctor was flushing out the wound with some syringe full of fluid that burned. Her eyes met Chase's and she flashed a smile—*that* smile, the one just for him.

It was second, maybe third grade when they'd first met. Chase and his family had just moved to the house behind Meg's. He seemed pretty shy, but during recess on his first day of school, he ran for the slide and had reached the top step when Peter Sidell pushed him off. He wasn't hurt, but he came up ready to fight. So Meg ran up and pounded Peter the second his light-up sneakers touched the rubber mat. He ran off crying while Chase just stared at her, kind of the way he does now. So she gave him a cookie.

Maybe that's what did it. That's when they'd both fallen with a splat.

Something stabbed her, tearing her right out of those daydreams. Jesus, the doctor was injecting something right into the gash itself. "Talk to me, Megan," Chase demanded. "What painting are you working on now? Oils? Watercolors?"

"Acrylics." She pushed the word through gritted teeth.

"Acrylics. I'm not very good with acrylics. They dry so fast."

"That's why I like them," she said. "I can change stuff if I don't like how it comes out the first time." Her voice rose and fell with the pain.

"What about watercolors? Are they hard?"

"Yeah, I like tube color better than pan paints. But I never get the same color mixed twice."

"I guess that's the point," Chase said.

Her eyes met his, surprised. "I never thought of that. That's a good point." She considered that for a few minutes—how each artist mixes and layers her colors. And then the pain flared again.

"What about working flat? You can't use an easel with watercolors, right?"

Again, she looked surprised. "How do you know so much about this? I didn't even know you liked art until this weekend."

Chase shrugged. "You like it. So I've been…uh, studying."

"Why would you bother?"

He didn't answer.

"That's it. All done," the doctor announced, and she saw Chase's eyes shut in relief. "Thirteen stitches, some inside, some out. We'll get a sterile dressing on it, and you'll be good to go." The doctor left and Meg lifted her hand to examine her wound. A line of stiff black threads followed the angry red trail in the webbing between her left thumb and index finger. Slowly, Meg flexed her hand.

"Easy, Megan. You'll tear," Chase's dad reminded her.

"Relax. You're right-handed. You can still paint. For everything else, I'll help you and so will Bailey," Chase promised.

To her profound embarrassment, she burst into tears.

"Jesus, Megan! It's okay. We'll take care of you."

"Bailey won't!" Meg shook her head. "It's her fault this even happened."

"What are you talking about?"

Meg shot a glance at Dave Gallagher.

"Um…I'm going to step outside and try calling your mom again." Dave jerked his chin toward the corridor.

Chase nodded gratefully. When his dad left, Meg couldn't stop herself from venting.

"The underwear. She told everybody I wet my pants in first grade. Posted it on freakin' Facebook! Chase, it was horrible. Every class, even in the hallways, people kept throwing their underwear at me."

"Hey, rock stars live for that shit," he offered with a grin, and she knew it was a lame shot at making her laugh.

She rolled her eyes. "I'm not a rock star!"

His smile faded. "So Bailey's mad at you, huh?"

Meg shrugged and then winced in pain. "I'm tired, Chase. Just so tired. Every time she meets a new guy, she pulls away from me. She never hears me when I tell her how great she is. But she listens to them. A guy she never met said I told him she threw up all over our teacher. I never told him that. I wouldn't do that. But she believes him."

When Chase didn't say anything, Meg let her head fall back against the gurney and shut her eyes.

"I'm sorry for spacing out on you," she said quietly.

Chase huffed out a breath. "I don't know why you didn't call us. You could have passed out on the street, been snatched up, run over, or just bled to death."

He took her good hand in his and Meg felt him shake. She shifted over. "Sit. You look worse than I do."

He moved without hesitating. Meg felt warm with him beside her.

"I'm sorry about what I said on Saturday. It wasn't fair. I know you're only trying to protect Bailey."

She fidgeted. Looked down at her stitched-up hand. Looked back into magic eyes. "Forget it."

"How's your head. Are you dizzy?"

"No, not anymore. Just tired." Her stomach let out a low rumble and she laughed weakly. "And hungry."

Chase jumped up. "I'll find a vending machine. M&M's?"

She breathed deeply, shut her eyes. Chase had found her. She didn't know how he knew that she'd needed help, but she was so happy he'd came. He was right. She wouldn't have made it. She hadn't realized how close she was to passing out until he'd settled her into the backseat of the car. She could hardly hold her head up. The IV in her hand was doing a lot to clear the fuzz from her brain. The drugs the doctor had pumped into her wound had killed the burn. What was Mr. Gallagher talking about before with that Peeping Tom stuff? Maybe Chase watched her the way she watched him. She'd have to remember to close the blinds.

She felt soft lips brush her forehead and she jerked, blinking into Chase's eyes. "What?"

He shook his head. "You fell asleep. Here. Have some sugar." He spread out his haul and she moved straight for the M&M's. He smiled when she tore the package open with her teeth, tilted half of it into her open mouth. That did surprise him.

"Oh...sorry. Want some?"

"Yeah, if you're sure I won't lose a finger if I try." He laughed when she shot him a glare and held out his hand. They popped M&M's and Dave rejoined them.

"I finally got a hold of your mother. They want to keep you here overnight—"

"No!"

Dave raised his hands. "Easy, easy. She said the same thing, so the doctor agreed to release you into *my* care."

Chase made a strange strangling sound and Meg blinked at both of them. "What does that mean?"

"It means you're coming home with us for the night. No arguments," he added when her mouth opened to protest.

Meg shut her mouth and remained quiet while the doctor removed her IV, provided some instructions for caring for her wound, and sent them on their way. Chase held her elbow while she walked to the car. She wanted to wrestle away but knew she was too weak to walk a straight line by herself. She climbed into the backseat and stretched herself out before he could join her and let herself drift on the meds the hospital had pumped into her veins.

Chapter 28
Bailey

Bailey huddled into her shearling jacket and jogged across the street to Meg's house. She mentally rehearsed the apology she'd make to Meg, even though Meg didn't really deserve it and was totally overreacting to stuff and should just mind her own damn business. She was in the middle of her speech when she came to an abrupt, jaw-dropping halt.

Toilet paper hung from every branch on every tree. Rolls of it—some down to the cardboard tubes—littered the lawn. Fruit of the Looms hung like deflated Christmas balls from the porch rails and diapers covered the porch near the front door. Holy cannoli! All this from one little Facebook post? Meg must be so pissed. Bailey hadn't seen her at lunch and figured she was just sulking, but it was obvious she really did owe her that apology now. She took a step up Meg's path when the sound of slow clapping had her spinning around.

"Chase!" She pressed a hand to her racing heart.

"You come to admire your work?" He stalked toward her, picked up a toilet paper roll, and thrust it into her hands. As if the sight of her made him sick, he turned his back and furiously shook out a large green trash bag.

"I didn't do this!"

"Yeah, Bay, you did." Chase shoved cardboard tubes into the bag. "You posted that bitchy comment online and the entire school ganged up on her. You even conned *me* into hurting her."

She caught her lip between her teeth and looked away. God, she'd thought that was hilarious this afternoon. Now it made her feel like...well, used toilet paper. Oh, poor Meg! She'd only wanted to get her to back off Ryder, not embarrass her. Okay, she did want to embarrass her too for telling Ryder she'd thrown up all over her teacher, but not this much. Meg would hate her forever and it was all her fault. She spun and ran up the porch steps, knocked quickly on the door.

"Don't bother. She's not there." Chase pulled clumps of tissue off tree branches and stuffed them in the bag.

"How do you know?"

"Because she's at my house, asleep in my bed."

Bailey's eyes went round, and she hurried down the steps, determined to get every juicy detail out of Chase. But he only rolled his eyes and went back to picking up the litter. "Nothing happened, Bailey. Not like that. Because of your little stunt today, she never ate lunch. She decided to cut up an apple after school and nearly bled to death when the knife went through her hand. My dad and I took her to the hospital. She got thirteen stitches and practically passed out." He stalked toward her. "Because of *you*."

Bailey shook her head and pressed her hands to her mouth. "Oh, no! God, I'm sorry. I'm so sorry, Chase!"

"And then we get home and see this," Chase said and waved a hand in an arc over the front yard. "Why did you do that to her? Are you guys like *not* friends anymore or something?"

Bailey took an edge of the trash bag and tried to hold it open for Chase, but he yanked it from her hands. "I don't know what we are anymore. She makes me so mad! She told Ryder I threw up all over Miss Monroe in first grade. Then she pretends she doesn't know why I'm mad. I like this guy, Chase. I really like him and he likes me! Why would she tell him those things?"

Chase moved around the shrubs, grabbing the briefs hanging from them. He probably wasn't listening, which meant he wouldn't be talking to her anymore either and probably wouldn't want to help her with her game anymore and—

"So…what? You wanted to get even? She told one guy something silly about you, so you thought you'd tell the whole freakin' Internet something silly about her?"

"It wasn't the *whole* Internet, just…you know, my Facebook friends."

Chase threw his head back and stared at the sky for a long moment. "Yeah, all two hundred of them plus their friends and their friends' friends. Christ, Bailey, we're lucky they're not driving here in buses to trash this house."

Bailey sniffled and walked up the steps to the porch, started collecting the diapers. Thirteen stitches! Oh, God. Meg wouldn't be able to paint. That was going to torture her. It would be like not being able to play video games or do her hair or put on makeup. The tears fell and Bailey vowed to make it up to Meg, starting with the apology Ryder insisted on and then being her slave until the stitches came out.

"Damn it." Chase's sigh of frustration sounded right behind her, and when she looked around, he opened his arms. She fell into them with a sob.

"I'm so sorry! I didn't mean to hurt her. Well, crap, that's not true! I did want to hurt her, only a little, not a lot. Not like this, I swear."

"Okay, okay. I believe you. Just…help me finish this up before her mother gets home, okay?"

Bailey wiped her face with her fingertips and worked with Chase to clean up the yard. It took nearly an hour, and he had to give her a boost into the tree so she could pull tissue from some of the higher branches. Bailey stuffed the last of it into the trash bag, figured they'd picked up at least fifty or sixty rolls, trying to think of ways she could earn Meg's forgiveness. The first thing she'd do would be to update Facebook with news of Meg's injury so everyone would be nice to her tomorrow, and then she'd wake up extra early to make Meg breakfast. Oh, she would probably need help getting dressed, so Bailey decided to get up even earlier so she could go to Meg's to help Meg shower and do her hair *and* make her breakfast. Wait, Chase said she was asleep at his house. She'd have to go there tomorrow. He couldn't help Meg in the shower, though she was sure he wouldn't mind one bit. Then again, if he tried, Meg would probably deck him with her good hand. She swallowed a grin, imagining it all.

"What time do you get up?"

Chase bent to pick up another diaper. "Around sixty-thirty. Why?"

"I'm coming over to help Meg get dressed."

Chase snapped up, turned, and stared at the front door. "Right. She'll need help. Come on. Let's pack her a bag." He walked up the porch steps and tried the front door.

Locked.

"What time does her mother come home?" Chase asked.

Bailey shrugged. "It depends if she's at work or at school."

"She goes to school?"

"Yeah, she's getting a degree in accounting. She works at the diner on Main Street too."

Chase sighed. "You got any clothes that'll fit Meg?"

Bailey frowned, mentally inventorying her closet. Meg was taller and thinner than she was but wore the same size shoes. "Yeah, I think so. Come on. I'll pack you a bag."

"Nah, I gotta get back. Just come over at like six-thirty."

"The bus comes at six-forty."

He blinked. "So?"

Bailey rolled her eyes. "You're such a guy. Girls do a little more than roll out of bed, tie on shoes, and leave."

Chase held up his hands. "Okay, okay. Come over whenever then. I'll be asleep on the couch, so I'll hear you knock."

Chase took the stuffed trash bag and headed home. Bailey walked back across the street and ran upstairs to her room, deep in thought. She flicked on the light, sat at her computer, and opened Facebook.

> Hey, just heard Meg Farrell got like 13 stitches in her hand. Everyone should be nice to her tomorrow.

There! That should stop the potty-training jokes. Her computer pinged, and she saw a chat window from Ryder.

Ryder West
• Hey. Just saw UR post. How bad is it?

PATTY BLOUNT

Bailey Grant
- Not sure. I haven't seen her. But she's really mad at me.

Ryder West
- I would be. Why did u do that, B? I thought the story was cute.

Bailey paused, hating the very thought of Ryder upset with her.

Bailey Grant
- Pls don't be mad at me. I went over to apologize, but she wasn't there. Our friend Chase took her to the hospital, so she's sleeping at his place tonight.

Ryder West
- Is he the one who's totally in love with her?

She beamed, ridiculously happy that he remembered what she'd said.

Bailey Grant
- Yep, he's been in love with her for years, but she pretends she doesn't know.

Ryder West
- And she's sleeping at his house? Sucks for him LOL.

Bailey Grant
- He never gives up. It's cool.

Ryder West
- It's cool UR not giving up on me. I'm trying, I swear.

Bailey Grant
- I know.

Bailey didn't know that—not for sure—but a tight little ball of guilt curled in her belly when she thought of Meg bleeding and all alone and upset.

Bailey Grant
• I have to go. I have to take care of Meg.

Ryder West
• B, don't leave me.

Bailey Grant
• Not leaving you, just being a good friend.

Ryder West
• She h8s me. Please don't listen to her.

Bailey Grant
• OK, what's going on? You said I should apologize, and now you say don't listen to her.

Ryder West
• B, I like u. A lot. I shouldn't have said a word. That was lame, and I'm really sorry.

Bailey chewed a nail for a moment, wishing she could ask Meg what to do. Meg would probably hold up her middle finger and then stand with one hip out, cross her arms, and say something totally supportive like, "He had his chance and blew it. You deserve better, Bay. You deserve someone who will adore you."

She slipped her phone in her pocket and started going through her clothes for stuff that would look good on Meg.

Chapter 29
Meg

Meg shifted and stretched, her eyes popping open when the searing pain in her hand protested her movements. She struggled upright, blinking at her surroundings. Her hand was wrapped in a thick gauze bandage and burned like the time Bailey slipped with the freakin' hair straightener.

The blood.

Chase.

Her mind spun when the day's events came rushing back. She remembered Chase and his dad driving her to the hospital but not much after that. Her hand wasn't the only body part throbbing; her stomach was pissed off that she'd missed lunch and apparently dinner. She scanned the room. It was 1:00 a.m., according to the clock beside the bed.

Not her bed.

Holy crap, she was in Chase's bed.

She flung the covers off and froze when her feet hit the floor.

He'd tucked her in. God! Was it even humanly possible for a guy to be this sweet?

She'd never been in his room. She'd seen it from her window, of course. It was a cool room. He liked movies. DVDs spilled from the shelves he had on one wall. His desk was littered with video game components. He had a bunch of controllers, one in pieces, a few handheld games, and even an ancient Game Cube system strewn across his desk. In a pile on the floor beside the desk, he had art books—sketch pads, history texts, boxes of pencils and charcoals. But it was the pictures stuck to the mirror behind his door that grabbed her heart. Pictures of his parents, his grandparents, his brothers—and two of her that she didn't remember taking. The bed smelled like Chase—a mix of his sports-scented body wash and sweat—and she stood up to escape its power only to be clobbered with a pressing need for the bathroom.

She found her battered old canvas shoes next to the bed. She slipped them on but couldn't find her sweatshirt anywhere. Her phone and house key were in the pocket. No matter. She shrugged. She could jog around the block and climb in the bathroom window. With a slow twist of the doorknob, she was at the door to his room but couldn't resist turning back for one last look.

It was the only time she'd see it.

In the dim hallway—they'd left the light on for her—she crept down the stairs to avoid waking up the rest of the family. Tomorrow, she'd bake them brownies to say thanks, but right now, she needed to pee and eat and sleep… in that order. Tiptoeing across the first floor, she'd just reached the front door when a deep voice rasped, "Where the hell do you think you're going?"

She spun with a hand to her mouth to cover her startled shriek. "Chase! Oh, my God, you scared me to death."

He was stretched out on the sofa in the living room, a thin knit blanket barely covering his lean torso. He tossed it aside, got up, and met her at the door, naked to the waist. Meg tried hard not to notice. He reached for her bandaged hand, examined it from every angle, and muttered, "Yeah, I guess we're even then. You gave us a damn good scare tonight."

Meg tugged her hand back. "Yeah, about that. Um...thanks."

Chase frowned down at her. "No problem. Go back to bed."

Her eyes popped. "What? Here? I can't! I have to go home."

He was shaking his head before she finished her sentence. "Uh-uh. You heard the doctor. He released you into our care." He angled his head and slowly ran his eyes up and down her body. "How do you feel? Any headache or nausea?"

"Um, just a little dizzy, but that's because I'm hungry."

That rallied Chase into action. "Right. Come on." He grabbed her good hand and walked toward the kitchen, but she dug in her heels.

"Chase, I have to—"

"Eat. You have to eat. Come on. I'll make you something."

Eat? How could she possibly eat with him wearing nothing but sweatpants and staring at her with stormy green eyes? "Fine. But after that, I have to go home."

"You're not going anywhere except back upstairs. You try, and I'll wake up the whole house."

The threat got her feet moving before she could think of a convincing counterargument. She must be more tired than she thought. In the kitchen, he pulled out a chair and practically shoved her down into it while he found bowls, cereal, and milk. Without asking, he grabbed a banana from a huge bowl of fruit on the center of the table and sliced it over Rice Krispies.

"Uh—"

"What?"

"I need to—" She waved a hand around, hoping he'd get the hint.

"Oh! Yeah, sure. It's that door."

Meg escaped into the small powder room in the hall that led to the kitchen, flipped on the light, and stared at her reflection. Her hair stood on end. Her face was pale and her eyes were all red and puffy. "Kill me."

With one hand, she fumbled with her jeans and managed to tug them down. That wasn't so bad. Getting them back up after she'd finished and flushed—yeah, so not happening. She tugged and shimmied, and when she let out a frustrated grunt, Chase knocked.

"You need a hand? I'll close my eyes, I promise."

Meg smirked at the door. He totally would. That was the thing about Chase; he did what he said. She had to admit that she needed the help. "Yeah, keep your eyes shut." She opened the door, unsurprised to find his eyes clenched.

"Okay, just take my hands, show me…uh, you know, where you—"

"Yeah, I got it." She directed one of his hands to the waistband of her jeans, currently stalled at hip level. "Can you just maybe pull them up?" In the mirror, her face was a flaming red, and she thanked God he couldn't see.

Chase slipped his fingers through her belt loops, his knuckles grazing her bare skin, and Meg jumped.

"Oh, God, did I hurt you?" He snatched his hands back and covered his eyes.

"No! I'm fine, good. Your hands are just…um, cold."

"Sorry." He rubbed them together and reached for the loops again. "Better?"

Better? Meg held her breath and shut her eyes, but that just made it way too easy to imagine Chase sliding his hand lower. She forced her eyes open and managed to mumble a weak "Yeah" and held her breath. If she opened her mouth, if she so much as twitched her lips, they'd fuse to Chase in a kiss that would swallow them both whole.

Chase gave a tug that lifted her jeans and then her to her toes. Before she could say anything, he shifted his hands to her fly, fastened the button, and raised the zipper.

She waited for him to move, but he just stood there, his hands on her waistband, his eyes closed, half a smile on his lips. She could see the pulse pounding under his jaw. A second later, he stopped breathing too. If he'd pull her closer, she would go. If he'd curl his fingers tighter into her pants, she would not stop him. If he'd lower his mouth to hers—

Her stomach growled.

Chase's eyes flew open. His hands fell to his sides and he took a step back.

"Your cereal is getting soggy."

She shoved her way past him and spooned cereal into her mouth like it was the first time she'd seen food. After a few minutes, Chase did the same. When she'd swallowed the last bit of puffed rice, he poured her a second bowl without a word.

She ate that one too and only then looked up into Chase's furious face.

"Talk," he demanded.

This time, she arched an eyebrow at his authoritative tone. She didn't take orders, not from anybody, especially not from Chase. As if he read her mind, his face softened and his hand reached to her uninjured one. "I thought we were too late, Megan. I really thought you were dying on me."

His eyes trapped hers under their spell, and she gasped at the tension rolling off him. He cared. That was obvious. That she cared he cared scared the hell out of her.

"It was a really crappy day, Chase. I was upset. And tired. And hungry. I tried to use an X-Acto knife on an apple instead of walking back downstairs to get the right knife. This is my fault."

He let go of her hand and pulled away from her. "I get why you didn't call Bailey's grandparents. But you damn well should have called us." His eyes burned with that same palette of pain and betrayal and disappointment she'd practiced painting for so long.

She straightened her spine. "I didn't think it was that bad."

His frustrated sigh told her otherwise. "You know, I used to think you were the smartest girl in the world, Megan."

Her blood simmered. "And now?" she asked before she could feign disinterest.

"And now I think you're the most scared. What I can't figure out is why."

"I'm outta here." She bolted from the kitchen table and got about three feet before Chase's strong arms caught her and carefully turned her around.

"Guess again."

She struggled until she realized Chase was much stronger than she'd imagined, so she gasped in pain, clutching her injured hand. Chase cursed and released her.

"Jesus! Are you okay?"

She darted past him and made it to the living room. This time, he grabbed her and pulled her to the sofa where he'd been sleeping, pinning her there with his own body. She couldn't resist the taunt. "Not bad for the girl who *used* to be the smartest one you knew."

His lips twitched, but he didn't smile. "You that desperate to get away from me?"

"Okay." She surrendered. "I'm sorry. Let me up."

"No, I like it here." This time, he did smile.

"Chase, I'm serious. Get off me." She wrestled under his weight and he went still. His mouth dropped open, and his eyes went from green to damn near black in the space of a few heartbeats.

"Megan. Don't move," he ordered through clenched teeth.

There was tension in his voice, not to mention his body, and after a second or two, she figured out why. In one sudden move, Chase was up and under the blanket, sitting at her feet, his face flushed.

After a moment, she nudged him with her foot. "You okay?"

He shot her a glare. "Awesome. Go back to bed. It's late, and I'm cranky if I don't get enough sleep."

"I can't sleep here."

Chase groaned and flung his head back against the sofa cushion. "Megan, you're not going home. You're going back upstairs to my room and going to sleep. You can't even button your own pants! What are you going to do if that starts bleeding again and you're alone?"

"I'll call you. I promise this time, I'll call."

He shook his head. "Forget it. My dad would kill me."

Meg blew out a loud a sigh. "Look, Chase, this is so incredibly weird. I can't stay here in your bed—" she snapped her mouth shut before *weird* morphed into *creepy*.

He turned to face her, took her good hand, and held on. Meg's pulse skipped once, twice, and then settled into a fast pace when he circled his thumb over the back of her hand, his eyes peering into her soul. "You feel it. I know you do, so don't bother trying to lie to me. It's intense. It's deep and it's real. Not weird."

Meg lowered her eyes, stared at their clasped hands, pulled in a slow, careful breath, and prepared to stab deep. "I'm sorry, Chase, but I don't feel that way about you."

She braced for his reaction. A frown. A sigh. An argument…or something. Instead, his eyes glinted with humor.

He leaned closer.

She pulled back.

He grinned, flashing a smile that was purely predatory, and before she could form any protest, he kissed her. Damn it! She knew what he was trying to do. His lips teased hers. Well, she was not going to play—oh! His fingers skimmed softly down her arms, carefully around her injured hand. No, she was stronger than him—God! His hand reached her thigh and squeezed and she couldn't remember what she wanted to say, couldn't remember her vow until he whispered in her ear.

"Bull."

Meg opened her eyes, found Chase back on his side of the sofa, looking all smug. In half a second, her scattered thoughts, her erratic breaths, her fluttering belly—it all collided, leaving her someplace halfway between angry and hurt. She tried to get up, to run, but he was ready for that and grabbed her hand.

"Meg, stop lying to me. I want us to be together." The arrogant grin disappeared, and his grip on her hand tightened. "Why don't you want me? Tell me the truth this time. I think I deserve that much."

Her eyes burned, her hand throbbed, and her head spun, but damn it, he was right.

He was right.

He did deserve the truth. Any guy who'd clean up his room and tuck her in his bed and pull up her jeans (without peeking or copping a feel) and make her Rice Krispies deserved so much more than *her*. She shut her eyes, let her body sag, and blurted out the thing that weighed heaviest on her heart.

"I don't want you stuck having to love me."

Chapter 30
Bailey

Tuesday morning dawned gray and cold. Bailey had been up for forty minutes already. She quickly finished her morning routine so she could make it over to Chase's house to help Meg get ready for school. She headed downstairs, reached for the granola bars, and changed her mind.

Pop-Tarts. Definitely. Meg loved Pop-Tarts.

She popped one of two different varieties into the toaster and texted Chase while they warmed.

He didn't reply, so she wrapped the hot pastries in paper towels, slung her backpack and her bag of stuff for Meg over her shoulder, and left. Across the street, she paused to examine Meg's front yard. It looked good. No more toilet paper or diapers had appeared during the night. She smiled happily and resumed her walk around the block.

"Bailey. Hi, Bailey!"

Bailey turned and saw Meg's mom frantically waving her over from the front porch. "Hi, Pauline!" Meg's mother hated being called Mrs. Farrell. Her mom also liked being called by her first name, but Bailey couldn't ever remember a time when Meg had said, "Hey, Nicole!"

Meg was funny that way.

Bailey walked back to the steps that led to the porch. "What's up?"

Pauline wore sweats and no makeup and looked like she hadn't slept in a week. "I packed some things for Meg. Could you run them over to her at Chase's house? I have to get a few hours' sleep."

Bailey took Meg's backpack plus the gym bag Pauline gave her and swung them over her other shoulder. "Sure."

"Thanks."

Bailey made it down the path before Pauline stopped her again. "Is it bad? The cut on her hand? There was so much blood in her room."

"I didn't see it." Bailey looked away and shivered. She was a horrible friend who made her best friend cry. It was her fault that Meg got hurt in the first place and had to spend the night with the guy who loved her forever but who she couldn't love back because she was stubborn and…and…just *wrong*.

"So much blood."

Bailey's head snapped up. "I'm sorry. I'd better go. I don't want Meg to be late."

"Tell her to call me. If she's in pain. I'll come right away. Tell her please?"

In Pauline's wide brown eyes, Bailey saw exhaustion and worry and bit her lip. "I will."

With one last wave, Bailey walked quickly down the street and around the corner, juggling four bags and two Pop-Tarts and the weight of her own guilt. She knocked on Chase's front door, waited a moment, and finally heard the scrape of locks turning. Chase opened the door, rumpled, shirtless, and majorly depressed.

"Hey, cutie, what's wrong?"

He didn't answer. He did open the door wider to let her in. Bailey took a few steps inside, dropped all her gear near the staircase, and spotted Meg on the sofa, her hand resting on a throw pillow, a dark brown stain on the bandage that almost swallowed her whole hand.

She gasped. "Oh, God, Chase. It's still bleeding? Is she okay?"

He nodded and yawned. "Bad night. You got this? I'm gonna get dressed."

"Yeah."

While Chase climbed the steps, Bailey shook Meg's shoulder. "Meg! Time to wake up."

Meg woke up with a jolt. "I'm up! I'm—*ow!*" She clutched her hand to her chest and winced. A few seconds later, her eyes hardened, and she glared at Bailey. "What are *you* doing here? Where's Chase?"

"He's upstairs getting dressed. I came to help you. Look! Pop-Tarts." She lifted a corner of the paper towel and waved the pastries under Meg's nose.

Meg ignored the Pop-Tarts, flung the blanket off her legs, and stood, cradling her hand. "You did enough."

Bailey's heart tightened. She put the Pop-Tarts on Chase's coffee table. "I'm sorry about that Facebook thing. I didn't mean for everyone to gang up on you and told them to stop. I came to help, Meg, and I brought a bag your mom sent. Do you want to shower? I brought a plastic bag for your hand if you do."

Meg stopped and stared at her. "Why? So you can take pictures of me and post those on Facebook? No thanks."

"Meg, I'm sorry! Really. The Facebook thing was totally uncool, and Ryder—"

Meg flung up her hands, grimacing with pain. "Oh, Ryder! I should have known he had something to do with this."

Bailey's blood heated when Meg got snarky. "Um...no. He told me to apologize."

Meg laughed once, but Bailey could tell she didn't really mean it. "Oh! You're sorry because he told you to be. Great." She picked through the bags Bailey left by the steps and grabbed the one her mother had sent. "You know, all I'm trying to do is make sure you don't get hurt, and somehow, I end up with thirteen stitches."

Bailey put her hands on her hips and frowned. "I said I was sorry. But maybe you shouldn't have told Ryder that I threw up on Miss Monroe or about the poem. You know I really like this guy, and you told him the most embarrassing stuff you could. What kind of friend does that, Meg?"

Meg paused on her way to the downstairs bathroom. "I didn't tell him that story. I didn't tell *anyone* that story." Her eyes went hard. "That's why you posted that comment on Facebook? To get back at me for something I didn't even do?" She shook her head with half a laugh. "What kind of friend doesn't believe a friend when she says she didn't do something?"

With narrowed eyes, Bailey stated the facts. "Ryder said you told him I threw up all over the teacher. He knew what grade. He knew the teacher's name."

Meg waved her unbandaged hand. "So you believe him? You've known this guy for like ten minutes. You haven't even met him in real life. And you've known me since kindergarten, but somehow, *I'm* the liar?" She stalked down the hall and shut herself into Chase's downstairs bathroom with the bag her mother had packed.

Bailey flung herself down on Chase's sofa, grabbed a Pop-Tart, and reconsidered everything that had happened. Ryder wouldn't lie to her—she was sure of it. He knew how much she loved Meg and would have to be smart enough to know that if he said Meg said something she never said, she'd find out about it. Plus, he just moved here, so how would he even know about second grade if Meg didn't tell him?

But if she thought it was for Bailey's own good, which was exactly what she'd said when she'd told her Simon was hanging out with Caitlyn, Meg *would* hurt her.

She stuck out her tongue and aimed it in Meg's direction.

Footsteps pounded down the stairs and Chase was back. "Where's Megan?"

His hair was still wet and he wore a black T-shirt with a gray hoodie, but somehow, those colors only made his eyes *beg* to be stared into, so Bailey did just that until Chase snapped his fingers in her face. "Oh…uh, bathroom." Bailey ate the second Pop-Tart.

"Alone? I thought you were here to help her."

"She doesn't want my help." Bailey crossed her arms and then crossed her legs, tapping the air with her raised foot.

Chase put his hands on his hips. "Bay, what the hell is going on with you two?"

"I apologized for what I put on Facebook. I got up extra early to pack some stuff for her and come over here and do her hair, but she won't apologize for telling Ryder I threw up all over Miss Monroe in second grade!"

Bailey waited for Chase to smile and tell her he'd talk to Meg and make everything all right, but he just stood there, hands on his gorgeous hips, staring at her like she'd forgotten to put on makeup. Wait. Her hands flew to her face. No, she hadn't forgotten her makeup.

A series of thuds on the ceiling overhead made Chase look toward the staircase with a frown. Loud giggles followed by shouts of "Butthead!" made him sigh.

"Look, Bay, in about twenty seconds, I'm gonna have to go separate my brothers. Can you just please try again? I can't help her—" He waved his hands up and down over her hips. "Not like that."

Bailey made a sound of disgust. If she were Meg, she'd be wrapped around Chase like a silk manicure and pretend her hand hurt so bad that he had to feed her every meal—one bite at a time—and then she'd lick his fingers clean.

"Chase! Come up here and rescue Evan! He's stuck in his pajamas again," Kelly Gallagher shouted from upstairs.

"Bailey!"

"Fine," she snapped and headed to the bathroom, where Meg had been locked for the past five minutes, and knocked on the door, even though Meg would probably slam the door in her face.

"What?"

"It's me. Let me in."

"No."

Bailey gritted her teeth and almost pounded on the door when she remembered this wasn't her house. When Meg was in a stubborn mood, the only way to get her to listen was to appeal to her logical side. "Megan, come on. We're in everyone's way. Chase's little brothers are up and need help, so he can't help you. I'm it."

The door clicked open. "Fine," she snapped, and Bailey wondered if she'd sounded that bitchy a few seconds ago when she'd said the same word to Chase.

She didn't think so.

Bailey squeezed past Meg into the tiny room. Meg had already managed to change shirts and was trying to wrestle a pair of sweatpants on.

"Just pull them up. I can manage the rest."

Bailey grabbed a handful of material and tugged the pants on. When Meg shut her eyes and turned red, she blinked in confusion. "Relax, Meg. They're on."

"Oh…right." She fumbled with the drawstring, waving Bailey off when she reached out to help. "I got it."

"Shoes we'll do in the other room. What about hair and makeup?"

Meg rolled her eyes. "Forget it."

Bailey gasped. "Meg, are you crazy? Do you want Chase to see what you really look like in the morning?"

"Bailey, I don't care how I look. I don't care how Chase thinks I look. I just want to get out of here. Are you gonna help or not?"

Bailey scanned Meg's flat hair and pale face and surrendered. "Fine. What's next?"

"I need to brush my teeth. Can you just hold my hair out of the way?"

Bailey nodded, and Meg finished the task in record time.

"Let's go."

The girls opened the bathroom door and found the entire Gallagher family in the kitchen, all talking at once. Chase poured milk over Dylan's cereal. Connor elbowed Evan who then shoved Ethan. Dave Gallagher was just sipping coffee when the tussle reached him. "Hey, hey, the next kid who makes me spill my coffee gets sold to pay for my new clothes."

The twins froze in place, and Dave mopped up the spill.

"Hi, girls. Breakfast? Coffee?" Kelly hurried in, wearing jeans, sneakers, and a hoodie with her hair pulled up in a ponytail. Nicole wouldn't be caught dead with her hair in a ponytail, but Bailey thought it was sweet and practical. And besides, there was no way Kelly Gallagher looked old enough to have all these kids anyway, so it didn't matter.

"Megan, sit down." Dave held out a chair.

With her mouth in a tight line, Meg took the chair he offered. She shot Bailey a "help me" look, but Bailey could only shrug.

"Megan, the next time you hurt yourself while you're home alone, you are to call this house immediately. Understood, young lady?"

Wow. Bailey shuddered in sympathy for Meg when her mouth fell open and her eyes popped, but Mr. Gallagher wasn't done.

"I don't care if it's a paper cut or a broken nail. If you're hurt, you call us. You do not tie a towel around a gaping wound and wait for it to stop bleeding, and you damn well do not try to walk to the hospital by yourself in the dark. Are we clear?"

With her eyes pinned to Mr. Gallagher, Meg nodded. Bailey swallowed a giggle. She'd never seen Meg so...so...so stunned before. Who knew it would be so much fun?

"And another thing, Chase tells me you lost your job. Since he's abandoning us for lacrosse," Mr. Gallagher said with a glare at Chase, "I need help at the store. You can start after school until the stitches come out. Then I'll need you at dawn on Saturdays. It pays ten dollars an hour."

"Hon, you're scaring the girl," Mrs. Gallagher said.

"Yeah, well, it takes a village and all that—" he retorted and then searched for Chase. "Chase! Get your girlfriend some juice."

Bailey almost forgot Chase was there. She followed Mr. Gallagher's gaze and found Chase hiding behind one of the twins, eating cereal out of the box. His head shot up. "She's not—"

But with one look from his dad, Chase snapped his teeth together, opened a cabinet for a glass, and poured Meg some orange juice, which was some kind of code for the twins to unfreeze and return to their breakfast battles. Chase poured cereal for himself. Mrs. Gallagher started the lunch-making assembly line. It was total chaos, and Bailey wanted the Gallaghers to adopt her. For a moment, she indulged herself, imagining how *her* dad would have handled Meg's injury. Of course, Meg would have called her. They'd have rushed right over, driven her to the hospital. Meg would have slept at her place.

"You get that yard cleaned up?" Mr. Gallagher asked Chase, putting a pin in Bailey's little thought bubble.

Chase stiffened and turned his furious face to Bailey. She shrank under the glare he shot her. "Yeah, it's clean."

Mr. Gallagher nodded. "Good. That's one less thing for Megan to worry about today."

That got Meg's attention. "I'm sorry…what?"

"Dad, I didn't—"

"Don't worry about it, Megan. Your place was toilet-papered last night, but Chase took care of it."

Meg raised her glass and glared at Bailey over the rim for a moment and drained it all in a single gulp. "Thanks for everything, Mr. Gallagher. I promise I'll call if I get hurt." She stood up and took one step toward the kitchen door before Mr. Gallagher stopped her in her tracks.

"Hold it. Where do you think you're going?"

"To school," Meg said it like she was talking to one of the twins.

"Not by bus. Give me ten minutes and I'll drive you guys. Or Chase will drive, and we'll sit with white knuckles—"

"Dad!"

"Kidding." Mr. Gallagher held up both hands and grinned. "Finish that. We'll meet you outside." He and Chase headed out to the car.

"Time for the bus!" Mrs. Gallagher called out, and two of Chase's brothers scrambled for jackets, backpacks, and lunch bags, while the twins ran to the window to wave good-bye. Five minutes later, there was total silence in the kitchen. Mrs. Gallagher sank into a chair with a loud groan. "Sorry, girls. I'd like to say it isn't always so insane around here, but that would be total fiction. How's your hand, Meg?"

"Um…okay, I guess."

"Does it hurt?"

Meg shrugged. "A little."

"Here. Take these." She stood, grabbed a bottle of Tylenol from the cabinet over the sink, and opened it for Meg. "Oh, girls, I'm sorry. You must be hungry, especially you, Meg! You were sleeping like a baby when Chase carried you up the stairs."

Bailey smirked when Meg's face went pink. "I'm good. Chase made me cereal around midnight."

"I had Pop-Tarts," Bailey added, earning another glare from Meg, which was funny because Mrs. Gallagher was staring at Meg while Meg was busy staring at Bailey and never saw the little smile on Mrs. Gallagher's lips or the way her eyes went misty.

"I'm glad Chase took good care of you, Meg. Did he tell you dinner on Sundays at three o'clock?"

Meg's face froze in place for a few seconds, and Bailey thought she heard a strangled "Help!" squeak out of her mouth but couldn't be sure because she wasn't even sure Meg was actually speaking to her, so she ignored it. But Mrs. Gallagher waited patiently for Meg to say something, so Meg finally gulped and shook her head.

"Um…no, he didn't mention that. Thanks, but I won't—"

"Of course you will! You're Chase's girlfriend, so that means you'll have dinner with us. We have big, noisy, messy family dinners here every Sunday. His grandparents are dying to meet you, not to mention the godparents and cousins."

Bailey hid her grin when Meg's face went from pink back to paper white while she swayed a little on her feet and wished she could pull up one of the chairs at the table and watch the drama unfold. But Meg stunned her.

"No, I'm not his girlfriend, Mrs. Gallagher. I'm not anybody's girlfriend, and I really have to get to school. Please thank everybody for taking care of me last night." She turned and left the kitchen, leaving Mrs. Gallagher twisting her hands.

"Bailey." Chase's mother turned to her with fire in her eyes. "Did I miss something here? The way those two watch each other, there's definitely something there, right? I'm not just getting old and seeing things?"

Bailey laughed. "No, you are definitely not old. Chase is crazy about Meg, and she's just as crazy about him. She just won't admit it."

"Oh, boy." Mrs. Gallagher covered her face with her hands and sighed. "Poor Chase."

Bailey nodded. Poor Chase. Poor Meg. And poor her! Surrounded by all this love nobody wanted—nobody but her. She'd kill to have someone adore her. She stared at her hand, wondered just for a second how much it would hurt if she slashed it. A horn honking outside jolted Bailey from her crazy thoughts. She called a hasty good-bye to Mrs. Gallagher and caught up to her friends in Chase's driveway, climbing into the backseat next to a barefoot Meg.

"Ewww, what's this?" Bailey held up a brown-stained towel.

"Um…blood."

Bailey dropped the towel and took Meg's kicks. "Give me your foot."

Meg dutifully lifted her feet while Bailey put on her shoes but said nothing. Chase was also unnaturally quiet. Bailey sat back and watched while Chase adjusted the mirrors and reversed out of the driveway. The drive to school was silent and tense, and it took Bailey the entire trip to figure out why.

Chase was giving up.

Chapter 31
Meg

Meg's hand burned with the fury of a dozen sunburns.

When they were twelve, Bailey thought it would be fun to slather baby oil all over their bodies and bake in the sun. It wasn't. For two days, Meg couldn't get dressed. For three days after that, she looked like a snake that couldn't figure out how the shedding process worked.

She stared at the bandage on her hand. Ten days before the stitches could come out, the doctor had said. She winced and hoped she could survive this burning for nine more days. With her head down and her hand cradled against her chest, she slipped through the corridors. Nobody threw underwear at her, so the day would have been better than yesterday, except for one thing.

Chase.

She'd divulged way too much information and she needed to regroup. It would be easy to blame the trauma of getting hurt or the drama that had led up to her injury or even the meds they'd given her in the hospital. Who knows? Maybe all those things *were* to blame—at least in part. But the truth was that Chase was way too easy to talk to.

He'd asked her why she didn't want him. And she'd told him the truth.

Just blurted it right out. She didn't want anyone, especially him, to feel like he had to love her. Oh, sure, at first, he'd scoffed and tried to laugh it off, but she wouldn't let him. He'd wanted the truth and he'd deserved it.

So she gave it to him. She told him how her parents never really wanted kids. How tight money was—and still is—since she'd been born. How it was her fault her dad died. Her fault that her mom worked twenty out of twenty-four hours, collapsed in bed, and then got up to do it all over again. She'd told him it was her responsibility to grow up as fast as she could, get out on her own, take care of herself.

He'd tried to hand her all the reassurances and promises he thought would solve everything, but she'd heard them before, heard them every time, every *single* time her parents had the same fight. She fell asleep with him still trying to talk her into believing him. Or believing *in* him.

Either way, she'd let him down.

He was different today. Around her, around Bailey, around everyone. It was obvious the truth changed him. She tried to justify it, but she couldn't. So then she tried to forget.

She answered the few people who expressed interest, even though they disguised it as concern. By lunch, the medicine Kelly Gallagher had given her had worn off, and the burning in her hand worsened to a steady flare. She sat at an empty table with a turkey sandwich, one of the few things she could eat with one hand. She had a bottle of water but couldn't open the cap, so it sat on her tray while she thought about her home test for the Cooper Union. With her left hand injured, now was as good a time as any to begin work on her ink project. India ink or stylus? She clicked her plain old ball-point pen and doodled on a notebook page, the turkey sandwich forgotten, until a shadow passed through her light.

She glanced up at Chase. Without a word, he took the bottle of water, unscrewed the cap, and handed it back to her. Then he turned to leave.

"Chase, wait."

He turned back, shot out one hip, impatience sizzling.

"What happened last night? Your dad said my house got trashed?"

Chase's jaw tightened, and he jerked his chin at something behind Meg. "Ask her."

She glanced over her shoulder.

"Hi, Meg! How's your hand feeling?" Bailey sang.

Meg glared. "It hurts." *Duh.*

Bailey's sunny smile faded. "Yeah, do we need to…um, clean it, put medicine on it, or something?"

Meg nearly laughed. Bailey almost hurled when she got her ears pierced. If she saw the angry black line of sutures across Meg's hand, she'd probably fall to the floor in a dead faint. "Thanks, but I can manage."

Bailey sat uninvited at Meg's table and Meg supposed that was because in Bailey's eyes, things between them were once again smooth. That things were not smooth in Meg's eyes usually didn't occur to Bailey unless she pointed it out.

"What happened at my house last night?"

Bailey forehead crinkled, and she looked ashamed for a moment. "A bunch of people toilet-papered your front yard. But I didn't put them up to it, I swear!"

Not directly, Meg thought.

"After you and Chase cleaned up, what did you do?"

Bailey shrugged. "I went home, posted what happened to you on Facebook, and told everyone to leave you alone."

Meg's eyebrows shot up. "Thank you so much for calling off your troops."

"Oh, Meg, they're not my troops, and I didn't call anybody off just like I didn't put them up to it in the first place."

"You did, Bailey. You did as soon as you told my secret."

Bailey's wide eyes fixed on hers and she pouted. "Only because you told one of mine first."

"I *didn't*," Meg insisted. "I never told anybody, not even Chase, any of your secrets. I didn't talk about you throwing up. I didn't talk about that poem you stuck in Jordan's locker, and I didn't even mention what almost happened with Mr. Milner back in ninth grade." Meg's dark eyes flashed.

Bailey's eyes went wide, and she whipped her head around, looking for eavesdroppers. "Shit, Meg, will you shut up?"

"Why should I? If you're gonna punish me for things I didn't do, I may as well as—you know—*actually do them*."

Bailey's darting eyes caught sight of a teacher bearing down on them. She held up her hands, tried to make peace. "Well, I *thought* you did, and I was wrong about that. And I said I was sorry."

"Only because Ryder made you," Meg sneered.

"No, not only. Chase did too. And I didn't need either of them. I was already on my way over to your place on my own."

Meg wasn't so easily convinced. "If you'd trusted me, you wouldn't have to apologize. I can't believe you trusted him over me."

"I didn't. Not at first. I even texted you, but you ignored me."

Meg frowned. That could have been true; she'd ignored a message that day. She huffed and crossed her arms and tried to wrap herself up in her anger. It hurt. So she sighed and gave up. "Okay. There's only one way we're gonna get past this."

Bailey looked at her with a raised eyebrow.

"We need to meet Ryder. Up close and in person."

Chapter 32
Bailey

Bailey was a bundle of raw nerves. She'd promised Meg she would not go anywhere alone with Ryder. They would meet in a public place, arrive separately, and leave separately. She promised Meg she'd insist on it and set it up for later that evening.

But that's not what Bailey did.

Bailey texted Ryder and arranged to meet him at the food court at the mall right after school, when Meg would be happily working the counter at the Gallaghers' bakery.

When she finally met Ryder West, it would be only the two of them, looking into each other's eyes.

It had taken her almost all of the next period to text Ryder without getting caught by her teacher and convince him that it was time to meet. It was now exactly 3:30. Bailey stood in the food court at the mall.

Alone, though she was surrounded by a few hundred strangers. She may be going behind Meg's back, but she wasn't dumb enough to totally ignore her warnings. And now she'd been here for fifteen minutes already with no sign of him.

It didn't mean anything, she tried to assure herself. She wasn't worried, not one bit. He was probably just running late, or he'd gotten into another fight with his aunt or something. And the place was totally jammed. He could be here and how would she even know? He never did send her a picture...or post one on Facebook. His profile shots were all video game avatars.

She checked her reflection in a store window. She'd rushed home after school and changed into her cutest outfit—jeans with black boots, a skimpy sweater that showed off her belly. She paced in front of the food stands, but nobody approached her. Nobody even checked her out. She finally snagged an empty table, took out her cell, and texted Ryder.

Bailey: You here yet? I'm sitting in front of Hot Wok.

A few minutes went by before the phone buzzed.

Ryder: No, I'm so sorry. Still at work.

Bailey tossed her phone to the table and fumed. Meg's smart-ass voice played in her head. She tried not to listen. She told the Meg voice that Ryder couldn't be a psycho serial killer or a sixty-year-old pervert or he'd definitely be there, chasing her through the Gap with a bloody ax or something. So there. Meg was wrong! That was something at least.

Still...he wasn't here. He wasn't coming. He'd blown her off again, and Gran wasn't coming back for her for at least an hour or so. She stared at her phone, willing it to buzz.

"Hey."

Bailey jolted back to reality and found a pair of gorgeous blue eyes looking down at her. He was here! Oh, God, he was here, and he was everything and more than she'd imagined. She'd worried, obsessed really, about letting him down easy if he wasn't cute, which was going to be so hard since she liked him so much. But that didn't matter now. His face, oh, it was a face she'd have dreams about. Those pouty lips and sculpted jawline. And his body! He was tall and built and he was *here*.

"You came," she managed to squeak out.

The god standing in front of her looked at her like she had spinach caught in her teeth and Bailey's little bubble of hope burst. "You're not Ryder?"

"No, I...uh, just want your table. You done or what?"

Bailey forced a smile. "Yeah. No problem." She stood up, turned away, and collided right into Simon.

"What are you doing here?" she snarled.

"Uh, walking," he snapped back. He was wearing regular clothes instead of all his usual fancy designer stuff, blond hair perfect as always. Bailey moved around him, but he blocked her way.

"Where's Caitlyn? Out getting her flea and lice treatment?"

Simon's nostrils flared. "Where's Meg? Out buying you a ring?"

Bailey's hands curled into fists, and she marched away before she used them. Safely enclosed in a stall in the ladies' room, she fell to pieces for a few minutes and then bravely fixed her makeup. She would not let Ryder's betrayal touch her, and she would definitely not go running to Meg to tell her how right she was. And she would most definitely not waste another tear on Simon. She blew her nose on some scratchy toilet paper, washed her hands, and walked with her head up high to the game store. She always went to the game store when she felt down.

Guys loved gamer chicks.

She spent a relaxing hour debating what the new *Assassin's Creed* game would be like with some poor slob who had no idea who he was dealing with and then met Gran outside.

"He didn't show, did he?"

Bailey slouched in the front seat and merely shook her head. Gran said nothing more.

Later than night, Bailey blew a curl out of her eyes and stared at her Facebook updates. She hadn't felt like eating dinner, and now her stomach was complaining. As she stared at the volume of Likes and comments her little Facebook story about Meg had earned, she knew her stomach was feeling a lot more than just hungry.

Okay, so maybe she shouldn't have posted the story about Meg wetting her pants. She would apologize again tonight. After she found something to eat. After she did her homework. And after Meg had time to paint, which Bailey knew would go a long way toward calming her. Maybe she would hold Meg's palette while she painted. Meg would like that.

Her cell phone buzzed. She glanced at the message and tightened her lips.

Ryder: Hey, u busy?

It took her a few minutes, but she finally decided on an appropriate reply. Her first few attempts were entirely too snarky.

Bailey: I'm not at work, so why would I be busy?

A new message came through instantly.

Ryder: I get that UR pissed off. I can explain.

Pissed off? Pissed off didn't even come close. She twisted a curl and thought of Meg. If Meg were here, she'd roll her eyes and yell, "Are you crazy? He blew you off! Don't give him a second chance to hurt you." But Meg *wasn't* here. And besides, he did say he was working.

> **Ryder:** Please?

A slow grin spread across Bailey's face. He was cute or…well, seemed cute and so determined to make things up to her.

> **Bailey:** No problem. I get it. Something came up. Whatever.

She would hear him out. But she wouldn't make it easy for him.

> **Ryder:** Bailey, I know it sounds lame, but I screwed up at work and had to fix it. That's why I was late.

That's it? Working late? She rolled her eyes. He was really going to have do better than that.

> **Bailey:** Bull. You never showed up. I was there until 5. I'm not stupid. You don't want to see me, fine. I don't need you.
>
> **Ryder:** B, I was scared. U happy now? I didn't show up because I was scared.

Bailey read the text message twice. It didn't make sense. Why would he be scared? Was he ugly or horribly deformed or something?

> **Bailey:** Scared of me? I look exactly like the pictures online.
>
> **Ryder:** No, not ur pictures. UR really cute. It's because of Meg, Bailey. I don't want to come between u guys.

Bailey's temper spiked so suddenly that she actually stomped her foot. Gran yelled at her from downstairs to stop dancing. As if! Meg was ruining things for her without even trying.

Bailey: Look, I'm the one who made Meg mad. I kinda blew her off yesterday, and she took it out on you. Nothing to do with you.

Ryder: She's just looking out for u. I get that. How mad at u is she?

Bailey wondered that very same thing.

Bailey: Total cold shoulder today.

Ryder: U should go talk to her. I don't want her to h8 me.

She frowned and typed back.

Bailey: Why? If she hates you, so what?

Ryder: I don't want u to hate me, so GO TALK TO HER!

Bailey laughed at his shouty text.

Bailey: I will! I promise. Later. She's painting now and hates being interrupted.

Ryder: Good. TTYL. XO

Bailey beamed. He'd texted a hug and a kiss. That *had* to mean he liked her and not just a little. She wrapped her arms around herself and twirled around her room. Gran yelled up at her again to stop dancing.

She couldn't wait to tell Meg.

Chapter 33
Meg

Alone in her room, Meg twisted the neck of the Pixar lamp clamped to her easel and angled it at her canvas. She switched it on and froze. Chase looked back at her, eyes blazing from under the hair that was always in his face. Blood dripped from his lips down his jaw and throat, making him look like a vampire out of a romance novel, and she couldn't tear her eyes away.

She ran a finger across his parted lips and her own tingled. She noted the slight flare around his nostrils and her breathing went shallow. She leaned closer and swore she could smell the faint scent of vanilla that always clung to him. His eyes locked on hers from under his lashes. When she felt her lips lift in *that* smile, she threw a cover over the canvas and sank to her bed. She hadn't painted his hands but imagined they'd be clenched into fists while he tried like hell not to reach out and grab her. She'd painted him the way he'd looked last night after he had kissed her—and that had been hours *after* she'd finished this portrait.

God, she was losing her mind. It was a painting! Nothing more than a few globs of paint, she assured herself. She pressed a hand to her chest and pulled in a calming breath. The computer on her desk caught her attention. She powered it on and found some unanswered emails from the weekend. One from Ryder on Saturday.

> **From: Ryder909@mail.com**
> **Subject: Chill out!**
>
> ---
>
> Meg, WTF is going on between you and Bailey? She's all upset. Could you please back off? I told you I won't hurt her. I'm trying to arrange my work schedule so I can meet her and prove to you that I am who I say I am, so please stop screwing with her head.

Before that, one from Bailey, whose subject line read, "BACK OFF!!!!!!!!!!"

> **From: gamerchic16@mail.com**
> **Subject: BACK OFF!!!!!!!!!!**
>
> ---
>
> I told Ryder how you wet your pants in second grade and had to wear boys' underwear the rest of the day. He laughed. He thought it was the funniest thing he ever heard. He thought it was so funny that I should put it on Facebook. I hope Chase sees it and laughs at you.

Meg winced. It was like they were six all over again. She'd never told Ryder that story. How could Bailey doubt that?

There were several from a bunch of classmates, all teasing her about her bladder control issues. She deleted them, unread. Then a second one from Bailey.

> **From: gamerchic16@mail.com**
> **Subject: How could you?**
>
> ---
>
> Megan, how could you do that? How could you tell Ryder what happened in second grade? OMG, I'm so embarrassed!!!! You swore you wouldn't tell anybody that story. I know you don't like Ryder, but seriously, Meg, this really sucks. I thought we were friends. I really like this guy, and now he'll probably never want to talk to me again because of you. Back off!

Her anger reignited, and she pounded out a new message to Ryder.

To: Ryder909@mail.com
Subject: You slime

Ryder, I don't know what you think you're doing, but I'm on to you.
You're a liar and a player who obviously knows us, and I'm going to
track you down. So what's the deal? You want to get back at me for
something? Fine. Be a man and face me in person instead of from
behind your computer, you slime.

She clicked Send and seethed for a moment or two, and then her phone
buzzed with a text message from Bailey. Her hand screamed with pain. With
a sigh, she called her.

"Hey."

"Oh, hey! Why didn't you text me?"

"Because it hurts."

"Oh…right. Sorry," Bailey said. "So I'll be over in like fifteen minutes? I
thought it might be easier to get you showered at night. Then in the morning,
all you have to do is change clothes, you know?"

Meg's eyebrows shot up. That was actually a really good idea. "Um…
yeah, okay."

"Did you eat?"

Meg glanced at the clock. It was after nine o'clock. "I forgot."

"I'll bring you some ravioli that Gran made. See you in a few."

Meg closed her phone and gathered the things she'd need for her shower.
Clean underwear, elastic-waist sleep pants, and a tank top were perfect.
What could she tug on tomorrow with one hand? She searched through her

closet and found a skirt Bailey had made her buy a few months ago. She made a face and nearly put it back but then reconsidered. It had looked nice on her. It was a long, flowy skirt in a soft brown fabric. She could wear it with ballet flats.

In the bathroom, she readied soap, shampoo, conditioner, towels, plus the plastic bag she'd found in the bag Bailey had packed for her. It covered her hand up to the elbow and should keep everything dry. When the doorbell rang, she was already halfway downstairs.

"Hey!" Bailey bounced in and headed for the kitchen. "Gran says to heat these only for like a minute in the microwave or—" She put a plastic container on the counter and made an explosion sound, emphasized it with a hand motion. "Hungry?"

"Yeah, but I can wait until after I shower."

"Cool. Let's go."

Upstairs, Meg kicked off her canvas shoes and then tugged off her shirt. With Bailey's help, Meg was soon under the hot water stream with her plastic-covered hand outside the tub. It took her twice as long to shampoo, condition, rinse, scrub, and shave, but she did it and felt tons better.

"Here. Put this on." Bailey wrapped her in a robe. "You need help with the clothes?"

"Nah, I can manage."

"I'll be in your room if you need me."

Meg was smiling when she finished getting dressed. Her hand wasn't throbbing anymore and it felt good to be clean. The clothes she'd chosen were perfect—easy to get on with one hand and comfortable for sleep.

Chapter 34
Bailey

Trust was fragile, Bailey thought when she tossed Meg's cell phone on her bed. She didn't want to believe Ryder and she didn't want to doubt Meg, not after everything that had just happened. But there it was—proof right on Meg's phone. She'd contacted Ryder just like he'd said she did after she had told her, promised her that she would stop interfering.

"Excuse me?" Meg said in that oh-no-you-didn't tone she'd perfected back in second grade, but Bailey wasn't backing down. Not this time.

"Ryder says you emailed him."

Meg's jaw clenched. "Yeah. So?"

"So I told you to stay away from him." Bailey stood up, glaring.

Meg shook her head. "I want to know why he's telling you lies."

Lies! Bailey rolled her eyes. *We're back to the Ryder's a liar song.* "You're putting him in the middle and he doesn't want that. Why can't you just stay out of it? I know what I'm doing."

Meg shot out a hip and snorted. "You never know what you're doing. Remember Mr. Milner? You could have gotten him fired."

Bailey's face went hot, and she shot up a hand. It was so…so Meg to bring up the past. "That's not fair!"

"Fair? I don't give a crap about fair. I just don't want him to make a fool out of you, embarrass you, hurt you."

Meg's words only made Bailey madder. It was her life, not Meg's. Honestly, she was like a prison guard. "Megan, I really like this guy. He's incredible. He's smart. He likes gaming and is helping me build my video game."

"Oh, please!" Meg flung out her hands. "You'll never build that game and you know it. It's just another scheme to get guys to like you. Maximum points!"

"It is not! I like video games. I'm going to build it and sell it no matter what you say!"

"No, Bailey, you won't. You'll just get some guy to build it for you. You tried Simon and then Chase and now Ryder. You're just using him."

"No. No, that's not true. I like him, Meg. I really like him. I don't want you to ruin that like you—" Bailey suddenly clamped her teeth together and turned away.

Meg flinched. "Like I what, Bailey. What were you gonna say? Like I always do? Is that it? You blame me for all your breakups?" She sank to her bed, blinking back tears.

"Meg, I just want you to mind your own business! I told you to back off. I told you I really like this guy. What is your freaking *problem*?"

"I don't trust him."

"*I don't care!*" she shrieked and stood for a moment, blue eyes hot and wide. "Look, I'm telling you for the last time. Back off, or we can't be friends anymore."

Meg gasped. "You...you don't mean that."

"Oh, yeah, I do," Bailey said with an emphatic head nod. "I'm sick of this, Meg. It's my life, and if Ryder's a mistake, I want to make it! I don't keep shoving *your* mistakes in your face."

"What mistakes?"

Oh, my God, are you really this clueless? "Chase! The way you keep treating him is sick, Meg! But do I constantly remind you of that? No."

"Yes, you do."

"I do not! All I do is treat him like the friend he's always been. You want me to cut him out of my life so *you* don't have to deal with your feelings for him, and that's just mean, Meg, so I won't do it. I know that pisses you off, but I don't tell you every second of every day that you're making a colossal mistake, even though you are. And I wish you'd stop doing that to me."

"Wait...what?"

"Oh, shut up, Meg! Just shut up and stay out of my life. I'm going home. I hope your hand feels better." She stomped downstairs and out the door before Meg could close her gaping mouth.

Back at her grandparents' house, Bailey looked for her mother, but Nicole was out on another date. Gramps was home, but she couldn't talk about girl stuff with him. He took it too hard and always threatened to get his shotgun if anyone hurt her. He didn't even have a shotgun. She'd told him that once, and he'd said, "For you, baby girl, I'll get one." Gran wasn't home either. *Oh,* she thought as she pounded up the stairs to her room, *time to make more friends.*

She considered a video game but wasn't in the mood to play by the rules. She flopped on her bed, opened her cell, and tapped out a quick text to Ryder.

Bailey: You there? I need you.

Ryder did not reply. Tears threatened, but she wasn't ready to sob into her pillow. She logged into Facebook and skimmed her Timeline. Her hands curled into fists, and her face crumbled. It wasn't enough that she'd texted Ryder after she'd promised she wouldn't. Meg had posted a brand new update on her Wall.

> What do all these guys have in common? Simon Kane, Chase Gallagher, Ryder West, Jordan Clark, Tanner Hayes, Jonathan Pritchard, Elliot Nielson, and Mr. Milner—GO!

What little she'd eaten earlier bubbled in her belly, and she gulped to make sure it stayed down. She pressed a fist to her mouth. Jonathan Pritchard wrote, No comment ;). Jordan posted, Uh oh! A girl in her English class said, They're all hotties! Another girl asked Oh, Bailey, how did you get an A from Mr. Milner?

It wasn't the Likes the Wall post was collecting, and it wasn't even the comments, even though they all pretty much implied she was the school's biggest slut. No, what hurt the most…what drove the knife through her back was that Meg was the one who posted it.

Chapter 35
Meg

Meg opened her front door with a snarl. "What?"

Chase all but seethed, his green eyes glinting in the glare of the porch light. "What the *hell*, Megan?"

She flinched but did not cower. "You saw Facebook."

"Yeah. Saw you stab a friend in the back. And you used me to do it."

His voice was quietly cold—no small feat considering how furious he was. She stared at him, speechless. He waited one more beat. "You don't even deny it?"

"Um, I believe it's called fighting back."

"Really?" Derision practically dripped from the word. "It sounds a whole lot more like getting even, and that's not you."

Her eyes went round and she leaned toward him. "Oh, I thought you knew me so well, Chase! That you loved everything about me. Guess you were wrong. You *don't* know me, and you can't possibly love me, so just go home and leave me alone."

She tried to slam the door, but it bounced off the foot he stuck in its path. She took a step back. Chase stole the opportunity to walk in uninvited, and her face went red. He angled his head and narrowed his eyes. "You think I don't know you. You're wrong. Under all this mad, you know what I see? You're in pieces. Bailey took a cheap shot, and you're hurt. I get that. But this—" He jabbed a finger upstairs toward her room and finished, "is low."

She shook her head. "Why don't I get a shot? She came after me first, and worse, she got Ryder and even you involved. I keep telling her not to trust this guy, and she actually *believes him over me*."

The sound of her voice bounced off the walls of the living room. Chase took another step.

"Delete it, Megan. Right now."

She folded her arms and shook her head. When he cursed, her eyebrows shot up.

"Damn it, Megan. You don't hurt people like this, not on purpose. Delete the post before it ends up with another TP'd front yard or a knife through a hand. Please."

"No, Chase. Not this time."

He met her gaze. "Fine."

If she'd expected him to walk out and leave her to suffer alone, she'd underestimated him. Instead, he picked her up by her elbows and moved her out of his path to stalk upstairs to her room. He strode into her bedroom and came to a complete and utter stop when he saw her easel. Right behind him, Meg saw his face the second he caught sight of her easel, and her heart skidded to a stop. He ran his thumb over the streaks of blood that dripped from the likeness of his face. That cold fury was gone. In its place, she saw wonder and something that looked a lot like pride.

She shoved past him, tossed the cover over the painting.

Grinning, Chase pulled it back off. "Too late. I can't unsee it."

Meg fought desperately for something to say, something to explain it away, but she couldn't when the truth was staring at them from a twenty-by-seventeen-inch canvas.

"Bailey told me, but I was too afraid to believe it," he murmured.

Bailey told him? "Oh, God. Told you what?" she asked, letting her eyes slip shut.

Chase turned, the expression on his face making her knees buckle. "That you paint me all the time."

She bit her lip. Of course she did. Bailey was all about revealing secrets lately.

He stepped closer. "She also said that you're obsessed."

She stepped back.

"That you feel the same way about me as I feel about you."

He took another step.

She felt the bed behind her legs. He grinned, and she cursed. He knew she had nowhere to go.

"I love you, Megan. I've loved you for so long. I can't remember not loving you."

She swallowed thickly and blurted out one word. "Why?"

He moved closer still. "Why?" he repeated. "Lots of reasons. One day, when you're ready to hear them, I'll give you the list."

Her eyes softened. He had a list.

"You know what I love most of all?" he asked. "You have the most loyal heart. The way you defend and protect and love Bailey amazes me and makes me jealous because I want to be loved that way. I want to be loved *your* way."

She stared at him, certain she was going to burst into flames. She wasn't sure when it happened or why she chose that moment to stop denying it, but she loved him. Oh, God, she did, even though her father had warned her. And the words played on her lips, but when she opened her mouth, nothing came out. She nodded and smiled her Chase-only smile, and it was answered with one of his own. He took her hand and her pulse skipped, but he only moved it over her mouse.

"Okay, okay. You're right." She deleted the bitchy post. "Happy now?"

When she turned back to Chase, his smile thawed her heart, and for the first time in her life, she told her dad's memory to take a hike. "You have no idea."

Her hand still under his on the computer mouse, she asked, "What now?"

He shook his head. "I don't know, Megan. Let's just start with tomorrow, okay? Wait for me. We'll go to school together."

Together.

Meg really liked the sound of that.

Chapter 36
Bailey

Wednesday morning dawned bright and warm, but still, Bailey feigned illness. Gran didn't buy it. She did, however, drive her to school, which was cool because Bailey didn't have to face Meg or deal with the rest of the kids on the bus.

Her relief didn't last long. The second they pulled into the school parking lot, a group of boys hooted and whistled as she got out of the car.

"Bailey," Gran called as she was about to close the passenger door. Bailey turned back. "Hold your head up high, sweetheart. You have nothing to be ashamed about."

Bailey nodded, wondering how Gran always knew exactly what was going on, and waved as she drove off.

Meg's little Facebook post hadn't gotten the same reaction hers had. Instead, it created buzz. Bailey walked down the main corridor, and heads came together to whisper behind hands. Fingers pointed. Eyes assessed.

She tried so hard to look at the positive side. No one was throwing their underwear at her, so that was good. And they wouldn't be toilet-papering the house, which was even better.

"Hey, Bailey."

Startled that anyone would actually dare address her after Meg's Wall post, Bailey looked up into the face of a senior named Matt Benson. "Hi, Matt," she answered with her trademark bright grin.

That's when Donna Gantry pounced.

Suddenly, she stood directly in front of Matt like a human shield—like highlighted hair and lip gloss will save you!—and waved a French manicured fingertip in Bailey's face. "Back off, skank. He's *mine*."

Bailey did not stay long enough for the nervous laughter and the collective "Aww" that was sure to follow the hush spreading through the corridor. She hurried down the hall to her first class, only to collide with someone large and solid.

"Jesus, Bailey."

She jolted at the sound of Simon's voice. She hadn't talked to him since that day at the mall. He had the best voice. She always thought it sounded the way melted chocolate tasted. She knew that was silly—voices couldn't sound like food—but God, she really missed it. "I'm sorry!"

He frowned down at her and then looked quickly away. He moved past her and then turned back. "Hey, you okay?"

She'd always loved how tall he was. She managed a brave smile. "Sure."

"Good." He took another step away and stopped with a frown. "No, you're not." He shut his eyes and shook his head. "Look, it's none of my business, but I saw your post about Meg and her post about you. Just hang in there, okay? You guys are best friends." He cracked the smallest of smiles and took off at a jog.

She shook her head and whispered, "Not anymore." She dragged her feet down the hostile hallway, refusing to make eye contact with anyone. She made it all the way to her locker when something made her look up.

She froze in the middle of the east wing, a gasp stuck in her lungs.

Meg walked in her direction. And she was holding Chase's hand.

For a minute, she forgot to be mad, forgot to be hurt, forgot to be jealous. For a minute, she felt the most amazing happiness that Meg had finally—after all this time—opened her eyes to see what was right in front of her. For a moment, she forgot the ugly things she'd said and everything was perfect— everything was the way it was supposed to be.

And then she remembered Meg's Facebook post, and suddenly, *nothing* was the way it was supposed to be. The entire school thought she was a whore. Ryder kept blaming himself for ruining her friendship with Meg and even Chase—good old solid and reliable and dependable and sweet Chase shot her a glare. Something ugly twisted inside Bailey and then it ate her alive.

She clenched the muscles in her bubbling stomach, forced her hands to her side, and pulled in a deep breath. Meg had spotted her and halted in the center of the hall, waiting. A hum of anticipation ran up and down the hall when all the haters stopped minding their own business to watch hers. Bailey ignored them and started walking.

Meg had the decency to look apologetic. "Bay, I'm—"

Bailey's hand shot up. "Don't even. I don't want to hear it. I only want to warn Chase."

His head whipped around. "Warn me about what?"

"Her." Bailey jerked her head toward Meg. "She's not what you think. She's sure as hell not what I thought."

Meg's face trembled. "That's not fair, Bailey. You started this—you and Ryder. All I asked was for you to trust me, but you couldn't. And I still gave you another chance."

Another chance? Bailey's teeth ground together when Chase swung an arm over Meg and pulled her close to his side. Meg had no idea—no freakin' clue how many chances Bailey had already given her, but when...when exactly had Meg ever done that for her? Okay, after her snarky post and the resulting stabbed hand, Meg *had* forgiven her. But what about all the times Meg had stepped all over Bailey's opinions and feelings? Meg had been glossing over her, rolling her eyes at her for years—even the idea for the stupid video game was hers. And now she gets the guy when Ryder—oh, God, Ryder—just thinking his name made her chest tighten. He wouldn't even man up enough to meet her in person.

The crowd had grown. Bailey saw the glow of cell phones as people started recording the floor show. She took a step closer and angled her head. "I don't know what made you open your eyes and finally say yes to Chase, Meg. But I am curious. Does he know the reason you kept saying no? The *real* reason, I mean."

Meg went pale, and there was a part of Bailey that cheered at the sight.

"Bailey," Meg whispered. "Don't. Please."

Bailey blinked and couldn't resist the urge—the *need*—to hurt Meg, to make her suffer the way she did. Still was. "You're dumber than I am if you think you can hold him without telling him the whole story."

Meg shook her head. "I don't think you're dumb. I never did."

Bailey scoffed. "Yeah, right. And how many times was it that you told me not to trust Ryder? More than I told you Chase was right for you. You finally listened."

Meg looked down at her feet but said nothing.

"Bailey, just leave it alone." Chase tried to break things up, but Bailey was too furious.

"No, Chase. You need to know. Why don't you ask her? Ask her why she wouldn't be with you sooner?"

Meg's eyes popped when Chase turned hurt green eyes to hers. "Chase, please...don't listen."

"Tell him, Meg! What's the big deal. You love him, right? And he loves you right back. Don't you trust him?"

"Of course I trust him!"

"Then say it. Tell him why you said no over and over again."

"I was scared, Bailey! He knows that. I told him."

"Tell him why, Meg. Tell him why straight A's mean so freakin' much to you."

Chase pulled her by the hand that wasn't bandaged. "Come on, Megan. Let's just go."

Bailey's heart constricted. "I was scared too, Meg. But that was never good enough for you. You kept hammering me, and when I didn't listen, you went after Ryder. For my own good. Right, Meg? It was for my own good."

Meg's eyes overflowed, and Chase kept pulling her away, glaring furiously. "Yes, Bay, I don't want you hurt."

"So you hurt me yourself by calling me a slut on Facebook."

"I deleted it!"

Bailey rolled her eyes. "Eventually." And a thought crossed her mind that made her heart cry. "Because Chase told you to, didn't he?"

Meg didn't answer. She didn't have to.

"It's okay, Meg. I get it. I know why you were so scared. It's about your dad. Tell Chase. If he loves you, he'll understand just like I did."

"Bailey, please—" Meg begged.

"Megan, what the hell is she talking about?" Chase tugged on her elbow.

Meg shook her head and wrestled away.

"Tell him!" Bailey shouted.

"No!" Meg screamed back. "For God's sake, Bailey!"

"For your own good, Meg."

Meg looked at Chase and quickly turned away. "I hate you, Bailey. I hate you for this."

Bailey didn't blink. "I know." She turned to Chase and revealed Meg's biggest secret. "She killed her father."

The pain in her chest was big, too big for her alone. Meg needed to feel it too.

Chase's eyes popped. "What the hell is she talking about?"

"Come on, Meg. Tell him! Tell him why you're scared!" Bailey screamed over and over again.

Meg was crying now, but Bailey didn't stop. She couldn't stop. "Tell him!" It was for her own good. Meg's hands came up to cover her ears and Chase kept trying to pull her away, but Bailey wouldn't let up. "Tell him what you're afraid of!"

"You promised, Bailey. You swore!"

"Just like you did, and we all know how great you keep your promises. So now it's your turn."

"Bailey, shut up—"

"No, Chase! You need to know. She's going to kill you. Right, Megan? Isn't that the messed-up truth?"

Meg's knees folded, and she went down to the floor. "Yes! Are you happy now? I killed my dad, and I'll kill Chase too." Meg hid her face. "I hate you for this. I hate you."

Bailey didn't feel a thing. "I know. That's why you posted every one of my mistakes online—and the poem—and even Miss Monroe. Because you're not a friend. All you are is the daughter of a dad who never wanted you."

Meg's head snapped up, and for one horrible moment frozen in time, their eyes met. Meg broke first and tore her gaze away with a sound halfway between gasp and sob. She stumbled to her feet and ran.

The bell rang, but still, no one moved except for Bailey. She turned and walked to the nearest exit with her head high just like Gran told her to.

Chapter 37
Meg

Meg ran.

She couldn't go home.

Chase would look for her there, and she couldn't face him. Not yet.

Her chest burned and her stomach pitched, but she kept running. Pauline was at work and would probably flip out if Meg called her, but she needed her mother. Meg ducked into the Starbucks near the high school and called her mother.

"Megan, what's wrong?"

"Mom." She managed to squeeze out of her burning chest. "Oh, God, Mom."

Thirty minutes later, Pauline had Meg tucked onto the couch in the living room, a cup of hot cocoa in her hand.

"Megan, let me see your hand."

Meg stared at her hand for a moment.

"Does it hurt?"

She flexed it and felt the answering burn. Right. "I...um, forgot about it."

Her mother gave her a tired smile. "Yeah, I guess you would. So when did all this start?"

Meg caught her up, finishing with that morning's performance in the main corridor.

Pauline reached out and tucked a lock of hair behind Meg's ear. "Honey, I owe you an apology."

Meg's eyes went round. "For *what*?"

Her mother lowered her eyes and lifted a shoulder. "The last time we talked, I told you to stop overreacting to this thing between Bailey and Ryder. I was wrong, and you were right. And I'm so sorry."

Meg handed her mug to her mother and buried her face in her hands. Pauline put the cup on the table and stroked Meg's hair until she fell into a restless sleep. It was hours later when she jolted awake, still in her mother's arms.

"Mom! What time is it?"

Pauline glanced at the clock on the TV cable box. "About noon."

"You didn't go back to work?"

"No, you needed me more." Pauline stood and headed into the kitchen with the now-cold cup of cocoa. "Hungry?"

"Need the money, Mom."

Meg scraped out a chair and sat at the kitchen table.

"We don't need money that badly." Pauline took the can opener to the top of a tuna fish can.

"I'm sorry. I shouldn't have called you."

"Meg, honey, I am so glad that you did. You needed me. You never need me."

Meg pressed her lips together and looked away. "I'm sorry," she repeated. "I didn't want you to worry." *I didn't want you to leave me too.*

"Give me your hand." Pauline washed her hands and started unwrapping the layers of gauze to the black row of puffy stitches between Meg's thumb and index finger. "So much blood. I cleaned up what I could. But your painting is ruined."

Meg's head shot up. "Did you move it?"

"No." Her mother held up her hands. "I know better than to touch your work."

Her mother's smile and raised eyebrow made Meg shift uncomfortably. When she was little, her mother used to clean her room and move her paintings while they were still wet. Meg had stomped her little feet and shouted and raged until her mother promised never to move one of her "masterpieces" again.

Meg's lips twitched. "I was so full of artistic temperament back then."

"Was?" Her mother laughed and reached for her handbag. She pulled out a drugstore bag, emptied its contents on the table. Fresh gauze, antibiotic ointment, tape, analgesic cream, and one last item that made Meg laugh out loud: Hello Kitty bandages.

"I bought all this the other day. Remember these?" her mother asked.

"Yeah," she nodded. It was a lifetime ago. When she was little and skinned her knee, her mother always put a pink Hello Kitty bandage over her wounds when she got home from work that night. It was all Meg ever needed to feel better. Then her father died, and nothing held that kind of power again.

She stopped laughing. "Thanks, Mom."

Her mother squeezed antibacterial ointment over a gauze pad and glanced up at her with a smirk. "You never told me—how did it go at Chase's house?"

Meg flinched. "Fine."

The smirk spread to a grin. "That's it? Fine?"

"Mom, seriously. He tucked me into his bed—"

"He tucked you into *his* bed?"

"Relax! He slept on the couch downstairs." Meg's face burst into flames, and she forced her hands not to fan it.

"It's wonderful that you have someone who cares about you so much."

Meg forced her gaping mouth shut and fought the urge to check her mother for alien implants or something—anything—that could explain her comment. It was...well, it was downright romantic, and her mother was, as a rule, *not*.

"I love him, Mom. It's...it's confusing and annoying and distracting and exciting and scary, but I can't help it." She spread her arms apart. "I haven't been able to tell him that yet."

Her mother's tired eyes lost their glint of humor before they once again fell to Meg's injured hand. She quietly wrapped the medicated pad with a few more layers of gauze and taped it in place. "Meg, I think it's wonderful. You're such a bright and talented girl. Chase is lucky to have you." Pauline went back to the tuna and mixed in a little mayonnaise.

Lucky?

Cursed was more accurate.

"Where is he, by the way?"

Meg shrugged. "At school, I guess."

"Hmm. I'm surprised he didn't call or text or even follow you. You were hysterical before."

Frowning, Meg tugged her phone out of her pocket. No texts.

She stared down at the tuna sandwich Pauline slid across the table, her stomach revolting at the thought of food. "Mom, what if he...you know, changed his mind?"

Pauline smiled grimly and ran a hand over Meg's hair. "It happens, honey. Better you should find out before—"

Meg understood what her mother left unsaid. She took her sandwich to her room and tried to work on her portfolio, which was hard because everything in it was Chase. She kept staring at her phone.

It insisted on remaining spitefully silent.

Chapter 38
Bailey

By the time school ended, Bailey had been laughed at, pointed at, and yelled at so many times that she was sure she couldn't possibly feel any more humiliated even if she'd gone to school in Gram's old bell-bottoms. She escaped to the privacy of her room and texted Ryder for the hundredth time.

Bailey: Where are you?

She waited and waited, but the only signs of life her cell phone displayed turned out to be a "Message Not Sent" error that claimed Ryder's number was unassigned. It was wrong. The phone company was wrong. Her brain was stuck on the same song: *He wouldn't do that to me. He just wouldn't do that to me.*

Her eyes burned. Her head spun, but she ran to Facebook. Her Wall was covered in comments, even though Meg did delete the post that had started the rumors. She didn't bother to read them all, just kept scrolling and scrolling. Finally, she searched her Friends list for Ryder.

A link beside his name made her gasp.

 Add Friend

Oh, God. He'd unfriended her.

Defeat was a punch to her gut. Tears dripped and she picked up the phone. She would find him. It wasn't true. It couldn't be true. She wiped her eyes and pecked out a text, but the phone stayed silent. A new post caught her eye. Someone had posted video of her confrontation with Meg. It had been edited down to only the big reveal. The *She's going to kill you* part was looped.

Her notebook laughed at her from the corner of her desk. She ripped the pages out and shoved them in the trash. The sketches Meg did of her characters were next. She tore them to shreds. She turned her back on the computer and powered up her Xbox.

WyldRyd11 was not online. WyldRyd11 could not be found. She tried his email. It bounced back. There was only one thing left. She called Information and got the number of the big warehouse store where Ryder said he worked.

"Sorry. Nobody by that name works here."

A chill walked slowly up her spine while the truth grabbed her by the hair and spit in her face.

She was right. Oh, God, Meg was right. Ryder wasn't real.

He never was.

But the pain—oh, that was real. And there was only one person she knew who got off on it. She should have seen it, should have known it was coming. Caitlyn had told her right to her face that getting her was *fun*, but no, she'd never had a clue.

Bailey swallowed hard, the truth tasting bitter on the back of her tongue, and underneath it all, there was the dull, steady throb in her ear whispering that Meg was right.

Meg was right.

Meg was right.

She fell to her bed and sobbed.

Chapter 39
Meg

Meg spent the rest of her unscheduled day off sketching ideas for her portfolio. Google led her to various home test examples that taught her how to devise themes in her work. She snorted. There was only one theme, and its name was Chase, but at least she managed to find some alternatives worthy of further exploration.

At three o'clock, she put aside her stylus and sketch pad and headed to work. She did not text Chase again. If he chose to believe Bailey over her, then her mother was right—better she discover who he really was now. She opened the front door and cursed.

Chase was sitting on her porch steps.

"Damn it, Chase. You scared me."

He looked up at her and then back toward the street. "Yeah, we're gonna talk about all the things that scare you but not now."

She wanted to run back upstairs and hide under her covers like the little lost girl she used to be, but she forced herself to meet him on the steps. "What's wrong?"

He turned toward her again, his eyes flashing with barely restrained fury. "I'm outta here, Megan."

He was leaving her. No! Her heart fell out of her chest with a *splat!* to the ground at his feet.

"I can't stay here. I gotta get out now while I can, and I want you to come with me."

She heard his words but couldn't quite connect them. "You're leaving."

"Yes!" He lurched to his feet and paced. "My parents are—they're…Jesus, they're forty-year-old teenagers, and I've had enough. I need to leave before they buy me a goddamn minivan with vanity plates!" He shoved his hands through his hair and stopped pacing to stare at her. "Well? Are you gonna say something?"

This didn't make sense. It…it didn't compute. Bailey outed her like some psycho, but he was yelling about minivans? "You're not leaving because of me?"

His face lost its color, and he moved to her side so fast he practically blurred. "No. No, Megan. I'm not leaving you. I don't care what Bailey said. I am *not* leaving you. Please, please come with me." He took her hand. "I want to talk to a recruiter, find out what my options are."

His touch calmed Meg, resuscitated the rational part of her brain. "Chase, tell me what's wrong. I don't understand this minivan and recruiter talk." She waved her hands.

He covered his face with his hands and groaned. "Mom's pregnant, Megan. Another Gallagher's on his way—number six. I think my parents are shooting for their own TV show."

Meg laughed once. "I think it's kind of cool. I always wanted siblings, and you'll have five of them."

"Pick some! I'd gladly give you Connor or the twins. I'm keeping Dylan.

He's finally cool now that he's older." He lifted his head and shook it slowly. "I was so close, Megan. Now they say I can't leave. I have to turn down the scholarship so I can help." Suddenly, he was on his feet again. "It's not even my fucking kid, and I get stuck raising it!"

"Scholarship? What scholarship?"

He slapped a hand to his head. "I forgot to tell you yesterday. I heard from Manhattan College. Full scholarship, Megan. All I have to cover is living expenses. The guys already got a lead on a decent apartment. My share of the rent would be cheaper than the room and board in the dorms." He shook his head. "And now they're saying they need me home. They want me to turn it down. So I'm going to enlist."

No scholarship and the army? No way. She'd finally caved in to his magic eyes. He couldn't leave, not now.

"Okay, I get why you're so upset. But you need to calm down and think about this. You only have a few months until graduation. You can't leave now. You need them."

He stopped pacing to stare at her. "I don't know, Megan. Damn it. I don't know anything anymore." He blew out a loud breath. "Except that I need you. You help me focus." He took a few steps toward her, tugged her to her feet, and wrapped her in a hug.

His words made her go weak and warm all over, so she squeezed him back.

"Come on. I'll give you a ride." He led her to the old station wagon parked on the curb. "I'll tell you one thing. I am *never* having kids, swear to God. I've already changed more diapers than most guys will in a lifetime."

Meg went still.

She was five—maybe six years old—when her father didn't come home one night. She was in bed but not asleep. She could never sleep when her mom cried. It was very late, and only the sound of her mom's sniffles broke the silence when she heard his key click in the lock. Her mother ran down the stairs. "Where were you?" she'd shouted. "Away from here!" he'd shouted back. They screamed and yelled and broke stuff, and Meg pulled the covers over her head but still heard every word. "I never wanted kids in the first place!"

She'd cried then. It was her fault. She'd always known that of course. Always known that they fought because of her, but her mother always dried her tears and rocked her long after her father was asleep.

"Megan, you ready?"

She jerked, blinking into gleaming green eyes, and suddenly, she saw a little girl with dark hair and the same gleaming green eyes hiding under her covers while Chase shouted, "I am never having kids, swear to God!"

She turned away. "I think I'll walk."

He ran around the car, took her by the shoulders. "No! Goddamn it, Megan, don't do this, not now!"

She slapped his hands away, forgot about her stitches. "Stop. I can't do this, Chase. I can't." Her voice was level, her tone even. She watched the light go out of those watercolor eyes of his.

And then she turned and walked alone to the bakery. *Alone*, she thought. *The way it would always be.*

Chapter 40
Bailey

The next morning, Bailey walked to school, unwilling to risk the whispers behind hands, the tweets, the giggles. She felt it throughout the day yesterday, like a current of electricity humming under the classroom noise. She walked alone with her bitter thoughts, hardly aware of the car that pulled up beside her until the driver honked his horn.

"Bailey!"

She jolted out of her thoughts, saw Chase's dad leaning over to shout through the passenger window. "Hey, Mr. Gallagher."

"You seen Chase? He never came home last night." His face was almost gray.

"What? No, not since school yesterday."

"Ask around and call me if you hear anything, okay? Anything!" He drove off with a squeal of tires.

Bailey frowned after him.

Maybe he and Meg ran off to Vegas and got married. Like she cared. She stalked all the way to school, the fuel of her anger burning slow and strong. She shrugged a shoulder when anyone did find the guts to ask her if she knew what was going on. She turned her head away when the whispers reached her ears and only jerked once at the words "missing since yesterday and "suspected in his disappearance." As soon as the bell rang, Bailey ducked into the closest bathroom and checked her cell phone. She thumbed past the texts from her social network feeds, ignored the ones from minor acquaintances, and stopped to read one from Meg that had arrived that morning.

Meg: Have you seen Chase?

Bailey rolled her eyes. Chase follows Meg around like a lost puppy, and she was asking *her* where he was? She continued scrolling through messages and bit back a curse when she saw none from Ryder. There was one from an unknown number though. She opened it and covered her gaping mouth with a hand that shook.

Unknown: UR dad's name is Matthew Schor. He went to Madison High School, graduated in '96. I'm so sorry.

Ryder! It had to be. He always abbreviated *your* like that. She called the number, but it just kept ringing. She ended the call and tried again. Nothing. Why was he doing this? She folded her arms around her body and folded up, swallowing back a sob that hitched on every breath. It wasn't fair! She'd tried so hard, but all she'd done was wreck everything with Meg and with Chase. She wished she were home so she could throw herself on her bed and cry. Slowly, she sank to the toilet in the stall where she hid and forced herself to breathe deeply.

Matthew.

She put a hand over her heart. She had a name. Her father's name. She started to text the news to Meg and then deleted the message. She couldn't text Meg. Not anymore. She held her breath against the pain that slashed deep, rolled her shoulders, and let it out. She didn't need Meg. She was a big girl. She'd do this on her own. She'd do a ton of research when she got home, and if Ryder's message could be trusted, well, she'd remember him without hating him.

Her nerves once again steely, Bailey left the girls' bathroom and headed to her next class just as the bell rang. She'd just opened her notebook when a knock on the door called the whole class's attention to the corridor. Mrs. Tyrell had a brief conversation with someone she couldn't see and then turned to her. "Bailey, collect your things. You're wanted at the principal's office."

As she stood and left the class, the whispers escalated to murmurs that spread across the room at warp speed. She refused to lower her eyes or hang her head. She was the victim here, not the bad guy. She stepped out into the hall and was met by a security guard who took her elbow and marched her down the corridor.

"What's going on?"

"Just come with me, Miss Grant."

She wrestled out of his grip but walked beside him down the stairs to the main hall and to the principal's office, where three people waited for her. She recognized Mr. Giovanni, the principal, and Ms. Christiansen, her guidance counselor. But the third person, a woman in a black suit with her hair pulled ruthlessly back, was a stranger.

"Bailey, have a seat." Mr. Giovanni waved her to a chair at the small conference table in the corner of his office. "This is Detective Powell. She has some questions for you."

Bailey turned to the tall woman. She reached into her suit jacket and pulled out a badge. "Bailey Grant, I'm Detective Powell, Nassau County Police Department, Special Victims Section. Do you know why I'm here?"

Bailey shook her head.

The detective removed a leather-bound notepad from her pocket, flipped it open, and clicked a pen. "You're friends with Chase David Gallagher, age eighteen, of Twenty-two West Highland Drive?"

"Yeah. Why are you—"

"And you're also friends with Megan Elise Farrell of Seventeen Park Slope Street?"

"Yes." She looked from Ms. Christiansen to Mr. Giovanni back to the detective. "What's going on? What happened?"

Detective Powell glanced up from her notes but did not answer the question. "When did you last see Chase Gallagher?"

"Uh—" She'd seen Meg earlier, but not Chase. God, he really *was* missing. "Yesterday. Yesterday before first period."

"Yesterday. Before first period. Did you argue?"

"With Chase? No." Not exactly. Bailey bit her nail.

Detective Powell turned to the principal with a sharp nod. "Mr. Giovanni?" The principal rotated the computer monitor on his desk so that it could be viewed from the table and clicked his mouse, and then a video began. The sound of her own voice played through the tinny speakers.

Tell him!

Oh, God.

No! For God's sake, Bailey!

The agony on Meg's face tugged at Bailey's heart, and she had to look away.

Bailey, shut up—

No, Chase! You need to know. She's going to kill you. Right, Megan? Isn't that the messed-up truth?

Detective Powell crossed the room and paused the playback.

"Is this you, Miss Grant?" She pointed to the image paused in tirade, and Bailey trembled in her seat. My God, was that girl with the icy eyes and rigid posture really her? Her stomach churned and she could only nod.

"And who is this?"

"It's…that's…uh, Chase. It's Chase Gallagher."

"And was this argument the last time you saw him?"

She nodded. "Yes. Why are you asking me these questions?"

Detective Powell glanced at Mr. Giovanni before she answered. "Chase Gallagher failed to return home last night. His parents are worried, so they called us." She paused, checked her notepad again. "At about four o'clock yesterday, Mr. Giovanni called us to report that a number of parents were upset over a video—*this* video—in which a boy, the same boy who didn't go home yesterday, is threatened. I don't think that's a coincidence. Do you?"

Bailey twisted her curls and tried not to cry. Oh, God! What did she do? What did she do? Chase didn't go home, and everything she said yesterday was up on YouTube, and now the police were—

Her head snapped up. "Wait. You think I hurt Chase?"

"Did you?"

"No! It wasn't him I was mad at—"

"That's right. You were mad at Megan Farrell. When was the last time you saw her?"

"Yes…yesterday." She pointed to the monitor.

"Did she hurt Chase?"

"What? No! Megan wouldn't hurt anybody."

"Are you sure? Because on that video, you said Megan Farrell was going to kill Chase Gallagher just like she killed her father." Detective Powell stabbed her finger in the air toward the screen.

The door opened with force, and Nicole Grant stalked into the principal's office, Gran trailing behind her.

"Bailey! Don't say another word." Her mother swept her eyes around the room settled on Detective Powell. "My daughter is a minor, and you can't question her without me present."

Detective Powell turned dark sharp eyes on Nicole. "Actually, Mrs. Grant, I can. I'm required only to notify her parents, which I did. She can either answer my questions here or I can read your daughter her rights and take her out of here in handcuffs to continue this at the precinct. Your choice."

Bailey reached for Gran's hand, gripped it tight. What happened? How the hell had everything gone so wrong? She shut her eyes tight and rocked in her chair.

"I want to know what's happening here and what happened to Chase Gallagher." The detective scraped back her chair and directly addressed Bailey. "Will you start at the beginning and tell me everything that led up to that video?"

Gran squeezed her hand. "Sweet girl, these are your best friends. Tell the detective everything."

Bailey knuckled tears from her eyes, took a deep breath, and did just that.

Chapter 41
Meg

Meg never slept last night. She was in the middle of her second-period class, math, not that she'd heard a word. She sat with her chin propped in her hand, forcing her eyes not to close. With half a laugh, she wondered why it was so hard. Chase's words were still stuck on an infinite loop playing in her mind. *I am never having kids, swear to God.*

She'd run from him. She'd just admitted she was in love with him not a minute before. She'd been ready to revise her entire plan for him because maybe—just maybe—her father was wrong, and it *was* possible to love someone and be loved in return and not ruin her entire future in the process. *I am never having kids, swear to God.*

Her gut twisted again, but she was used to it now—almost. The pain spoke to her in her dad's voice. *I told you to focus on your plan!* It attacked every time she thought about Chase—the slump of his shoulders, the set of his jaw, the never-neat mop of brown hair hanging over furious unearthly eyes.

He'd had a plan that had been all shot to hell. She shook her head and winced. What the hell good did it do to make plans? All that time, all that work and for what? Another revision? Another course correction? For a spotlight on the disappointments? For a giant red X over the failures? Maybe Bailey had the right idea all along. The pain returned for another go at her whenever she thought of her former best friend—the bounce in her step, the ever-ready giggle.

She heard the whispers and saw the fingers pointing at her and slouched lower in her desk, wishing for invisibility. The teacher was discussing sine, cosine, and tangents, but her mind circled right back to Chase. She'd been right there—right on the edge of tearing up The Plan. No revisions this time, no course corrections, but a totally new plan, one with Chase right smack in its middle. She'd finally believed him when he told her she could have it all.

Swear to God.

"Megan Farrell?"

Swear to God.

A hand tapped her shoulder and she jerked. "Megan Farrell, you're wanted in the vice principal's office."

Her heart stopped, restarted with a jolt, and then tried to pound out of her chest. She swallowed hard, grabbed her stuff, and followed the security guard. She couldn't remember walking down the halls, two flights of steps, and the main corridor to the office. Suddenly, she was sitting in a hard metal chair at a small round table in the corner of Mr. Poynter's office. He stood by the window, holding a steaming paper cup of coffee. A cup of water was pressed into her hand, and Meg looked up and saw one of the guidance counselors sitting next to her.

Funny—she hadn't noticed her.

She looked into the cup of water, saw her reflection shimmer and ripple. Even the distortion did nothing to hide the pain in her eyes.

They sat for minutes or hours—who knew? Who even cared? Her hand throbbed. Had she cleaned the wound today? She couldn't remember. What day was it? She couldn't remember that either.

Swear to God.

She cradled her head in her hands and then pulled them away. They shook.

The door opened and a woman walked in, a battered laptop open in her hands. She glared at her with hard dark eyes over a thin mouth. Her hair was coiled up in an elastic, a ball-point pen stuck in the bun. She put the laptop on the table and dragged out a chair. Meg shivered at the screech.

Swear to God.

When the woman sat, her jacket opened, and Meg saw a badge on her belt. "Miss Farrell, I'm Detective Barilla, Special Victims Section. Do you know why I'm here?"

Meg only stared at her with wide dark eyes. The woman slid the laptop around so Meg could see the screen. "Do you recognize this?"

Meg wiped the tears from her eyes to clear her vision and peered at the machine. "It's my Wall."

"Your Facebook page, correct?"

Meg nodded.

The woman leaned over and scrolled down. "I want you to look at something."

Meg bit her lip. Like she had any choice?

The woman clicked a link to a video someone had posted. As soon as it played, Meg's stomach pitched and she clapped a hand to her mouth.

Bailey's voice, thin and shrill, filled the room. *"Tell him!"*

"Oh, God!" Meg clutched her ears and shut her eyes.

"Open your eyes. Watch," the woman commanded.

Meg didn't need to watch. She'd been there. She remembered every gut-wrenching minute right up until the end. *"I'll kill Chase too."* Her voice sounded raspy, even desperate. Her eyes looked tortured. Chase kept tugging on her arm, but she wouldn't go with him.

"Is this you? Did you say, 'I killed my dad, and I'll kill Chase too?'"

Meg shook her head. "I…I didn't—"

"No? No, that's not you, or no, you didn't threaten to kill Chase Gallagher?"

Her heart skidded to a stop, and she stared at the detective. "I didn't threaten him."

"Miss Farrell, I'll ask again. Is that you on that video stating, 'I'll kill Chase too?'"

"Yes, but—"

"Where is Chase Gallagher? When did you see him last?"

"I don't know."

"You don't know where he is, or you don't know when you saw him?"

"I don't know where he is. I saw him yesterday."

"Yesterday when?"

"After school. He was angry."

"Did you argue? Did you threaten him again?"

Meg shook her head frantically. "No! It wasn't like that. He was mad at his parents, not me."

A sharp knock on the door sounded. Meg snapped her head around. One of the secretaries came in and spoke to Mr. Poynter too quietly for her to overhear. Meg's lip trembled and her stomach rolled. "Please tell me what happened. Why are you asking me these questions?"

Detective Barilla looked at her sideways, and a moment later, she nodded. "Your classmates seem to think you're a danger to them. A time bomb about to go off." Barilla scrolled to another comment.

> Meg looked ready to strafe!
>
> Wouldn't surprise me LOL
>
> She's a badass; she'd totally shoot.
>
> She paints death all the time ;)

"Word spreads, Miss Farrell. Fast and far. Classmates talk to other classmates. A parent overhears and calls a few more parents. Someone calls the school. Your principal was concerned about this video and later, the 'strafe' term, so he called us. Who were you going to 'strafe'?"

Oh, God! Meg rocked on the hard chair, shaking her head.

"Do you have a gun, Megan? Are there weapons in your house?"

There was a gun once. Suddenly, Meg was six years old again, gripping her ears and staring at her father's body, blood pooling on the tile, chunks of…of *stuff*…clinging to the walls of the master bathroom. *I never wanted kids! Swear to God. Swear to God.*

"We tried to talk to Bailey Grant and Chase Gallagher. Only Chase is gone. Nobody's seen or heard from him since yesterday. And Bailey seems to think you're the reason why." Detective Barilla leaned in. "Did you hurt Chase Gallagher, Megan? Did you kill him?"

Oh, God, Bailey. Oh, God. Oh, God. "No!" She shook her head vehemently. "No, I swear."

"You swear, Megan? The video shows you clearly saying, 'I'll kill Chase too.' Who else did you kill?"

"Please," she begged. "Please let me go home."

I never wanted kids!

"Who did you kill, Megan?"

I never wanted kids! "Shut up!" she screamed. "Shut up, shut up! I killed my father! Is that what you want to hear?"

Swear to God.

Chapter 42
Bailey

"Bailey, you need to tell Detective Powell everything. Do you understand? Your cooperation in this situation is critical," Mr. Giovanni said.

Cooperation with what situation? Bailey wished they'd get to the damn point. "I already told you. Meg didn't threaten anybody."

"That's not what that little video says. You accused her and she admitted it." Mr. Giovanni shook his head.

Oh, God! She was only mad. Why was everyone making such a BFD out of it? "No, she didn't mean that. We were fighting and—"

"Fighting?" Detective Powell walked back into the room. She reminded Bailey of Steven Seagal with C cups. "About a boy."

"Yeah." Bailey shrugged. "I was mad at her." She twisted a curl. "That's it."

Ms. Christiansen's head jerked up. "This isn't a game, Miss Grant. Did you read the stuff your friends, your classmates, are saying? They're worried. Their parents are worried. Mr. Giovanni is worried. We're worried. The only one who's not worried is you."

"Because there's nothing to worry about. It was a fight, just a stupid fight."

"Okay. Why don't you tell us what the fight was about?" the detective demanded.

"I already told you. Meg wouldn't butt out of my friendship with Ryder."

"Oh, right. Ryder West." She flipped through the pages in small black notebook.

Nicole looked at her sharply. "Who's Ryder West?"

Bailey shot her a look. Really, Mom? Bailey had been talking about Ryder West for weeks, and this was the first time she actually heard his name? "Ryder's the guy I like."

"Where did you meet?" Powell asked.

"Online."

"Where online?"

"Xbox. We played *Call of Duty* together."

"And what do you and Ryder do when you hang out?"

Bailey examined her fingernails. "Um…play video games. Text. Chat on Facebook. Work on my game."

"Your game?"

"Yes, my video game."

"What does that mean?"

She rolled her eyes. "It means I'm creating a video game. He's helping me."

"Why would he do that?"

If there was a point anywhere in all these questions, she really hoped they'd get to it soon. She was starving and nobody would let her eat.

"Bailey, answer the question."

Oh, now it was okay to talk? Bailey blew a curl from her eyes. "Uh, because he likes me? He's trying to impress me."

"Trying to impress you by texting and chatting and playing video games. Is that it?"

"Yes, that's it. I told you this already."

"Okay, Bailey. Tell us where Ryder West lives."

Bailey's eyes dropped. "I can't."

Powell's eyebrows went up. "Miss Grant, I wasn't asking."

"I heard what you said, and I can't. I don't know where he lives."

"You've never been to his house?"

"No."

"Where did you meet him?"

Bailey flung out her arms. "I told you! Online."

Powell angled her head, her pen poised over her notes. "Wait a minute. Are you telling us you've never physically met this boy?"

Nicole's eyes snapped to hers, and Bailey's shoulders sagged. "Bailey?"

Slowly, she shook her head.

"Oh, my God. You've been carrying on with a boy you aren't even sure is a boy?"

"Oh, my God, Mom!" Bailey echoed. "Now you sound just like Meg. Why can't you be happy that I finally met a guy who likes me? I mean, *really* likes me?"

The detective put up her hand. "Wait. What do you mean 'just like Meg'?"

Bailey tensed in her hard metal chair. "Meg wouldn't leave it alone. She kept nagging and warning and ordering me not to trust Ryder. Every time he made an excuse not meet in person, she was convinced he had to be some sixty-year-old sex offender living in a trailer park with nothing but beer and cigarettes! I kept telling her she was wrong, but she wouldn't shut up, and when she started texting him herself—"

"Megan Farrell texted your boyfriend?"

"Yes!" She punctuated the word with an emphatic nod of her head because Detective Powell sounded like she understood. "She threatened him, told him to back off, and even told him my most embarrassing story ever—all so he'd stop liking me."

"She threatened him how exactly?"

Bailey crossed her arms. "Why don't you ask her?"

"Because I'm asking you," Detective Powell shot back.

"That's enough." Nicole put up her hand. "My daughter answered your questions. I'm taking her home." She stood up, so Bailey stood too.

The woman frowned. "We're not done here." She pointed at the hard metal chairs.

Nicole crossed her arms and glared. "Are you arresting her?"

Detective Powell returned the glare. "Not yet."

Nicole smiled hard. "Then we're going home." She led Bailey out of the office.

"*I* didn't do anything!"

The sudden shout had everyone's heads whipping toward the double doors that led to the main corridor. They burst open and two security guards shoved Simon Kane through. His designer clothes were wrinkled and his face was blotchy with outrage. As soon as he saw Bailey, he clamped his mouth shut and just stared. Bailey stared back. What was he doing here?

Detective Powell walked over to one of the guards holding Simon's elbows and took a sheet of paper from him. Bailey squirmed under the weight of Simon's stare.

"Well, Miss Grant, you may find this interesting." Powell waved the paper. "Mr. Kane, I'll give you a chance to tell her before I do."

Tell me what, Bailey wondered. It's not like Simon posted that video or called the principal or—

"Bailey," he said and looked at the floor. "I'm so sorry, Bailey."

"Three seconds, Mr. Kane."

"Okay! I'll tell her!" Simon swallowed once. "It's me, Bailey. I'm Ryder. I made him up."

She covered her ears and shook her head. She would not listen to this. If she didn't listen, she couldn't hear. If she couldn't hear him, then she couldn't get her heart broken. If she couldn't hear him, then she wouldn't have to admit Meg was right.

Tears dripped down her cheeks and someone kept pulling her by the arm. It wasn't true! Ryder was funny and talented and seriously loyal and…and liked her. He really liked her.

A motion captured her attention. Meg stood in the door of the vice principal's office.

Bailey hated to look, knowing, dreading what she'd see on Meg's face: the look that would just scream, *See? I told you so.* But Meg only cried. And that— oh, that was so much worse.

Bailey didn't even wait for Nicole. She ran.

Chapter 43
Meg

Simon is Ryder. Meg repeated the words a few more times until they lost any meaning. *Simon is Ryder. Simon is Ryder.* Oh, Bailey. She began to cry and hated herself for it. Her heart didn't understand that it no longer needed to care for or worry about or love Bailey. Guess it wasn't easy to break a lifetime habit. As if she'd heard her thoughts, Bailey swung blue eyes wide with shock to hers and then ran. Meg took two steps after her and had to remind her feet that Bailey was no longer their concern.

Should-haves ganged up on Meg until she reminded her traitorous conscience that she'd done everything—right up to risking her friendship—to make Bailey listen.

"Megan! Meg, oh, honey," her mother rushed into the office and crushed her in a hug, but Meg didn't react. She could only see Simon flanked by two guards. She searched his face, expecting to find that same old arrogance. But she swore she saw regret there when Bailey ran. So...why? Why, damn it, why?

Detective Barilla was back. She took Meg's arm, but Pauline protested. "Mrs. Farrell, you can wait here. We're not done yet." She led Meg back to the table in the corner of the VP's office and shut the door. "Megan, I know you're upset. But I need to hear the truth from you. Tell me about this video." She clicked a button on the laptop, and again, she heard Bailey shrieking at her to tell Chase. Again, she heard her own voice—bordering right on the edge of hysterical—blurt out her darkest fear. *I'll kill Chase too!*

She folded her arms on the table and lay her head on them. If they could arrest her for thinking bad thoughts, she was going to need one hell of a good lawyer. The thought almost made her giggle. She could just imagine telling Pauline. "Forget college tuition. I'm gonna need you to remortgage the house for bail."

"Talk to me, Megan."

Talk about what? About the friend she'd lost? About the boy she was never meant to love? And the mother who cried for her lost love and lost life alone in her room—every damn night?

"I was supposed to be an abortion," she spoke into the table. "My parents never wanted kids. When my mom got pregnant, she couldn't go through with the abortion and kept me. She quit school to be there for me. My dad really hated that." She raised her head but could not meet the detective's eye. "I didn't know it. I thought he loved me."

She heard Detective Barilla's sharp breath.

"There's this show on FOX that everybody at school watches—you know, the one with the talking dog?" She didn't wait for Barilla's answer. "I can't stand it. There's a 'Meg' on that show too, and everyone just craps all over her. 'Shut up, Meg,' they say. Or, 'Who let you back in the house, Meg?' That kind of thing." She finally looked up to find Detective Barilla hanging on every word. "You probably think that's really dumb—identifying with a cartoon character, but—" she trailed off, wiped more tears from her face. "That's why Chase calls me Megan. Because of that show." A sob escaped and she swallowed back the ones that wanted to follow.

"I thought I was so special. My dad played with me, brought me to daycare, picked me up, even made me breakfast in bed. I adored him. But he had problems. He used to cry a lot. I didn't know why. I was too little. He told me all the time I had to have a plan for my future because the only person I could ever count on was myself. I needed to get good grades, go to a good school, get a good job so I could be self-sufficient. I thought he was looking out for me. I thought he was telling me all this plan stuff because he loved me so much and wanted to make sure I would be okay." Meg wrapped her arms around her middle, suddenly freezing.

"It was all a lie."

She shut her eyes and could almost hear his furious voice all over again. She told Barilla everything, reciting it the way she might read a grocery list.

"One night, when they thought I was asleep, my parents had a horrible argument. He'd been out late, and when he came home, it was without the car. He'd lost it in a card game. Mom screamed at him that he had to grow up, he had a child now. Dad screamed right back that he'd never wanted a kid in the first place, that it had been her idea to keep me instead of getting an abortion like he wanted."

The heart in her chest had cracked that day, and she didn't even know what an abortion was.

"The next day, he picked me up. I went running up to him like I always did. He didn't say anything. He just took me home, carried me all the way upstairs to his room. He opened the top drawer of his dresser and pulled out this big black thing."

She shut her eyes and covered her ears, but the sound was etched too deeply in her memory not to hear.

"I never saw a gun before and didn't know I should have been scared. He took me into the bathroom, sat me on the edge of the tub, and told me he loved me so much, more than he ever imagined he could. That made me happy. But then he admitted he'd never wanted to have kids and was so mad at my mom for keeping me. He said she made her choice and it was time he made his. He put me down, and right before he told me to get out, he made me promise to stick to The Plan. I was scared, so I ran. When I heard the shot, I stopped and went back. There was so much blood."

She shivered and ran her hands up and down her arms. "I don't remember much after that. Mom came home and found us, and we had to leave for a few days. When we got back, the bathroom was clean, but I still know where every drop of blood was.

"He left us deeply in debt. I didn't know how bad it was until I started hearing my mother cry every night when she thought I was sleeping. I'd sneak down the stairs and hear her on the phone with bill collectors, begging them for help, but it never worked. She got a job and then another and even a third. I spent all day in school and then in an after-school program and then with various neighbors until bedtime. Some days, I even had breakfast with the neighbors. She told me she loved me all the time, but when I found their wedding video, I knew she was lying too.

"I watched it every day, as many times as I could. My father was so handsome and Mom was so beautiful. She looked like a Disney princess. Dad was laughing and Mom had shiny hair and sparkles in her eyes. I never saw them like that. I watched them put rings on each other's fingers and make promises and dance and laugh and kiss. They were so—" A fresh wave of despair crushed her. "Oh, God, they were happy, and I ruined it."

She stopped talking when the door opened. A secretary walked over to Mr. Poynter and whispered in his ear. He shut his eyes in relief and then motioned to Detective Barilla. They moved to the window and had a brief whispered conversation. Megan curled her knees into her chest and wrapped her arms around them. It was funny. Now that she'd started talking, she had to finish the story. She *needed* to finish the story. As soon as the secretary shut the door, she did.

"A year later, Chase's family moved to our block. I think I fell in love with him on the school playground. He has magic eyes. But I couldn't let him love me. I killed my dad. I'm slowly killing my mom. I don't want that to happen to Chase. So I paint him. That way, I can still be with him. Bailey's the only one who knows this—any of this. I was in the middle of a big oil painting the day I sliced my hand open. I just…worked through it."

Detective Barilla blew out a slow breath. "Okay, Megan. Okay." She stood up, closed the laptop. "You can go."

Meg blinked. "That's it?"

"That's it," the detective echoed.

Meg felt the old familiar pain claw through her gut, swallowed it down, and rose on shaky knees.

Oh, sure. That's it.

"Meg." Pauline's tired eyes were red and filled with tears. Oh, God, she'd heard. She'd heard every word. Meg flung herself into her mother's arms.

"Let's get you home." Her mother put an arm around her and led her to the exit.

"Megan."

She froze at the sound of Chase's voice.

No. No more. She couldn't bear any more. But she looked up anyway. At least this time, there was no stupid smile. That was some consolation.

"Mr. Gallagher? Why don't you come in and tell us where you've been all night?" Detective Barilla said.

Chase ignored her and spoke directly to Meg. "I'm sorry. I'm so sorry. Please believe me, Megan."

She wanted to. She wanted to so badly that it hurt, but she didn't...she couldn't, not completely.

And he knew it.

Chapter 44
Bailey

The days passed. Bailey had not spoken to Chase or Meg or Ryder or Simon or her game buddies or even her family. She hadn't gone to school, even though Gran had been dropping her off in front of it every day for the past week. That's because every day for the past week, she'd been hiding in Starbucks, the movie theater, or the library until the last bell.

She tugged on the hood of her sweatshirt, tucking her ponytail under it. *A ponytail*, she thought with an eye-roll. She'd always hassled Meg about her messy ponytails but had to admit it was nice not having hair fall in front of her eyes and really good at keeping people from recognizing her. She kept walking, wondering if her stomach would ever *not* twist into a ball whenever she thought about Meg. Or Ryder. Or Chase. Or even her mother.

Probably not.

She kept walking.

She walked until she reached the enormous house with the windy driveway with closed gates and a little intercom built into the post. A camera mounted high on a tree swept left and right and back again. Even the stupid tree was designer. She stabbed the call button and stuffed her hands in her pockets while she waited.

"Who is it?"

"Bailey Grant. I'm here to talk to Simon."

There was a long silence. Bailey glared at the camera every time it panned by.

"I'm sorry, but Simon's lawyer doesn't think—"

"Yes, *my* lawyer agrees with Simon's lawyer, but I came here anyway because I need to talk to him."

Another long silence. Finally, Bailey leaned on the call button.

"Miss Grant, you'll have to leave. Simon is not permitted—Simon? Simon! Get back here!"

Off in the distance at the end of the windy driveway, Bailey could see the front door open. A tall figure jogged her way. It took him almost five damn minutes to reach her.

"What are you doing here, Bailey?" He stopped on his side of the gate.

"Needed to talk to you."

"You could have texted."

She shook her head, still under its hood. "You. Not Ryder."

Simon winced. That scored him a few points in Bailey's eyes.

"So is he the reason you're here?"

"No. Yes." Bailey shut her eyes. "I don't know. I guess that's why I'm here—to figure it out."

Simon lowered his head. "You want me to apologize again? I will if you want me to, but it doesn't really change anything. I can't undo what I did."

"No."

His eyes snapped to hers, and she had to take an extra breath. It was his eyes that she'd needed to see. Even when he was shooting off his big mouth, trying to be cool, Simon was never able to get his eyes to follow his mouth. They couldn't lie. Like Abraham Lincoln. She could design a whole character around him in the video game if she still had it. Maybe it wasn't too late. Maybe she could recover everything she'd deleted and—

"Then why?" he demanded.

She stepped closer, wrapped her hands around the cold iron bars. "Okay, look. I don't have very good luck when it comes to guys. Meg always said I tried way too hard. The horseback riding, martial arts, NASCAR racing, video games. She says I'm never just me."

"Meg's right."

Wow. Judging by the way he clenched his jaw when she mentioned Meg, Bailey figured it must have really hurt him to say that. It actually kind of hurt to *hear* it. She stared at him and he rolled his eyes.

"Come on, Bay. It's obvious, isn't it? You try on lifestyles like they're outfits at the mall. Do you really think I believe you actually liked stamp collecting?"

Bailey's lips twitched. "You didn't?"

"No! Hell, I'm not even sure I like it. I just tried it because my dad wanted me to. At first, I thought it was really cool that you were willing to do things for me. But it got old really fast, Bailey. Your heart was never in it."

"I really liked you, Simon." She ran her thumb over a rust spot on the iron bar and watched bits flake off and float away.

"I really liked you too, but you were just pretending to like me, just like everybody else in this freakin' neighborhood since the money came in." His words were like a whip, and she jumped.

"Is that what you thought? Is that why you weirded out on me? I thought—"

"I never cheated," he shouted. "I never even looked at Caitlyn before that day Meg happened to see us. But you trusted Meg more than me."

Damn it, his eyes weren't lying, and suddenly, she realized *that's* why she was there—to look into Lincoln blue eyes and know without a doubt what was the truth and what was insecurity and fantasy and wishful thinking and... and a lost cause.

"You're right. I did, and I'm so sorry. Meg and I—we've been friends for so long, and it's just so hard *not* to believe her, you know?"

"Oh, trust me, I do."

Bailey's eyes widened. "Is that why you did it? To play us against each other?"

A muscle in Simon's jaw twitched, and he wouldn't meet her eyes. "I wanted you to see what it's like."

Bailey's filled with tears. She blinked them back. She'd obviously made a mistake coming here. She heard a car approach and watched it disappear around a curve. "You know, it felt real. The only time in my life that it did, but the guy was fake." She laughed once. "That must be so funny to you."

He suddenly shook the iron bars that separated them, and she jumped back. "I'm not laughing," he shouted. "I tried to end it, end *him*. I was gonna tell you that day at the mall. I deleted all the accounts, but it was too late. Half the damn school watched you two fight like it's the Golden Gloves, and I'm—"

There it was again. A flash—a glimmer that lit his eyes for no more than a second.

"You're what?"

He tightened his lips and shook his head. "Forget it. It doesn't matter anymore."

"It matters to me."

"You should go. The Dream Team's gonna have a fit when they find out I talked to you."

"Simon, it'll be okay. You didn't murder anybody. Maybe I can help? Talk to them for you?"

He sneered. "Yeah, like you'd really do that for me."

"I would. Simon, I came here because I'm sorry. I just wanted you to know that."

"Yeah. Me too," he murmured, shoving his hands in his pocket.

Bailey curled her hands around the bars. "Simon, did you send me his name?"

He hesitated a moment and then turned away. "I gotta go." He ran up the windy driveway without waiting for her to reply.

Bailey started walking. But her steps were lighter, and a smile tugged at her lips.

For the first time in her life, Bailey had a plan.

Chapter 45
Meg

Megan stared at the computer monitor with blurred eyes, watching status updates scroll by like the credits at the end of a movie.

Or the end of a friendship.

It had been weeks since that end. Even the senior class's graduation didn't kill the buzz about her brush with the law in the main office, like it was a scene from that same movie instead of her life. The pain chewing its way through her heart still plagued her, though it had dulled. Guess she'd just gotten used to it.

She'd had plenty of experience getting used to pain.

She thought about her dad and shook her head with a sad smile. He'd been right all along. The only one she could count on was herself. He'd drummed that into her head over and over since she was born, but had she listened? First, she'd lost him, and that was the first set of teeth to gnash at her heart. Then there was Chase. Oh, she'd tried. She'd tried so hard to stay unaffected—to push him away—to protect herself, yet somehow, he'd sneaked in. *Nibble.* *Nibble nibble.* But the Bailey stuff—oh, she'd never seen that coming. She'd been so careful. She'd never sought popularity and social status and saw little value in having dozens of acquaintances. She'd allowed herself one friend. One really good friend.

And the loss of that friend was the final set of jaws to chomp through her heartstrings.

Abruptly furious, Meg jumped up and paced her room, sick of this pointless wallowing. She headed to the stack of canvases in the corner, found the portrait she'd done of Bailey with her game face on, thumbs blurring over the controller. She studied it critically, the oils she'd painted on a smoky blue background. Nailing the color of Bailey's honey-blond hair had been almost as hard as getting Chase's eyes right, but she'd done it—titanium white, burnt sienna, and burnt umber with pale blue for the highlights and violet for the lowlights. The hair looked like it could be brushed. It was beautiful. One of her best.

Meg fisted her hand, pulled back her arm, ready to smash through Bailey's face, and then changed her mind. She crossed the room, fished around in her closet for the small toolbox, and found a hammer, tape measure, a couple of D rings, and some wire. She measured and marked, attached the rings to the back of the canvas, and looped a length of wire to each. With a swoop of her arm, she cleared her bed of pillows and climbed on top of it, the hammer under her arm, a hook in her mouth, and the canvas in her hand. She nailed the hook into the wall over her bed to carefully suspend the canvas.

It would look down on her from that spot of prominence, a daily reminder of what can happen—what *did* happen—when she didn't listen to her dad.

She put the tools back in their box and the box back in her closet and then stared at the portrait, steeling herself against the burn. Easier all the time. She forced her eyes away, thought about watching TV, maybe reading a book, but neither held much interest. She could hear the clock ticking in the hall, a nagging reminder of her deadline, and knew she should paint. But even that failed to excite her. She wandered to the huge window and stared down at the Gallaghers' backyard. The lawn had been cut, she noticed. She supposed Dylan had done it now that Chase was gone.

She had to steel herself against that burn too. He'd graduated, and as he'd planned, he had moved to the city with his teammates. He never said good-bye.

Meg tore her gaze from the window and returned to pacing around her room. The monitor caught her eye again, and the burn in her chest flared white-hot for a moment.

Bailey had updated her status. A dozen, a hundred, a hundred dozen times, she'd tried to unfriend Bailey but couldn't click the damn button.

> OMG. I found him. I found my dad. His name's Matthew Schor. He's a Marine Sgt! He lives in the next town. Wish me luck, everybody! I'm heading there right now.

The burn in Meg's chest hit the redline and she gasped, trying to rub it away. She'd done it. Bailey found her dad. And in spite of all the pain, Meg smiled. The smile spread to laugh when she realized Bailey abbreviated because she couldn't be bothered to look up "sergeant." The on-screen activity sped up. People liked Bailey's post and wished her luck, and Meg's fingers itched to join in, but she willed them away from the keyboard. Bailey had made it damn clear she no longer cared what Meg had to say.

She was suffocating under the weight of all this *nothing*. She had to fill the hours with something, anything, that might bleed the pain and grief from her body. With a determined press to her lips, she shut down the computer and pulled sweats from her dresser. She needed to run. She changed clothes, tied on shoes, grabbed her iPod, and stuffed her ancient cell phone in her pocket. Outside, the air was sticky with a storm that threatened and matched her mood.

She ran down her street, away from Bailey's house, her feet slapping pavement in time with the driving beat of the music she'd chosen, a song called "Monster."

It also matched her mood. Storm Cloud Gray. Soul Suck Black. And when she let her guard down, a little Betrayed Blue oozed out, and none of it was inside the lines.

Sweat soaked her shirt. Her lungs wanted to explode, and the cramp in her leg hobbled her. She slowed to a walk and then gave up when a passing car honked at her. It suddenly hit her that she could die there—just fall down dead—and it would be hours, maybe even a day or two, before she was missed. Her mom would mourn and then go back to her jobs and her classes. For a while, she'd be the trending topic at school, and then she'd just fade away with not even memories left behind.

She rolled her eyes, climbed to her feet, and started walking.

It didn't matter. Nothing did.

Half an hour later, she was back inside her empty house with its ticking clock and suffocating nothingness and the echo of her father's last words. Her mom had been gone since six that morning. It was now close to eleven. She was due at the Gallagher bakery at noon and still had to shower. She flew around her room, pulling underwear and clothes from her dresser, shuffled into the bathroom, and stood under the hot stream of water until her fingers pruned. She made it to the bakery with mere minutes to spare.

"Megan."

Mr. Gallagher smiled when she stepped behind the counter, tying an apron around her waist.

"How you doin' today?"

She managed a tight-lipped smile and shrug. "Okay, thanks."

"Good." He patted her shoulder. "That's…ah, good." He turned to a tall bakery cart. "Fresh batch of bagels. Can you bin them please?"

Work. Yes, work would be a relief, something to lose herself in for a while. From the box of food service gloves, she grabbed a fresh pair and got started. To the bins in the display case, Meg added the fresh plain, sesame, and poppy seed bagels. An hour later, the bins were nearly empty. She was ringing up a sale for a dozen when Mr. Gallagher came out of the kitchen with his cell phone to his ear. "Yeah, she's right here. Megan? It's Chase."

Her heart stalled in her chest. She wanted to run, hide, stick her hands in dough—anything but answer that phone. But Mr. Gallagher had other ideas. He took her hand, slapped the phone into it, and muttered a terse, "Stubborn kids," before he strode away.

Meg moved just inside the kitchen, pulled in a gulp of air, and squeaked out, "Hello."

"Are you ignoring my messages now?" Frustration sizzled in Chase's voice.

"What? No!"

"I texted you like an hour ago."

"Oh, I went for a run and then showered and then came here. I haven't looked at my phone all morning." What would be the point?

"Look at it now."

"Chase, I'm working—"

"It's Bailey, Megan. Did you see her Facebook post?"

"Yeah, it's…um, great news. She found her dad." Meg tried to sound enthusiastic.

"Cut the crap, Megan. This is me." Something squeaked, like a chair he'd just sunken into. "She said he's a marine. Matthew Schor. From the next town. Megan, I sent you a link to a newspaper story I found. Sergeant Michael Schor was killed in action in Iraq."

Her chewed-up, spit-out heart plummeted down to her feet, and she fell against the closest wall.

"Are you there?"

"Yeah," Meg whispered. Poor Bailey. This news was going to crush her. And there wasn't a damn thing she could do about it.

"Well, what are you gonna do?"

Meg straightened up with a frown. "What can I do?"

She heard his muttered curse. "You can forget about all the crap that just went down and be there for her. This is *Bailey*, Megan. This is gonna devastate her."

He was right. Of course he was right. But what could she do? She had no car. Hell, she didn't even know where Bailey was heading.

"Megan, my dad's waiting for you. Go."

"Where? I don't even remember what town."

"He does. I already told him. She's been posting steadily."

Meg's mouth tightened into a thin line. "If she's texting while she's driving, I'll kill her."

"Kill her after you save her. And for the record, she hasn't posted since she left."

Her eyes slipped shut for a moment. "Chase, why are you doing this? You didn't even say good-bye when you left. I figured you never wanted to talk to me again."

He was quiet for so long she thought the call had dropped. "I'll tell you, Megan. I'll tell you everything you want to know on the way there. My dad's waiting outside for you. Go."

Chapter 46
Bailey

Oh, my God. Oh, my God. Oh, my God.

Bailey was actually going to meet her dad.

After all these years of not knowing, all the weeks of searching, she'd found him. She'd finally found him. It was like Christmas morning. No, it was like seventeen years of Christmas mornings. Even though it had totally upset her mom, signing up for that classmates site was the best thing she'd ever done. It was kind of cool seeing pictures of Nicole at seventeen. But when Ryder—no, *Simon*—had sent her the name he'd found, it wasn't hard to use the same site to find his yearbook. Matthew Schor.

Her father.

She'd even found pictures. His hair was curly like hers. And they had a dimple in exactly the same place. He played football and basketball and was voted "Best Smile." Maybe she'd win "Best Smile" next year. Maybe he'd want to adopt her and she could move in with him instead of Nicole's creepy soon-to-be-husband. *Oh, my God!* Maybe he was married with kids of his own and she'd have brothers or sisters.

Whoa. Head rush.

Matthew Schor.

She liked that name. It sounded so strong and, well, fatherly. She could have been Bailey Schor instead of Bailey Grant. That hot spike of outrage aimed at her mother surged in her core, but she battled it back. She wanted to remember every second of this precious moment with clear eyes. She wrapped her arms around her middle and squeezed out a big smile. At a red light, the driver of the car next to her kept turning to laugh at her, but even that couldn't kill her joy.

What would he be like? *Smart*, she thought. Of course, he'd be smart, like doctor or professor or lawyer smart. Or maybe he was artistic. Not like Meg. The smile froze in place when another little pang hit, and she pushed it away. She would not think of Meg. Not now. Not today.

She was meeting her dad. She tapped out another status update.

Oh my God, wouldn't it be cool if he's a computer programmer?

The light turned green, and she put the phone away. They could build her video game together—it would be a father-daughter project. She thought and dreamed and wished and imagined halfway to the address she'd found online. For the second half of the trip, she obsessed over what to say. She supposed she should have called first, but she didn't want him to hang up. She had to see him for herself. Although just knocking and blurting out, "Hi! I'm your daughter!" was probably not the best idea. She'd seen too many cheesy movies to not know that was the fastest way of getting a door slammed in your face. She revised and rewrote her script. She'd smile, give her name, and say she was looking for Matthew Schor to talk to him about her mother, Nicole Grant, and hadn't they gone out together when they were teens? He'd smile and nod and say "Of course I remember Nicole, the great love of my life. Whatever happened to her?" And she'd say that Nicole had had a baby and that baby was her and she was there to find out if her dad wanted to get to know her. He'd smile and cry and grab her in a big bear hug, spin her around and around, and never want to let go.

It was just a little past noon when she stood in the driveway of a huge house with red shutters and lots of windows, her palms sweaty and her heart pounding, and for a minute—just for a minute—she wished Meg was here to hold her hand. She swallowed hard and swallowed again and forced her feet up the walk to the front door, where she rang the doorbell with a hand that trembled.

Footsteps approached.

She wiped her hands down her pants.

The locks clicked.

Her heart stuttered.

The door opened.

She forgot to breathe.

There he was. Tall. Blond. Dimples. Older. With her heart swelling, Bailey just stared.

"Can I help you?"

She beamed.

The man's eyes popped. "Who are you?"

"I… I'm—are you Matthew Schor?"

The man's face fell, and he shook his head. "No. No, I'm sorry. I'm Josh, his brother. You knew Matt?"

Bailey's smile faded. "Um...no. I think he knows my mom. Nicole?

"Grant? Yeah, he knew her."

"I'm Bailey. Bailey Grant."

Josh took a step out the door and halted and then pressed both hands up to his open mouth. "You...you're...holy mother of God. Oh, wow. Christ. Jesus Christ. You'd better come in. Yeah, you should come in."

Bailey hesitated. If Meg were here, she'd do that frownie thing with her forehead, grab her elbow, and hiss in her ear that she was crazy to go into some stranger's house. But how could she not? She'd already lost so much time and to come this far without more? She stepped inside and waited for Josh to close the door. He led her to a comfy living room with a flat-screen TV hanging on a wall, matching sofas arranged in an L in front of it, and sank heavily into one. She scanned the room, her eyes greedy for any glimpse of the man she hoped to meet. There was a graduation picture on a shelf. A picture of a handsome soldier hanging on the wall.

He stared at her for a long moment. "Oh...um, please sit. I—God, I don't even know where to start."

"Is Matthew home?"

"No, he's not." Josh stared at his hands. "You're Nicole's daughter. I'm gonna take a wild guess here and say you're what? A little over seventeen?"

"Yeah." Bailey smiled, impressed. "My birthday's in February."

Josh scratched his head and nodded. "And you're here because you think Matt's your dad?"

"He is." Bailey leaned forward. "It took me ages to find him."

"Yeah, so does your mom know you're here?"

Bailey's eyes went round, and she shook her head. "No, she doesn't even know I figured it out."

"Figured—ah. Okay, look. Bailey, is it?" At her nod, Josh leaned forward. "I don't—the thing is—hell, this is hard. I'm just gonna say it. Matt's dead."

Bailey's ears rang. Dead. The word bounced around in her mind, taking turns with the *Oh, my God* chorus on repeat. Tears burned behind her eyes and her face crumbled. How…how could it hurt this much? How could she possibly feel this much pain over the death of someone she'd never met? She wrapped her arms around her middle and tried not to cry. She should have called first or…or maybe not come at all. All those years of wondering and imagining what her dad was like, all those weeks of figuring out who he was, where he was, and then nothing. *Oh, my God.*

"I'm sorry. I'm so sorry. I shouldn't have come. I really shouldn't have come." Bailey jumped up and hurried to the door before she lost it completely. She had her hand on the door knob when Josh stopped her.

"Wait! Don't go. I'm sorry. I shouldn't have blurted it out like that. It's just hard—would you…if it won't upset you, maybe you'd like to hear about him?"

The tears fell then. "Yeah. Yeah, I really would."

Fifteen minutes later, they were back in the living room, cups of hot coffee on the table in front of them beside a fat photo album stuffed cover to cover with pictures and mementos. Josh had asked her about school and her friends. She'd told him all about the video game and he told her that her dad was a big Xbox fan, which really made her cry.

"I knew it," she wiped her eyes. "I knew I was like him."

Josh flipped through the pages of the album. "Oh, look at this. Our fort! I think Matt was thirteen and I was fourteen. That's our friend Tim. He's a chiropractor now." Josh went through the album snapshot by snapshot for her. Through her tears, a picture emerged of the boy Matthew Schor had been and the man he later became—laughing, always laughing. Every picture showed him surrounded by friends, by family. Bailey traced the medals he'd earned in combat and read the letters from the Department of Marines and the White House and the obituary that ran in the local papers. Bailey wondered how she'd missed all this when she was researching the name Simon had sent her.

"He was on his third tour. He died saving a buddy from a live grenade. That's the way he was." Josh smiled, but his face showed nothing but pain, and Bailey wondered if her face looked the same.

"Did he…um, ever get married? Have other kids?"

Josh shook his head. "Nah, he never could settle on just one girl. But he'd have loved you if he'd known. Why did Nicole keep you a secret?"

Bailey nibbled her lip. "She won't tell me. She wouldn't even tell me my father's name. A few weeks ago, I found my mom's yearbook online. I checked around and finally learned about Matt, so I searched white pages until I found this address."

"Oh, this was his house. After he was killed, my parents moved in. Speaking of my parents, they'll be back soon. You should probably leave. They're…well, they're pretty mad at your mom. They blame her for Matt's death. If she hadn't broken up with him, he probably wouldn't have enlisted and—"

"He'd still be alive. I get it. I'll go." Like a fist to her gut, Bailey finally figured out why her mother never spoke about Matthew Schor. Had she loved him? Probably. But love wouldn't have been enough. No, Nicole would have wanted things a seventeen-year-old guy could never have given her. She chose not to settle.

Bailey stood, surprised her legs could hold her up. "Thanks...um, Uncle Josh."

Josh blinked and then smiled wide. "Uncle Josh. I like that. Jesus, I like that." He stood up and held out his arms, and she moved into them without hesitation, held on, and held tight.

"Thanks."

They broke apart, and Josh closed the photo album and put it back in its box with all the other stuff. "Take it," he held it out to her. "Take it. Bring it back when you're done and I'll tell you more."

"Deal," Bailey squeaked out.

She had no idea how she was going to drive home. In her plan, her father was supposed to fall instantly in love with her and start clearing out a spare bedroom. She'd made it halfway down the street when the last of her strength ebbed. *Oh, my God*, she repeated again and again and again. He was dead, and he'd never taught her to ride a two-wheeler or tucked her in bed and read her stories or taught her how to drive or even scolded her about boyfriends and it was her mother's fault. He'd been right here in a town hardly twenty minutes away and she'd never known his name and now he was dead. *Dead.* Like never-coming-back dead.

Ever.

She fell against the car, his photo album pressed to her heart while the sobs shook her whole body. She barely noticed the hand stroke her back or the familiar voice tell her everything would be okay. Suddenly, she was in the car, and Meg was there beside her.

"Meg? How?"

Meg lowered her eyes. "I thought you'd need me. Mr. Gallagher drove me."

Oh, my God. Bailey shook her head slowly from side to side. It was like her dad had sent her himself. "You know he's dead?"

"Chase clued me in. Bailey, I'm sorry."

"Oh, Meg!" She flung herself into Meg's arms. "He was so, so good. He died saving his friend." Abruptly, Bailey straightened up, the words she'd just spoken tasting sour in her mouth. After everything she'd done, all the ways she'd hurt her, and still, Meg had come for her. "Why did you come?"

"We'll talk about all that later. Right now, I want to hear about your dad."

Bailey told Meg everything Josh had shared with her. Meg dug tissues from her pocket.

"Bay, I'm so sorry."

Her deep sigh squeezed Meg's heart.

"Bailey, talk to me. Are you okay?"

Bailey's eyes slipped shut for a moment. "I don't know. I think I'm feeling all the emotions in the world at the same time. I don't know what this means—any of this—and I really need to know, and I can't stop saying, *Oh, my God* in my head." She wiped her eyes. "I'm so mad at her, Meg. I don't know if I can ever forgive her for this. She knew. All this time, she knew he was one town over and she never told me."

Meg nodded. "She had her reasons. When you're ready to hear them, you will."

Bailey sighed and sniffled into a fresh tissue. Her phone buzzed, and she frowned at the caller ID. "Hey, Mom. No, I'm at his house. Yeah, it was hard. Because I needed to know. Okay…yeah, in a few minutes. Bye." She ended the call and smiled weakly at Meg. "Mr. Gallagher squealed. She knows I know and wants to talk."

"What do you want?"

Bailey crossed her arms and blew a curl out of her eyes. "To make her hurt the way I do."

"Bay? Maybe that's why she called. Because she already is."

Meg was always so practical and logical and smart. "Yeah, maybe she is. She said she couldn't marry him, knowing he'd never be able to stick. She *lied*. She never told him about me. I think I hate her for that." Bailey's face tightened, and she put all that aside for the moment. "So…what about us? It's so great that you and Mr. Gallagher came after me today. But I know you're still hurt. I can see it."

Meg thought about that for a moment. "You're right. I'm still hurt."

"Yeah," Bailey agreed. "Yeah, me too. So what do we do now?"

"Let's go home and talk."

Bailey searched Meg's face, but everything there told her she wasn't playing around. With one last look back, Bailey started her grandmother's car and drove them home. Half an hour later, they each sat on an end of the old lumpy sofa, the gulf between them the size of an ocean.

"I can't believe you did that." Bailey shook her head slowly. "I was wishing you were there to hold my hand. And then you were."

"I know what it's like to lose your dad. I wouldn't wish it on anybody."

"Not even your worst enemy?" Bailey asked with a smile, even though she wasn't joking.

Meg brought her knees up, curled her arms around them. "We're not enemies, Bailey. We may not be friends anymore, but we're definitely not enemies."

"Yeah." Bailey blew her nose. "*Friends* feels really far away."

Meg was quiet for so long that Bailey sat up and angled her head. "Okay, look. I hate this. This is so stupid. I miss you, and I know you miss me too. I know how we can fix this. If you're up to it."

"Yeah. Yeah, I'm up to it." The frown smoothed out on Meg's forehead.

Bailey tucked her legs under her and mirrored Meg's position. "'Mistakes were made.'"

"What?"

Bailey waved a hand. "Oh, sorry. Just some *Call of Duty* humor. But we really did make a lot of mistakes, and you know why?" Bailey didn't bother to wait for a reply. "Because we've grown up. We're not in second grade anymore and I'm too old for a babysitter. That means you have to find another way to be my friend. I broke up with Simon because you told me he and Caitlyn were together. I was crazy about him and I never even talked to him, never gave him a chance to explain. I just blindly trusted you."

"Bay—"

Her hand shot up. "Wait."

Meg snapped her teeth together.

"I shouldn't have done that, and then I realized I do that all the time. I hurt Simon. I hurt you. I hurt a lot of people because I listen to what other people say instead of trusting myself. All Simon was doing was talking to her."

Meg lowered her eyes. "Oh, God, I'm sorry," she whispered.

"I really liked that boy, Meg. And I blew it. I screwed things up so much. He created Ryder to get back at me and at you, and now he's in so much trouble. All I had to do was…was just *listen*, you know? I didn't then, but I am now. I went to Simon's house and we talked. And we've been talking ever since, and oh, God, Meg, I am so mad!"

Bailey shot to her feet, bounced around the room, waving her hands the way she always did when she was fired up.

"I mean, mad like a can of soda all shook up. I'm mad at you and me and my mom and Simon and Chase and I didn't even know it and that just makes me madder. I still really like Simon in spite of all the crap he did to us—" Her hand shot up again, but Meg didn't even think about interrupting. "And the thing is…I can forgive all that. I can forgive him because I did some pretty crappy stuff too, and so did you." She stabbed the air with a finger pointed right at Meg.

Meg got the point, but it ruffled her feathers. "You *told*, Bailey." She countered and made Bailey flinch. "Friends don't do the stuff we did. Jesus, Bailey…my dad? You actually told Chase about my dad. And then all that crap with the police." She squeezed her eyes shut, amazed that they could still find tears left to cry over that.

"Oh, come off it, Meg!"

Meg's eyes snapped open in time to see Bailey shoot out a hip and cross her arms.

"Friends don't tell potential boyfriends about the time you threw up on a teacher. They don't talk about the stupid seventh-grade love poems, and they damn well don't call each other sluts on Facebook." Bailey's eyes practically shot laser beams through Meg.

"I never did that! I never told him you got sick on Miss Monroe and I never told him about the poems! That was Simon, Bailey. All Simon. But you wouldn't even *listen* to me! You cared more about some guy you never met than me!"

Bailey looked Meg straight in the eyes. "Okay. You're right. I should have listened to you and I didn't and I'm sorry. But don't I get credit for trying? After you hurt your hand, I tried, Meg. But that wasn't good enough for you. You had to play the slut card. You knew all that happened with Mr. Milner was a stupid little girl's crush, and you put his name on Facebook."

Meg's face drained of its angry flush and she dropped her gaze. Bailey sank back to the sofa and shut her eyes. There was no point, not to any of this. No point at all. Ryder...well, Simon was in trouble, Chase was miserable. She was sad, and Meg—she opened her eyes to gauge her—she was just lost.

"I've been thinking a lot about the other stuff," she said quietly and waited until Meg raised her eyes. "Friends are there for each other. They hold their hair out of the toilet after that night when they swiped a bottle of Schnapps from their grandparents' bar and watch *The Vampire Diaries* together and then even when they're mad and hate each other's guts, they come—" She had to pause there. Swallow. Swallow again. "They come and rescue them when they find out their dad died."

Meg's eyes filled with tears, and she squeezed Bailey's hand.

"People screw up, Meg. All the time. And when they do, friends should make them face it and then give them the space to get over it, make it right again."

Meg managed a halfhearted smile. Bailey had gotten scary sick that night.

She, of course, had not because drinking Schnapps—even peach flavored—wasn't part of The Plan. "Friends also tell each other the truth. I want us to be friends again."

Bailey didn't give her the chance to say anything. "I want us to be friends again, but not the way we were, Meg. I'm not you. I don't have a master plan for my future. I'm just making things up as I go. And I need you to be okay with that. You can't pressure me anymore to do things your way. You can give me advice, but you need to know I'm not always going to take it, and that means you don't get to ram it down my throat even when it is for my own good."

"I don't—"

"Yeah, you do, and you have to stop."

"Stop?" Meg echoed. How the hell was she supposed to do that? Hold her breath? She frowned and stared at Bailey. "I don't know if I can."

To Meg's surprise, Bailey smiled. "Sure you can. Watch this." Bailey straightened her spine and cleared her throat. "Megan, I've decided I want Simon back, and you are *not* going to waste one word telling me what a mistake I'm making. You're going to smile and say, 'Bailey, I hope it works out for you.' And also, I've decided I'm going away to college next year. I won't go to a school anywhere near yours because I want to miss you, to look forward to seeing you and talking to you and texting you. And you're going to smile and say, 'I'll miss you so much.'"

"And what are you going to do?"

Bailey merely shrugged. "I won't post anything you did in second grade online. And I promise I won't drop you for a guy. And I'll even help you get Chase back. And that brings me to my third point. You can't live this ridiculous plan your father left you. You need help to deal with your dad's suicide. You need to go after Chase Gallagher like he's a freaking Olympic sport and you're the medal contender. Let's practice. I'll go first. Megan, I want Simon back."

"Um—" Meg looked ill. "Okay. I wish you luck."

Bailey giggled and rocked her head from side to side. "Not bad, but you can do better. Let's try another one. I'm going away to college. I've decided to study computer science and animation. I'm going to build my game myself."

Meg shot out of her seat. "Oh, my God, Bailey, I'm so—" When she saw Bailey's arched eyebrows, she calmed herself and tried again. "Uh, right. Okay. I'll miss you so much."

"Good job! Okay, last one." Bailey got serious.

Meg sucked in a deep breath, let it go.

"Meg, I think your father's whole plan is wrong. He was sick. Obviously, he wasn't thinking straight. I know you love him and you think you owe him, but you deserve to be happy. I'm seeing a therapist. I think you should too."

Meg stared at her for a long moment and then admitted with half a smile, "The counselor at school said the same thing. My mom already found somebody willing to work within our budget. I saw her once so far. She says I have to open up more, not let my parents' problems be mine." She lifted a shoulder. "It's hard work."

"Yeah, I have a lot of work too. Mine says I feel unloved, so I keep reinventing myself as the means to prove my worth." She made a face. "Or something like that."

Meg's lips twitched. "Um, I've also been doing a lot of thinking about Chase. You know, we had a really long talk today on the way to find you."

Bailey clasped her hands together. "And?"

"I think you may be right about him."

Bailey's eyes narrowed. "May be?"

"Well, I thought I should at least give him another shot. Just to be sure." She squirmed. "The thing is… I think I'm out of chances, you know?"

Bailey jumped from the couch. "Okay, you need to be sure. You can't do this and then freak out on him again. He doesn't deserve that."

Meg's lip quivered. "Bay, I've completely screwed everything up. I miss him so much. He…he never even said good-bye to me."

"Aw, Meg." Bailey squeezed her hand and then reached for her phone to check the time. "Okay. Here's what you're going to do. You're going to get dressed up, hop on a train, and go to him. Tell him how you feel. He won't be able to resist you."

"You think?"

"I know," she called over her shoulder as she hurried upstairs to Meg's room. Meg caught up to her just as she pulled open the closet door. She pawed through Meg's meager wardrobe and pulled a hanger out. "This. This would be perfect."

Meg blinked. "It's a dress."

"Duh. That's why it's perfect. It shows Chase you put some thought and planning into this."

Still not convinced, Meg took the dress, tugged it on.

"I was right. It's perfect. Now we just need a few more touches."

Meg groaned when Bailey tugged her into the bathroom.

Chapter 47
Meg

At the door to an old building sandwiched between a camera store and another camera store, Meg rang the buzzer for the second time and turned to head back to the subway.

Chase wasn't home.

It was nearly dark. She couldn't hang around too much longer. She'd let Bailey dress her up and drive her to the train station, and she'd traveled all the way to the city for nothing. She wiped a bead of sweat from the back of her neck and started walking, oblivious to the messenger bike that with a squeal of hand brakes, narrowly missed plowing into a parked car.

"Megan? Megan, is that you?" A familiar voice shouted.

She spun, found Chase in the street, bright yellow helmet on his head, standing beside a bike. His jaw dropped. So did the bike.

He left the bike where it fell and ran, pure joy in his mystical eyes. "Megan!"

She took a few steps toward him, stopping to clutch an iron rail in front of the building. She smiled his smile and never bothered to hide it, and it almost hurt it felt so good. When he reached her, he scooped her up in his arms and just held her, held tight. "Megan, what the hell are you doing here? Why are you wearing a dress?"

She pulled back—not away—just far enough to look up at him and try to understand the temper that heated his words. "Um."

"You here for me?" He pulled back, dropped his hands.

"I'm here for *me*. I think."

"What the hell does that mean?"

"Chase, I'm so sorry. For…for not trusting you and not talking to you and for…for all of it."

He crossed his arms over his chest. "We should talk," he said after a long moment. The smile faded from her lips, but she nodded.

"Come on." He retrieved his bike, led her through his door, and walked to the elevator. They rode in silence to the eighth floor, tension so thick it practically had its own heartbeat. He did not look at her. Finally, the doors slid open. He pushed the bike to the third door on the right, opened it, and stood aside to let her go first.

She stepped into a narrow hall that led from the front door to the living room, where the smell of old pizza lingered. He propped the bike on a rack and removed the helmet. She moved to the window, stared down. "Nice view."

"The one from my room back home was better." He flopped onto a secondhand sofa covered in threadbare brown fabric pushed up against the short wall. "I used to watch you, you know. All the time," he suddenly blurted.

She spun, the blue skirt swishing around her legs. "Really?"

He ran his hands through sweaty hair and then wiped his palms down his bike shorts. "It's…um, how I knew you hurt your hand."

She flexed it, and a long purple scar winked at him.

"I love to watch you paint. It's like…like someone kicked you into high gear. You're awake. You're moving, but damn, when you paint, you're—" He spread his hands, unable to find the word.

"Alive," she finally supplied and then laughed.

"What?"

She waved a hand. "It's nothing, just thinking how Bailey would go all gooey at that. She'd have said, 'Oh, my God, he's just like Edward!' and I would have rolled my eyes or something."

He scrubbed a hand over his face that had suddenly gone red but didn't say anything, so Meg lost her grin. "You must have thought I was crazy, painting you all the time."

Slowly, he shook his head and smiled. "No, all I saw were eyes, hands, a jaw. I was jealous. I wanted to be what got you fired up like that. And then the night you cut your hand, I found out I was. I thought I had it made." The grin faded when he shook his head and added, "I was wrong."

She moved to sit beside him at those words, but he jumped up. He crossed to the tiny kitchen and snagged a bottle of water. "You want something? Water, soda, iced tea?"

"What? Oh…no. No, thanks." This wasn't going as well as she and Bailey had planned. And then she almost laughed. She put on a pretty blue dress, let Bailey smear some makeup on her face, and thought what? That Chase would just heel like a trained pet? She'd hurt him. Hell, she'd *meant* to hurt him. To drive him away. She'd always believed hard work and perseverance were the keys to success. Her heart pinched, and she'd never wished to fail at something as hard as she did now. She ran her hands down her legs, felt the lump in the pocket of her dress, pulled out the folded square of paper she'd tucked inside. She held on to it for luck. For courage.

He cracked open the water bottle cap, tipped it back, and gulped. "So what do you think of our place?"

She noticed he didn't come back to the sofa. "Um, it's cleaner than I expected. How close is it to your campus?"

"A couple of subways."

It gave her a little pang whenever she thought about Chase living in Manhattan instead of in the big house behind hers. She smiled briefly. "You've got…what? Three roommates?"

"Yeah, it's nice not squashing one of my brothers' toys every time I sit down." Chase hesitated a moment and sat back down, settling against the cushions only to wince and immediately straighten up. He stuffed his hand between the cushions and pulled it back, holding the TV remote control. His face went crimson, and she laughed, but he didn't. "How'd you get here anyway?"

"Bailey. Um…she had your address, dropped me off at the train station. Then I took a subway."

He choked on his water. "You took the subway dressed like that? Which one?"

"Uh," she tried to remember. "I think the number six train."

He shut his eyes and shook his head. "I'll get you a cab back to Penn Station. You're not walking around in the dark like that." He put the water bottle on the floor, froze when he saw the paper clutched in her fist. His eyes shot to hers, held there. "You…is that? You kept this?" He took the paper, unfolded the sketch he'd done of them at I-CON. "Why?"

He smiled and it was real, and whatever kept pinching her heart finally let go. "I was wrong, Chase," she blurted. His eyes popped, a muscle in his jaw twitched. "I was so wrong."

He didn't say anything, so she tried harder. "Have you ever imagined not having your dad?"

Her question made him pale. It was a long time before he spoke. "I don't know if imagining that does any good, you know? I've had my dad my whole life. You haven't. I don't know if anybody can really understand something like that unless you live it."

She nodded, staring at her hands. "For as long as I can remember, he used to tell me to have a plan for the future. It was pretty scary sometimes. I was like…four, maybe five years old and he'd be telling me how short life is and that if I didn't have a plan, it would be over before I knew it." She tugged the skirt over her knees, abruptly cold. "I didn't even know what a plan was, let alone how to make one. So instead of bedtime stories, I got lessons on the future."

Something passed over his eyes. She thought it was sympathy and continued, "He told me how important it was to get good grades and go to college and get a degree, how important it was to be able to take care of myself so I'd never have to worry about money. He told me not to let anything or anybody sway me from my plan. And I didn't. Not until you."

He twitched beside her. His legs bounced, and for a minute, she thought he was about to run. Instead, he reached over, took her hand, and squeezed. She clutched it like she had the night in the hospital. "When I was little, I thought he was teaching me all about plans because he loved me." Her voice broke. He shifted closer. "But the truth is…he *blamed* me."

He made a sound of protest, but she cut him off.

"I was an accident. I knocked all his plans off course. Then he lost his job and the money problems just exploded. Everything that happened, everything that went wrong—it was all my fault. The night before he shot himself, I heard him arguing with my mother. He was screaming, 'I told you I never wanted kids!'"

She dropped his hand and covered her ears. "I swear that was louder than the gunshot."

Chase drew his hand back, put it on top of his thigh, and stared at the dingy carpet. "You're not five years old anymore, Megan. People have kids they didn't plan all the time and don't kill themselves. He was sick. It had nothing to do with you. If not you, he'd have found some other reason."

She winced at his tone. "Yeah, that's what my therapist says," she murmured, and his head snapped up.

"What?"

"Yeah, I'm seeing a therapist now. It was sort of Bailey's idea." She gave a tiny smile, and his eyes popped.

"You and Bailey are friends again?"

She rocked her head sideways. "We're trying. We have a lot of work to do. Therapy for both of us was part of the deal—along with a fashion intervention." She waved a hand over her dress, her face burning.

"So where do I fit into this plan?"

She almost winced at his choice of words. Instead, she took a deep breath and stared him right in the eye. "Chase, the time I spent being with you was so amazing, it was like I was painting even when I wasn't. And then when you told me about the new baby, I freaked out."

"Let me guess…this master plan you and your dad constructed…it has a spot for the 2.5 kids, a dog, and a white picket fence somewhere between age thirty and thirty-five?"

Her dark eyes filled with hurt. "No. No, Chase, you don't get it. I was going to live my life alone. College, career, financial independence. No one to answer to. No one to worry about. No one to sway me from my goals. The kids, the dog, the white picket fence, the minivan with vanity plates—"

His lips twitched into half a smile.

"All that showed up on my plan after you tucked me into your bed and made me Rice Krispies. I woke up the next day, and suddenly, I was part of this big noisy family expecting me for Sunday dinner. I was scared and unbelievably touched and confused and hurt with all the Bailey crap and then you dropped the baby news on me by asking me to run away with you and…and I couldn't stop thinking, *What if it was us? What if I got pregnant?* Damn it, Chase. It was all…all just too much."

Chase flung himself back against the cushions and stared at her. "I don't get why you're telling me all this now. Nothing's changed."

"Uh…yeah, it has." She retorted. "*I* have. Or…well, at least, I'm trying to. And that's why I'm here. I want us to be together."

That muscle in his jaw twitched again. "Megan, I don't have a plan. I don't know what I want, what I want to be. I don't know when or if I'll ever have kids. There are just so many possibilities, you know?"

She nodded once, swallowed hard, and shifted. It was time to leave. Maybe she never should have come. Just as she'd finally accepted that her father's life plan was wrong, it hit her that Chase's idea of no plan wasn't much better.

Bailey's last words as she dropped her off at the train station replayed in her head. *Just see what happens. Let it play out.* She'd done that. And supposed it was good to know one way or the other.

Even if it felt like a steel-toed kick to the gut.

"But I can promise you this. We can figure all these things out as they come." He waited a second. "Could you live with that?"

She didn't reply. Could she live with unknowns?

Instead, she stood up, held out her hand. "I want to show you something."

He didn't take the hand she offered but stood anyway. That hurt too, but she moved to the window. "Look. See that building over there?" She pointed west. "That's the dorm for the Cooper Union. That's where I'll be staying next year if I make it in." She turned, took his hand in both of hers. "But if I don't get in, I have to have a new plan."

He sighed, so she reached out and squeezed his hand.

"It's pretty short. It has room for kids some day—a whole bunch of them. I didn't even know I wanted kids until I woke up in your house. I know I want to paint. I want to surround myself with art. It used to be just a hobby, just something I did to keep myself busy. Now it's going to be my job. I don't know how yet. Artist, curator, appraiser maybe—I have no idea. So besides Cooper Union, I'm applying to a bunch of other schools. I may end up living at home, commuting to school, or, hopefully, staying right over there." She jerked her thumb at the window. "So there's a lot of wiggle room in The Plan."

"That's it?" He crossed his arms, angled his head.

Meg understood that part of her plan wasn't enough for him. She lifted a shoulder. It was time to reveal the next part. "No, that's not it. There's you.

You're part of The Plan. I mean, if *you* want to be." She managed a small smile. "I don't know how we can do this if we're in different towns, but we could try."

Chase stared out at the brick facade on a building a few blocks over and said "Binoculars."

"What?" She looked worried when he grinned.

"Nothing. Come on." He grabbed her hand and dragged her to the bedroom. He shoved a pile of dirty clothes off a metal folding chair by an ancient battered desk, sat down, and logged into Facebook. She watched him click his profile, tap a few keys. Finally, he looked up at Megan and said, "Okay. You sure about this? I'm not deleting it this time."

She turned her gaze from his monitor to enchanting green eyes and swallowed once. "Told you...I'm making this up as I go."

"I like this plan." Chase clicked Post and smiled when his status updated.

Epilogue

Forty miles away, Bailey's cell phone buzzed. She unlocked it, saw a new Facebook update from Chase, and clicked it.

💜 Chase Gallagher is in a relationship with Megan Farrell.

"Oh, my God!" she squealed and did a little chair dance, and this time, Gran didn't shout at her to stop.

TMI Discussion Guide

Questions about *TMI:*

1. What are *TMI*'s main themes?

2. Pick one trait that describes each of the main characters. Do you think the same trait still applies by the end of the story? Why or why not?

3. How do you think Megan's family life influences her? How does Bailey's family influence her? Compare the girls' families to Chase's family.

4. Why do you think Megan denies how she feels about Chase for so long? What finally prompts her to admit her feelings?

5. How others perceive us often determines how we act in certain circumstances. How do Bailey's decisions reflect the way others think of her? How do Meg's decisions reflect the way others think of her?

6. Why do you think Megan and Bailey are friends? Do you feel the girls respect each other? Why or why not?

7. Let's talk about Ryder. Why do you suppose Bailey trusted him? Why do you think she believed him instead of Megan?

8. Do you feel the characters changed by the end of the book? In what ways?

Questions about You:

1. Which of the characters is more like you? Would you be more likely to be Bailey's friend or Megan's?

2. Bailey blogs about secrets that girls have. Do you agree with her that secrets are the foundation of a friendship? Why or why not?

3. Consider the friendships you have. Do your friends know your secrets? How would you react if a friend revealed your secrets online?

4. What do you think it was like for Megan and Bailey to return to school after their secrets goes viral? Have you ever wanted to skip school because of an embarrassing moment?

5. How we perceive ourselves is often different from how others see us. Does Bailey think she is smart? What about Meg? How is people's perception of you different from how you see yourself?

6. Have any of your views and thoughts changed after reading *TMI*? Which ones?

Acknowledgments

We did it again!

I used "we" because even though it's my name on the cover, this was not a solo endeavor. Hugs, kisses, and head rubs to my guys, Fred, Robert, and Christopher, who picked up the household slack while I tried to complete *TMI* a few weeks after my mom passed away. Know this would never have been possible without you. An extra cuddle to Chris, who introduced me to *Assassin's Creed* and helped me nail many of the game references, and to Rob, who introduced me to a friend willing to beta-read.

To Kelly Breakey, Alex Newcorn, and @Alyssa-Susanna, big hugs for reading *TMI* so fast and providing the incredibly insightful feedback that helped me make Bailey into a character I am proud of. You all rock!

To all the members of the Long Island Romance Writers, RWA Chapter 160, *mwah*! Thank you for your support, advice, cheerleading, and sanity preservation as I juggled this project while I was saying good-bye to my mother. Special thanks to Jeannie Moon for not only reading early drafts of *TMI* but inviting me to join her and her own BFF under the guise of "research." I'm so touched that you shared your oldest and bestest friendship with me. *grins*

Enormous thanks to Aubrey Poole and the Sourcebooks team for giving me this opportunity, for the time I needed to mourn, and for making sure I'm not a one-hit wonder! *laughs* The Gallagher twins were named for my agent, Evan Gregory at the Ethan Ellenberg Agency, to whom I send extra special thanks for continuing to be a fount of wisdom, humor, and patience (especially patience!) as I learn the ins and outs of publication. I am so grateful to you. *high-fives*

Finally, love and gratitude and all the chocolate to my Twitter friends for your continued guidance, humor, and support, especially Ali Trotta, the sister of my heart (she knows why), and my Book Hungry ladies—Kelly Breakey, Abby Mumford, and Karla Nellenbach—for their cheerleading, feedback, and outstanding taste in books. *winks*

Thank you to Janet Reid, Brooks Sherman, and Jeff Somers, for rallying around this debut author in ways too big to ever adequately express my gratitude, and to Bill Cameron...just *because*.

About the Author

On a dare by her oldest son, Patty, who writes software instruction manuals during the day, wrote her first novel in an ice rink during his hockey practices. Though *Penalty Killer* was never published, Patty figured if she could do it once, she could do it again, and she finished several more novels. Her big break came in 2012 with *SEND*, a story about a former bully learning to cope with his guilt after one thoughtless click led to a classmate's suicide. *SEND* was published by Sourcebooks Fire in 2012. Fueled by a serious chocolate addiction, Patty is always looking for story ideas and wrote *TMI* after she read a headline about a fake Facebook account.

Patty lives on Long Island with her family and is currently writing a ghost story set there. Visit www.pattyblount.com for more information.